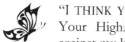 

"I THINK Y[...] Your High[...] against my hair. "Perhaps you need to help her find her voice."

"Hmm, yes, I think she's feeling quite shy at my finding her naked in bed with you. Again." His gaze lowered to my chest, causing my nipples to harden in response, my body alight with wonder and sensation and confusion. "Any suggestions?"

"Several." Titus's palm slid across my lower belly, the touch a brand against my skin as he pulled me backward. "I introduced Claire to fire play."

"Did you?" Exos stood, his fingers playing over his dress shirt, popping open the buttons with nimble fingers.

This can't be happening.

It has to be a dream.

"You two don't even like each other," I blurted out, then winced at allowing my thoughts to grace my lips. *Are you trying to ruin this?*

Exos grinned. "Maybe not, but we both like you, Claire." The fabric parted around his torso, revealing the toned physique beneath. He was leaner than Titus, but just as muscularly defined, almost in a regal sort of way. Fitting, considering his title. "It's not common for a Spirit Fae to take two mates, but it's not unheard of. Sometimes our affinity for a secondary element is strong, requiring an outlet. Clearly, you have a lot of fire in you." He finished removing his shirt, folding it and setting it on the nightstand beside the bed.

"I'm willing to work with it if you both are," Titus added, his thumb drawing a hypnotic circle around my belly button.

I resisted the urge to pinch myself, certain this had to be my unconscious mind indulging in this inappropriate scenario. But as the mattress dipped beneath Exos's weight, his eyes darkened with desire on my breasts, I realized I'd never felt more alive.

Elemental Fae Academy

Book One

Elemental Fae Academy

Book One

USA Today Bestselling Authors

Lexi C. Foss & J.R. Thorn

Elemental Fae Academy

Editing by: Outthink Editing, LLC

Cover Design: Sanja Balan of Sanja's Covers

Published by: Ninja Newt Publishing, LLC

Digital Edition

ISBN: 978-1-950694-10-5

This one is for our readers. We hope you enjoy Elemental Fae Academy.

#Dickwand

Elemental Fae Academy

Book One

PROLOGUE
EXOS

"HER BIRTHDAY IS NEXT WEEK." Elana sat back in her chair at the head of the council table, her silver-gray eyes brimming with expectation. "Allowing her to stay in the mortal realm is a risk we cannot allow."

"Then kill her," Mortus suggested, his tone flat. "She's an abomination."

"Hear, hear," Zephys agreed. "It'd solve several of our issues."

"But what if she's the one?" Vape was always the voice of reason in these meetings. He sat opposite Elana, his white hair pulled back in a bun, the lines adorning his face showing his near millennia of life.

"Oh, this again." Mortus shook his head. "The curse is a myth."

"Say that to the nearly extinct Spirit Fae," my brother said from his seat at the table. I stood behind him, leaving my seat at his side vacant. There were many who wanted me to join the Royal Council, to take my place in the Fae Court, but I never desired that life. I was a warrior by nature. Not a king, even though my blood indicated otherwise.

"Her mother caused that." A flame played over Blaize's fingers while he spoke. "Just thought I'd point that out. Again."

"We don't know that for a fact," Vape reminded, his tone stern yet gentle. Because this was a delicate topic, one several at the table felt strongly about. Especially Mortus—the fae who fought Ophelia Snow to the death. Ninety percent of the Spirit Fae perished on the same day. Some argued it was a coincidence. Others accused Ophelia of being the destructive force, her betrayal shaking the entire Fae Kingdom.

My instincts told me there was more to the story than met the eye, but I didn't know what.

"Oh, come on. We all know Ophelia was the cause, and this little terror is going to be just as much trouble." Zephys stood. "I don't even know why we're having this conversation. It's a waste of bloody time."

"Sit. Down," Elana commanded, her place at the head of the table affording her the authority of the room. As the eldest, and arguably the most powerful of the fae, she carried significant weight in this discussion. Despite the fact that she used to mentor Ophelia personally, providing her with a somewhat biased opinion.

Still, I believed everyone deserved a chance. Even Claire. "She should not have to pay for her mother's sins," I murmured, knowing my brother would agree. "I vote we give her a chance."

"Good thing your vote doesn't count, then," Mortus sneered.

"But mine does," my brother replied. "And I stand by my brother's words. Claire should not be punished for something she had no control over. We should bring her into the Fae Realm."

"And do what with her?" Blaize demanded. "Keep her in a cage? She's a Halfling. We don't even know what elemental skill she'll possess."

"Clearly spirit," my brother replied, his voice calm. "And likely one other." That was what set our kind—the Spirit Fae—apart from the others. While spirit was our primary element, we all maintained a secondary one. For me, that was fire. For my brother, water. Our kind used to hold the most power in the Fae Realm as a result, and still would if the majority of our species hadn't mysteriously collapsed and died in a single day.

Mortus snorted. "Right. She'll be weak with that mortal blood pumping through her veins."

"Or incredibly strong," Vape said in his raspy, old voice. "There's a prophecy depicting a Halfling of five elements. It could be her."

"You and your curses and prophecies," Mortus grumbled, shaking his head. "Show me the proof, old man."

"It's written in the stars" was his cryptic reply. Despite being a water elemental, he seemed to have a foresight ability, something no one else possessed. But for someone of his age, and with his experience, it almost made sense that he would be able to depict patterns in time, to predict an event before it happened.

"We should vote," Elana said, eyeing the parties at the table. Each element had three representatives, which mainly comprised of the royal bloodlines and a few high-ranking fae with stronger affinities to others.

Placards appeared, courtesy of an air elemental carrying them in off a subtle wind and scattering them around the long, oval surface.

"Should we bring her to the Fae Realm?" Elana asked.

Purple meant affirmative. Gold for negative.

My brother tilted his to the violet side, Mortus and Zephys immediately flipping to gold. Blaize surprisingly

LEXI C. FOSS & J.R. THORN

chose purple. "Call me curious" was his explanation. Several others followed suit, all maintaining a similar opinion, bringing the room to a unexpected agreement on allowing her into the Fae Realm.

"All right, then." Elana clasped her hands over the hard surface. "What will you do with her when she arrives?"

"Send her to the Academy." My brother's suggestion seemed to shock the room.

Mortus's cheeks actually tinged red. "To corrupt our youth? No."

Youth? I thought, nearly laughing.

The fae grew up faster than humans and didn't start attending the Academy until age nineteen. She'd fit right in with the crowd, apart from having grown up without access to her gifts for the last two decades.

Most fae began using their gifts earlier in life, but Ophelia had cast a charm over Claire to stall her elemental progression. It'd been one of the many atrocities the female fae had inflicted on others before her death. And had also been the reason the Council chose to let Claire remain in the mortal realm. She couldn't defend herself here, and there were many who wanted her dead.

Case in point, the furious Spirit Fae to my left—Mortus. I could feel the malevolent intents pouring off his aura. If allowed, he'd kill the Halfling himself.

Claire would need a protector, or several, to survive here. And unfortunately, if her powers manifested as they should, she'd be too dangerous for the mortal world as well. Leaving her rather… stuck.

"The Academy." Vape scratched his jaw, considering. "That would provide her with the ability to learn more about her gifts. She's enrolled in human university now, yes?"

"Yes," Elana confirmed. "But what sector would she attend? Spirit was disbanded after…"

"Her mother destroyed everyone?" Mortus offered. "You can't admit it out loud, but you'll allow her

4

abomination to attend the Academy? To play with the impressionable minds of our realm?" He stood. "This is ridiculous and you know it. I can't be a part of this conversation."

"Then leave," my brother said, his voice hard. Despite Mortus being the elder of our kind, my brother's royal blood superseded the elder male's authority. "My brother and I will represent our kind in your stead."

"You'd like that," Mortus said, his beady black eyes landing on me. "*Your Highness*." He bowed mockingly. "Enjoy playing with fate. Don't be surprised when she bites back." He stalked out of the room, leaving me sighing in his wake.

That bastard saw me as a constant threat to his position. As he probably should since he clearly couldn't behave as an adult of three hundred years. I wasn't even a tenth of his age, and I behaved more appropriately.

"What do you think, Exos?" Elana asked. "Should she attend the Academy?"

"It would provide her with the tools she needs to hone her elemental gifts," I said slowly. "But Mortus brought up a reasonable point. Who will help her learn about the most important ability of all—Spirit?"

She nodded. "I have an idea for that." A mischievous twinkle entered the elder fae's gaze, one that warned me I was not going to enjoy her suggestion in the slightest. "I'd like you to train her. In fact, I also think you should be the one to retrieve her."

"Why?" I blurted out, unable to hold the word back.

Elana's lips curled. "Because you're the most powerful Spirit Fae I've ever met. And if anyone can protect her, it's you."

"She's right," my brother agreed, glancing up at me with his piercing blue eyes—the same shade as my own. "You're the strongest amongst us. If anyone can control her, and train her, it's you." He lifted his hand to rest over mine on the back of his chair. "She needs you, Exos."

"It's a good pairing," Vape added. "Protection coupled with teaching. Assuming you're up for the challenge?" He raised a white eyebrow, his bottomless gaze boring into mine. The old elemental knew I couldn't turn down a summons, especially when he endorsed it.

I sighed. "Fine. I'll fetch her from the Human Realm. We'll discuss the mentorship when I return."

"Excellent." Elana held out her hands. "Then I believe we're adjourned for now?"

"When this all goes to hell, remember that I voted against everything," Zephys said, walking away from the table. "And if she dies, I didn't do it."

My brother squeezed my hand before releasing it. "You're going to need all the luck you can get, Exos. Try not to die on me."

I smirked. "Anyone who tries deserves their fate. Right, Cyrus?"

He returned my grin. "Right." We bumped fists as he stood. "Happy vibes."

"Happy vibes," I returned.

I'd need them, especially for the road ahead. Because there were very few places worse than hell, and the Human Realm was one of them.

Yeah, lucky me.

Chapter One
Claire

"TRUTH OR DARE?"

I nearly spit out my drink—some sort of fruity concoction my bestie had given me. Like strawberries or something. Really sweet. Totally not the point. "We're not playing this game, Rick."

"Oh, Claire Bear, we are *so* playing this game." Amie's lips pulled into a wide grin. "And the birthday girl goes first."

I tried to roll my eyes, but the room was already spinning. I wasn't drunk exactly. Just very tipsy. Or I thought that might be my current state. Honestly, I just felt really, really good. Like untouchable. Powerful. *Happy.* But this fruity drink in my hand was so blah. I needed something with more punch, like a shot or something. Maybe—

"Truth or dare, birthday baby?" Rick asked, flashing me one of his sexy-as-sin grins. Alas, he and I shared a preference for men. Not each other.

"Nope," I said. "Not playing."

"But I have the best dare for you," Rick said, a wicked glint in his dark eyes. I'd been on the receiving end of his dares several times over and knew better than to accept.

"Nope," I repeated. "My birthday, my rules." That was a thing, right? Yeah, it should be. "I'm making it a thing."

"What thing?" Amie asked, then shook her head, waving me off. "Ignore her, Ricky. She'll play. You know she will. Our Claire Bear can't deny a dare."

"Oh my God." I couldn't believe we were even talking about this. "We're twenty-one, guys, not sixteen."

"Are you saying we're too old for truth or dare?" Brittany sounded aghast. "I'm *not* too old for anything."

"Oh, we know, B," Rick said, patting her hand. "We know."

"And what's *that* supposed to mean?" she demanded, giving me a headache.

"You know what it means, baby girl." He pretended to toss his nonexistent hair, the gelled spikes on his head not moving an inch.

"No, I don't kn—"

"All right," I cut in, not wanting to be in the middle of a banter-fest on my birthday night. "I choose dare." Because it was the only way these two would shut the hell up. "What do you want me to do, Rick?"

"Him." He pointed to a boy—no, a *man*—in a leather jacket at the bar.

My jaw actually dropped. "*What?*" He was so out of my league that we weren't even playing in the same field. And I didn't feel that way due to a lack of confidence. No, I considered myself pretty enough, a solid B on the charts. But that man was drop-dead gorgeous in a bad-boy-rocker kind of way. Strong shoulders, lean waist, gorgeous white-blond hair.

I drew my thumb against my lower lip. Yeah, he was the kind of male women dreamed about, the type who could wreck some lady parts in the bedroom. Or, at least, that was what his confident exterior exuded.

As if he sensed my perusal, he glanced my way, causing me to duck my head.

"Yeah, him," Rick said, a grin in his voice. "He's been checking you out all night, Claire baby. You need to go lay one on him. That's my dare."

"You want me to kiss him?" I couldn't help the squeak in my voice. "At the bar?"

"Wouldn't be your first time," he pointed out. "What was the guy's name? Justin? Jack?"

"Jeremy," Amie supplied.

Rick snapped his fingers. "Jeremy. That's it. You had no problem sucking his tongue right out of his mouth. I want to see you do that to our gorgeous dude over there. Mainly because I want deets. I'm betting he's the dominant type, the kind who takes charge of the kiss and teaches your mouth a good lesson or two."

"Oh God." My face was on fire, my head already shaking back and forth. "Give me a truth instead."

"Nah, this is a good dare." He took a swig of his beer and relaxed into the booth, his free arm going across the back over Brittany's slender shoulders. "I dare you to kiss the blond bad boy. And then report back."

"If you don't do it, I will," Amie cut in, my bestie's eyes taking on an adoring gleam as she studied the bar. "He's *hot*."

Rick snorted. "I love you, A, I do, but the only one at this table with a shot is our Claire Bear. He's had a hard-on for her all night. Trust me. I've been watching."

"Really?" I asked, suddenly feeling far too sober. "He's noticed me?"

"Oh, yeah, constantly." Another sip. "Seriously, go over there and say *hi*. See what happens. It's not like you're dating anyone, C."

I pressed my clammy palms to my exposed thighs, my skirt feeling a bit too short for comfort. The man had returned to his drink, his broad back to me again. Even from behind, the guy oozed sex appeal. Amie was right. He was definitely hot with a capital *H*. "I don't know," I said. "I need another drink or five for that."

The hoop through Rick's brown brow glistened as he arched it. "Since when is this sort of dare an issue for you?"

Since you asked me to kiss what appears to be a god in a leather coat. "I got this," I replied instead. "I just need some more liquid courage. And it's my birthday. I shouldn't even have to ask, right?"

His gaze was knowing. "Yeah, yeah." He lifted his hand for the waiter—a male who'd been eyeing Rick with interest all night. They were totally going to fuck later. "My too-sober friend here needs a round of shots."

"Tequila?" the cute waiter—Drew—suggested.

"Perfect," Rick replied, looking him over. "Definitely perfect."

Drew smiled, his hazel eyes gleaming with interest. "Be back in a moment."

"I hope so."

Brittany scowled as Drew disappeared. "How do you always do that?" she demanded, sounding disgruntled. "Like, he's totally going home with you tonight, and you've barely said anything to each other outside of ordering drinks."

Rick shrugged. "The power of a glance, sweetheart." He winked at her. "Learn how to use your best assets, and maybe you'll perform better."

She grabbed her breasts. "Trust me, I'm using them. This top couldn't be any lower cut."

He eyed her substantial cleavage. "Sometimes revealing less is more. Take Claire Bear. That graphic T-shirt is clingy, showing off the curves without displaying them for the world. And she's grabbed the attention of several men tonight."

"Because she's blonde," Brittany said, gesturing to my long hair as if it were my only asset.

"She's also gorgeous," Amie added. "And tall, with those killer legs."

"That she's exposed beautifully in that skirt," Rick agreed.

My cheeks warmed. "Guys, I understand it's my birthday, but this is starting to get weird. Are you all hitting on me right now? Because I gotta say, none of you are my type."

"I'm totally your type," Rick argued. "You just can't handle my D."

I scoffed at that. "Yeah, that's the reason."

Another wink, this one for me just as our drinks arrived. "Another round, if you don't mind," Rick said before Drew had finished distributing the glasses. "Actually, two."

"On it." Drew was apparently more than happy to continue serving our table—exclusively.

Amie was right.

Rick had a magic touch, or look, or *something*, because this always seemed to happen when we went out.

He clinked his glass against mine, a devious smile flirting with his lips, and I shot the liquid into the back of my throat. It burned so good. I may have just turned the legal age to drink, but this was not my first time in a bar. Most of the clubs near Ohio State University's campus were eighteen plus, and several of them didn't card.

Two more rounds later, a warm, fuzzy feeling settled over me again, easing me back into a comfortable state, one where my reservations dwindled. Mr. Hottie still sat at the bar, not talking to anyone.

Hmm.

Okay. I could do this.

Just walk up to him, flirt a little. How hard could it be?

"Just a kiss, right?" I asked, taking a sip of the water Drew had brought for me.

"Preferably with tongue," Rick replied. "But you do you,

boo."

I nodded. "I got this."

"Damn right you do." He grinned. "Go get him, Claire Bear."

I swallowed some more water and stood, testing my heels.

The world spun just a little, but otherwise good. Adding three inches to my five-foot-eight height gave my legs a sexy appeal, lengthening my overall appearance. It also had the skirt at my hips looking indecently short, but it covered the right amount.

Unless I bent over.

Well, that would be one way to draw Mr. Hottie's attention.

I giggled to myself as I approached him. The stool beside him sat empty, giving me the opening I needed. I squeezed in beside him and the vacant seat, resting my elbows on the counter as if I wanted to flag down the bartender. My arm purposefully brushed his in my ploy, sending a zing of electricity across my skin.

Frowning, I glanced at him and met a pair of gorgeous sapphire eyes dusted in golden lashes. Wow, his face up close was a sight to behold. Chiseled perfection. His mouth seemed to beg me to taste him, drawing me in, consuming my vision.

Rick's dare appealed far more than it should.

What would this stranger do if I just laid one on him? Would he kiss me back? Push me away? Gasp?

I leaned closer, enthralled by the mystery of his reaction, addicted to the allure of his lips. He hadn't even said a word, barely even met my gaze, and already I would beg him for a night in bed.

"Who are you?" I marveled, completely in awe of his existence. I trailed my fingers up his jacket-clad arm, needing to touch him, to be near his energy, his pure presence.

He appeared equally as captivated, his throat working as

he swallowed. His ocean-blue gaze ran over my features, his tongue sliding out to slick the seam of his mouth. I eyed the movement like a woman starved, desiring him more than I desired to breathe.

What is happening to me?

This instant draw, this attraction, floored me, forcing me to lean in, needing him, *craving* him. I brushed my lips against his, enthused by the feel of him at first touch.

Oh God...

He grabbed my elbow, his grip tight, pulling me closer. Energy hummed between us as my side aligned with his, his warmth a blanket I didn't know I needed.

"Do you often kiss men you hardly know?" he asked against my mouth, his voice deep, seductive. *Sexy as fuck.*

I shook my head. "No."

"Well, that's something, at least," he whispered darkly, his peppermint breath hot against my tongue. I leaned in for another taste, but his grip on my elbow held me in place beside him. "You want to take a walk?"

The words came off as a demand despite the intended question behind them. "Where to?" I asked, completely under his thrall regardless of the warning bells sounding my head.

He's a stranger. Don't leave with him!
But he feels so familiar, so right...
That's the alcohol talking, sweetheart.
Or something else entirely.

Because I didn't feel drunk at all. The daze and confusion of the shots had already worn off, leaving me hot and needy against this too-strong male. His intoxicating scent was like a drug, infusing me with these urges I didn't understand.

"Outside," he suggested, his bottom lip teasing my mouth by remaining just a hairsbreadth away. I clenched my thighs, his deep tenor sending me into a pit of arousal only he could save me from.

"Who are you?" I asked again, completely lost to him.

13

My gaze held his, my breathing erratic. "What are you doing to me?"

"I could ask you the same, princess," he replied, his hand a brand against my elbow. "Let's go for a walk."

Definitely not a question now.

Yet I found myself nodding, accepting this bizarre proposal despite every logical instinct inside me rioting and demanding I say no.

It's just a walk.

You've lost your mind.

It's the right thing to do…

There was just something about him, something I couldn't quite identify. And my friends wouldn't let me go too far, right?

"Just a walk," I whispered.

"Yes." The word was a promise against my mouth, followed by the briefest of touches that left me *needing* more.

"For a kiss," I all but begged.

He arched a perfectly sculpted brow. "Another one?"

"The other didn't count." We'd barely brushed our mouths, let alone *kissed.*

His hand slid up my arm, leaving a trail of goose bumps in its wake. My chest burned with expectation, my legs shaking in anticipation. He wrapped his palm around the back of my neck, holding me tightly as if he owned me, and firmly pressed his lips to mine.

Fire licked through my veins, heating my body in a way I'd never experienced, the energy inside me roaring to the surface to meet his in a foreign mating I couldn't describe, only *feel.* His touch inflamed my very being, his hand anchoring me to him in the most delicious manner.

And then he cursed.

Loudly.

People around us were screaming.

I blinked, confused. Startled by the chaos erupting throughout the bar.

Then I noticed the scorched walls.

Smelled the scent of burning wood.

Felt the hot wave traveling over the crowd as an inferno surged across the room.

My lips parted on a scream, the stranger wrapping his arms around me, sheltering me from the tornado of sensation beating down upon us just as the world went black.

CHAPTER TWO
EXOS

"SHE BURNED DOWN THE BAR?" Elana's question felt weighted, accusatory. "What did you do to her?"

Oh, it wasn't what I did to her but what *she* did to *me*. "Nothing." I couldn't bring myself to tell the truth, to admit that I'd let her kiss me.

What the hell had she been thinking, anyway? Kissing a complete stranger? For fuck's sake.

Right, more importantly, why had I allowed it?

Because she was gorgeous.

Because she seduced me with her elemental gift for spirit.

Because I'd wanted to taste her plump lips all night despite knowing it was wrong.

I shook my head. "I managed to help most of the

mortals survive, but there were a few casualties." Including one of her friends, which I imagined would not go over well when Claire awoke.

Shit. I scrubbed my hand over my face, exhausted. It'd taken every ounce of my strength to mitigate the damage. My affinity for fire was negligible at best. And Claire had done a number on that bar, her power exploding out of her and diminishing the establishment to ash.

"Well, on a positive note, we have an adequate cover story for her disappearance." Vape lounged in a chair near the floor-to-ceiling windows of Elana's living area, his casual slacks and button-down shirt suggesting he'd been about to retire for the evening when I'd called.

I hadn't known where else to take Claire, Elana being the only Council member I truly trusted with her safety and the story of the bar. She'd brought in Vape, but no one else, and allowed me to lay Claire upstairs in one of the myriad of guest rooms.

Being one of the oldest fae, Elana owned an exquisite piece of land, her manor adorned in flowers and greenery, all animated by her inner Spirit. Our kind controlled life and death of all beings, including the fae. Unlike the others, like Vape, who mastered a specific element, such as water.

"Yes, we'll spin the bar story to claim her as one of the victims of the tragedy. That'll ensure no one searches for her." Elana stood near a master piano, her hip resting against the hard surface. Her youthful appearance belied her ancient aura. A human would think her maybe thirty, but I knew her to be closer to a thousand years old. It was her ties to Spirit that kept her looking younger, unlike Vape, who showed his age in the creases of his pale skin and the white coloring of his long hair.

"Can you train her?" he asked, his midnight gaze resembling a black pit of wisdom. "Or is she too dangerous for the Academy?"

Goose bumps threatened to pebble over my skin at the memory of Claire's energy. I'd never felt anything like it.

"She's powerful," I admitted, palming the back of my neck to diffuse the chill rising at the top of my spine. "But my Spirit can tame hers." It'd taken a great deal of strength—more than I'd ever used before—to temper her gift, but I'd managed it. "I can train her."

What I really meant to say was, *I'm the only one who can train her.*

Elana might be my elder, but my pure royal blood elevated my status, making me far stronger than she could ever be.

Unfair, yes.

But such was life.

Not even my brother could stand up to my affinity for Spirit, which was why the Royal Crown technically belonged to me. However, I'd chosen to abdicate my throne in favor of a warrior life, providing Cyrus with the opportunity to lead.

The arrangement suited us both.

"Then it's settled," Elana murmured, her silver-gray eyes glittering as she smiled. "I recommend the Fire Quad since that's her secondary strength, as well as your own."

"You wish for me to reside with Claire?" I asked, uneasy.

"She needs a protector. I think you're the only one suitable for the job."

I sighed, my hands in my pockets as I leaned against the tree in the middle of her living room. "I'll make the arrangements." Because she was right. Not only was I the only one who could keep Claire's abilities in check, but I also happened to be one of the few who preferred her alive. Most others would use the opportunity to kill her for the sins of her mother.

"She needs more than a single protector," Vape said as if reading my mind. "The girl requires an army of bodyguards."

"Which we don't have." Elana sounded frustrated, likely because our fae brethren were refusing to acknowledge and accept one of our own. She advocated for peace and harmony among the Fae Kingdoms, which was why she'd created the Academy—a place where all the Elemental Fae were forced to bond. Yes, they had separate quads and specific core classes, but there were numerous activities that brought the fae together, such as sporting events where gifts were not allowed and general education courses covering human studies and other useful, employable skills.

"That's a lot to put on one fae." Vape's tone suggested how he felt about that—unconfident. "An important fae at that."

"I volunteered for the job." Not exactly true—more that I was the only one capable of handling this task and wouldn't wish it on another. "I'll keep her safe."

"And what about you?" Vape countered. "Who will keep you safe as one of the two remaining royals of the Spirit lines?"

My lips curled. "I keep myself safe." And I dared anyone who thought otherwise to try to fuck with me. "I'm not concerned."

Elana smiled. "You're so much like your father, Exos. He'd be proud to—"

A shriek upstairs had all three of us straightening.

"Seems Sleeping Beauty is awake," Vape drawled, amusement in his expression.

Crash.

I darted to the windows, peering out into the early morning surroundings, the sun a distant pink on the horizon.

"She knocked down a tree," I said, my brow furrowing. "How the hell did she knock down a tree?" I would have felt her use of Spirit, my own energy having tied itself to hers days ago when I started tracking her. A whirlwind of water and air formed outside, uprooting several trees in its wake and heading toward the house. "Oh, *fuck.*"

I ran up the stairs without a backward glance, vaguely aware of Vape and Elana on my heels, and shoved open the door to the guest room.

19

Claire stood in the center of a room of roses and vines, her blonde hair tangled, her blue eyes wild as they darted around what she likely perceived as a garden of sorts. She stilled when she caught me standing in the doorway, her hands curled at her sides, her full lips falling open.

My Spirit reached for hers, stroking her with soothing vibrations meant to calm her inner turmoil. This was one of my personal skills—my ability to manipulate and persuade others, to lull them into a state of my choosing.

Calm down, I urged, eyeing the dissolving tornado outside.

Thank. Fuck.

It was working.

Her essence was, slowly but surely, responding to mine.

"Is this a dream?" she asked, her soft voice filled with wonder as her shoulders relaxed. She took in the life of the room again, the blooming flowers and the vines slithering up the walls and covering the ceiling in an earthy glow.

I glanced over my shoulder at Elana and Vape. "I'll talk to her."

Elana nodded, understanding that this required delicacy, or we risked overwhelming Claire. Again. "We'll be downstairs, should you need us," the elder murmured.

Vape tilted his head to the side. "One thing first. I sense water. And air."

Yes, I did, too.

And it seemed to be coming from Claire.

She blinked those big blue eyes at me, her brow furrowing. "Who are you?" she asked, her tone holding a hint of marvel. "Why am I dreaming this?"

Yeah, time to have a chat. "We'll be down in a bit." I didn't wait for Vape or Elana to reply before softly closing the door and locking myself in the guest room with Claire. We needed privacy for this discussion.

Claire twirled, her skirt riding high on her long, sexy legs, her arms loose at her sides. She tilted her head back on a smile filled with wonder and excitement. "Oh, it's beautiful

ELEMENTAL FAE ACADEMY: BOOK ONE

here. I feel so alive. So... happy." More dancing, her Spirit clearly drunk on mine. Apparently, I'd soothed her a little too much.

Right. Time to ground her.

"Claire," I murmured, sitting on the bed of flowers she'd awoken upon. The mattress beneath was made of earth, the bed frame crafted from the trees outside. I preferred more modern accommodations, but every fae embraced the elements differently. It seemed Claire liked this style of décor. She bent to touch the roots decorating the floor, her skirt lifting to reveal the curves of her ass.

"Claire." Her name came out a bit strangled this time, my need for her to, well, *stop*, taking over. "Can you look at me, please?"

"Oh, yes." She turned, her gaze traveling over me with unveiled interest. "I will happily look at you. But as it's my dream, I'd really prefer you without clothes so I know what I'm working with here."

I coughed as a jolt of heat seared my insides. "Okay, well, first things first. You're not dreaming."

"Riiiighhhhtt," she drawled. "We're playing hard to get. Is that it?"

"No, we're not playing anything. You're not dreaming. This is the Fae Realm, where I brought you after the fire."

Her brow furrowed. Then she burst out laughing and folded over from the force of it.

I supposed, in her shoes, I'd react similarly. The world around her was nothing like the one she'd grown up in, her version of a forest a destructed beast due to humanity's lack of understanding. Fae, however, embraced the wilderness, allowing it into our homes and living peacefully with nature rather than against it.

"Claire, I'm telling you the truth," I tried again, my voice soft. "I meant to ease you into this, to bring you here of your own free will, but burning down the bar forced my hand. Your powers are awakening now that the charm has finally worn off, and you need to be among your kind."

21

She laughed harder, sitting on one of the roots on the floor, her arms wrapped around her middle. "Oh God, seriously. This is the most fucked-up dream I've ever had."

"Because it's not a dream," I replied through my teeth. "You're in the Fae Realm."

"Uh-huh." She wiped at the tears beside her eyes. "Because fairies are real."

"Not fairies. Fae."

"There's a difference?"

"Yes. Fairies are a myth. Fae are real."

"Oh. Okay. That clears it up." She fought a smile and lost, her lips curling again as another laugh fell from her mouth.

Gods, give me strength and patience; I'm going to need it. "Let's try a new path," I suggested, thinking out loud. "Tell me about your parents, Claire."

All signs of mirth disappeared, her brow furrowing. "What? No. I don't want to talk about that at all."

"Too bad. I want you to tell me about them."

"And I don't want to," she countered. "Fuck off."

"Not a dream, Claire," I told her, yet again. "Can't just make me disappear. Tell me about your parents."

"No."

"Why not?"

"Because I don't want to," she repeated.

"That's a shitty reason. There are a lot of things in this life I don't want to do, such as be here with you now, but we all have a sense of duty, a purpose we can't ignore. And I want to talk about your parents. Specifically, your mother, Ophelia." A cruel tactic, yes, but it seemed to be breaking through some of the fog in her mind, because her pupils contracted, her focus astute.

"I don't want to talk about this," she whispered.

"What do you know about your mother?" I wondered, ignoring the petulant turn of her mouth. "I'm guessing not much since you grew up in the Human Realm." And her father died shortly after Ophelia's demise. "What did your grandparents say about her?" That was who had raised her in Ohio, the mortals seemingly oblivious to Claire's natural birthright. "Because you look just like her, Claire. Did they tell you that?"

"Stop."

I didn't. She clearly needed a push to realize this wasn't a dream, to truly grasp her surroundings and purpose. *To grow the fuck up.* "She placed a charm on you, a hex of sorts, that dismantled your true nature. It finally unraveled yesterday, on your twenty-first birthday. Do you feel it? The gift of energy flooding your veins? Your affinity for the elements? You asked me at the bar who I am, remember? You *recognized* my essence. Because you're one of us. You're a fae. Your mother—"

"*Stop.*" She balled her hands into fists, her gaze narrowed. "Just. Stop."

"I can't." And I wouldn't even if I could. "You need to hear this, Claire. You need to understand *who* and *what* you are. And unfortunately, I don't have a lot of time to ease you into this since you're already in the Fae Realm. Your mother—"

A blast of wind blew me backward into the wall, my head knocking against the vines with a snap that I felt all the way down my spine.

Claire gasped, her hand flexing before her. "Oh God, oh God, oh God." She jumped to her feet, tripping over the root behind her and landing on her ass. "Oh God!"

I wheezed, pushing away from the wall. *Definitely has an affinity for air, too.*

"This… this…" she stammered, her hands feeling around on the floor, her eyes taking on a wild gleam. "This can't be happening. This isn't real. I need to wake up." She pinched her side, causing me to frown.

"Does that ever actually work?"

"Stop talking to me," she demanded, hurling another blast of wind at me with her fingertips.

My jaw snapped to the left from the localized blast,

23

reminding me of a punch to the fucking face. "*Ow.*"

"Oh, fuck! I'm… Shit!" She scrambled toward me, then backward, then froze with her hands beneath her. As if that would stop her.

A knock on the door had her petrified gaze flying sideways as Vape's deep tenor floated through the wood. "Everyone all right in there?"

"Just getting acquainted," I replied through my teeth.

"Sounds like she's kicking your ass, son" was his reply.

I snorted. "Because I'm fighting with both hands tied behind my back."

Claire's eyebrows shot up. "Where am I?"

I couldn't help my resulting sigh. It wasn't like I hadn't said this about a hundred times already. "The Fae Realm."

"The *what?*" she squeaked, shaking her head. "That's not a thing. That's not real."

"It's very real and you're currently inside it." I massaged my jaw, stretching my neck to loosen it. She lifted her hand again, forcing me to add, "Hit me with another blast of air, princess, and I'll retaliate." I wouldn't hurt her, but I would pin her. Our first lesson? Control.

Her lower lip trembled, but her teeth audibly clenched. "What the fuck is going on?"

Did this woman have a hearing problem? Because I swore we just went through this. "It all relates back to your mother, Cl—"

Energy quaked around me, causing the bed to collapse to the floor, the headboard disappearing into a pile of ashes as flames erupted around us.

Claire screamed.

I cursed.

And tackled her to the ground.

CHAPTER THREE
CLAIRE

THIS ISN'T REAL.
This isn't happening.
Everything will be fine when I wake up.
I just need to—

"Claire!" The furious growl came from the man on top of me, his striking blue eyes glowing with fury. "Focus on me, on my voice."

I'd really rather not.

I just wanted to go home.

To wake up.

To escape.

To be anywhere other than here, with this man who kept talking about my mother, the woman who abandoned me as a child, who shattered my father's spirit. Grandma always said she killed my dad when she broke his heart. He never recovered.

I hated my mother, couldn't stand to hear anything about her. Childish, yes, but it was how I survived, how I escaped my reality.

My memories of my parents were nonexistent, having been too young when she left us, too young when my father *died*.

I shook, tears of the past clouding my eyes. Remembering hurt. Thinking about them *hurt*. I didn't want to be here. I didn't want to hear about *her*. I just wanted to wake up, to be done with this horrible nightmare.

"Breathe," the man on top of me demanded. "Come on, princess. Listen to me. I need you to calm down, to breathe, to *focus*. Search for the tranquility inside you, call on it, pull it into you and use it."

What the fuck is he even talking about? It could be a different language, for all I knew or cared.

"Claire," he whispered, his lips dangerously close to mine. "Please, sweetheart, I need your focus, or you're going to burn the house down. I'm still exhausted from earlier. Just close your eyes and think of a peaceful place. Describe it for me."

A peaceful place? I thought hysterically, nearly laughing. "Not fucking here!" I shouted, warmth flooding my insides, spilling through my fingertips and raging around me. "Let me go!"

"I can't do that," he said, his palms on my face, forcing me to look at him, to *see* him.

My eyes widened. "You're on fire!"

"I'm aware," he gritted out, wincing. "Just… breathe, Claire. Breathe for me. Slowly."

"You're on fire," I repeated, my heart galloping in my chest. How was breathing going to help? If anything, it'd make this worse, right? Smoke inhalation?

Except, nothing but clean air met my nostrils and mouth.

My brow furrowed.

How is that possible?

And why am I not burning?

I actually felt quite cold, not hot. Because the flames were so intense I was freezing? No, that couldn't be it.

"That's it," he whispered, his forehead falling to mine. "Relax."

"Relax?" Some strangled combination of a laugh and a cry escaped my mouth. "This is… *insane*."

"You're an Elemental Fae coming into her abilities for the first time." The words were low, his voice utterly calm despite the inferno soaring around us. "It's not normal for someone this age to access her elemental gifts. Most fae are taught as children. But I can help you, Claire."

I shivered beneath him, my skin slick, my throat dry. "Help me?" I whispered, my gaze flickering to the wildfire behind him and back to his face. "This is a nightmare. It has to be."

"It's not." The words were a breath against my lips, his body hard and heavy on top of mine. "Please, Claire. Let me help you."

"How?" I asked, unsure of all of this. Of him. Of this place. Of the erratic energy threatening to burst out of my chest. "*How?*"

His nose brushed mine, his fingers sliding into my hair, his mouth trailing over my cheek. His gentle caress set off a flurry of butterflies in my abdomen, a direct conflict from the warning rioting in my mind. The man was *on fire*. Yet he seemed perfectly at ease, his strong form a comforting blanket over mine.

What is happening to me?

My eyelids drooped, exhaustion taunting the edges of my thoughts.

I don't want to sleep.

"Picture your happy place," a deep voice whispered against my ear. "Somewhere that makes you feel calm, at peace. For me, it's the lake behind my old home. So warm and tranquil, and I swear the water tasted of the finest spring you could ever imagine. Swimming is my serenity, where I go when I need to think. What about you, Claire? Where do you go?"

"I…" I swallowed, hesitant. "Camping. Beneath the stars. I love the night sky." *Why am I telling him this?*

"The stars here are beautiful, too. You'll see them tonight." His lips touched my throat, my pulse soaring in response. "Where did you go camping, Claire?"

"In Ohio," I whispered, frowning. My grandparents used to take me to the woods, saying I needed to be closer to nature, to enjoy the fresh air and clear my head. I always loved it, feeling almost at home surrounded by the elements.

Wasn't that what this man had called me? *An Elemental Fae?*

"What's an Elemental Fae?" I asked out loud, my limbs tensing.

"It's what we are." He went to his elbows on either side of my head, causing my eyes to flutter open. He was no longer on fire, the room around us just as green as before.

What the hell is going on?

"Shh, stay in that calm place," he said, his thumb drawing a line across my cheekbone and down to the column of my neck. "I'm strong, but you… You're exhausting me, Claire."

My brow furrowed. "*I'm* exhausting *you*?"

"Yes." He cocked his head, his blue irises taking on a heady glow that stole my breath. "Your… *Ophelia*… was a fae. A pureblood of Spirit. That makes you a Halfling. A very, very strong Halfling."

"Ophelia?" I repeated, frowning.

"The given name of your…" He trailed off, raising a brow.

My mother, I realized. "My mother was a fairy?"

"A fae," he corrected, his lips curling down. "Fairies are tiny little figments with wings, and they don't exist. You're a *fae*. As am I."

28

"And fae are…?"

"Supernatural beings with affinities for the elements." He sounded so nonchalant, as if this type of topic were discussed every day. "Ophelia was a Spirit Fae, like me. And—"

"Spirit Fae?" I repeated. "What the hell does that mean?"

"A fae who connects with life and death." He balanced on one arm, lifting his palm. "Try not to freak out."

"Okay…"

He eyed me for a long moment, then refocused on his hand. It glowed, energy shivering over my skin, as a gorgeous lily appeared, blossoming into the size of my head, with big white petals.

"How did you do that?" I marveled, awed.

"Life," he said, tucking the flower stem behind my ear. "You, too, have access to the same gift. And with time, I'll teach you how to use it."

Uh, right. He'd lost me again.

"You're saying I can do that?"

"Yes," he confirmed. "In addition, it seems, to several other things." He stared down at me for a long moment, his gaze dropping to my mouth before flicking back up to my eyes. "I'm going to roll off of you now. Can you try to stay calm?"

He really enjoyed that word. *Calm. Relax. Breathe.* "Sure." I could feign calm if it kept the crazy man content.

A flower just blossomed in his fucking hand.

And I'm in a room shrouded in… forest.

I pinched my side again.

Nothing.

This can't be real.

But it certainly *felt* real.

"You're not dreaming," he said softly, clearly catching my not-so-subtle pinch.

I slid away from him, bracing my back against the tree—*yes, a fucking tree*—in the center of the room. "Fae Realm."

"Yes." He drew his knees upward, wrapping his forearms around them. "I know it's a lot to take in, and you still don't believe me, but you'll see."

"And if I want to go home?"

He shook his head. "You can't, Claire. Your powers are too much for the mortal realm. You destroyed that bar."

My brow furrowed. "What bar? When? I don't…" A vision tickled my thoughts. One of him in his leather jacket, sitting on a stool, his lips a hairsbreadth from mine. And then flames, like the ones that had adorned his back only moments ago, encircling us and expanding. "No… That… *No.*" That couldn't have happened. It couldn't be real. "Tell me…" I paused, swallowing. "Tell me that's not… Tell me it didn't…" But I felt the truth of it somewhere deep inside, heard the reminiscent screams as everyone bolted into the night.

Oh God…

"Tell me I didn't…" I couldn't finish, my hand covering my mouth. *Rick, Brittany, Amie…*

"I'm sorry," the stranger whispered, his expression one of sorrow. "Your power burst out of you too suddenly for me to anticipate. I tried to save as many of them as I could, but the destruction was too much."

"I destroyed the bar?" I whispered.

He hung his head, as if he blamed himself. "Yes."

"And my friends?"

His eyes lifted to mine, the answer lurking in his gaze.

"Who?" I demanded. "*Who?*"

"The boy," he said.

"*Rick?*" Oh God… I pinched my side again, but it was futile. I would *never* dream this. Not even in a nightmare. "I killed Rick?"

"It's not your fault, Claire. You didn't—"

"*Not my fault?*" I shrieked. "You said I burned down the damn bar!" I jumped to my feet, mindful of the roots in this stupid, tiny, forest-laden room. Such a lie. It felt like I was outside, but I wasn't. And the air closing in around me proved it.

I needed to be free.

To run.

To be in the clean air.

Not locked in this little greenhouse with…

Fuck, I don't even know his name!

Fae Realm.

Powers.

Fire.

Burned-down bar.

I spun, not hearing whatever he was trying to say beside me. Not caring to hear another word. This was too much.

I killed Rick.

Did I? What if he's lying?

Why would he lie?

I don't know. I don't fucking know!

His palm was too hot against my forearm. I twisted out of his grasp, needing space, needing *air*. And as if hearing my call, it whirled around me, blowing him into the wall again with a grunt. His pained expression struck me in the heart, causing me to falter.

I don't know him.

I don't belong here.

"I can't," I breathed, staring at the window, watching as the glass blew out with a breath from my lips. "I'm sorry." I followed the breeze on instinct, letting it carry me down to the grass below, not pausing to think about the how or the why, just needing to *run*.

There had to be a way home. A way back to the bar. A way back to Rick. To my friends. My family.

I couldn't stay here. This wasn't my place. This foreign land of endless trees and flowers and vines. *Oh God, where am I even going? It doesn't matter. Just run.* And I did, sprinting through the fields and beneath the canopy of leaves, then across and more fields, past lakes, and continuing into unending nature.

The sun moved overhead, illuminating my journey,

aiding my attempt to escape.

But nothing new crossed my path. Only more and more trees, denser with every step.

I whirled around, mystified, tears rolling down my cheeks.

"Where am I?" I breathed, falling to my knees in the thick underbrush. "*Where the fuck am I?*"

I collapsed to my side, my exhaustion finally overcoming me. My legs were bleeding, my feet aching, my heart… *broken.*

"I don't belong here," I whimpered, curling into a ball of despair. Leaves seemed to fold around me, cocooning me from the elements, soothing my spirit in a way I could hardly comprehend. But I allowed it. Because what else was I supposed to do?

"Who am I?" I asked, a sob ripping from my chest.

Claire… My name whispered on the wind, my vision blurred by the flutter of butterflies overhead. *Claire…*

I closed my eyes, not wanting to hear another word, refusing to acknowledge this insanity any longer.

This is not my home.

CHAPTER FOUR
TITUS

WHAT A FUCKING MORNING. My head spun from the aftermath of what felt like a dream that had me in a fog for hours.

Something strange was happening, causing the campus to come alive in excitement. And I wasn't in the mood for excitement, something most would say was out of character for me.

However, after my fuckup with Ignis last night, I had good reason. Sleeping with her had been a huge fucking mistake—not that I'd had much choice in the matter—and now she refused to understand the words *never happening again*. I didn't do relationships, especially not with the likes of her. I just wanted to be alone. Heading to the gym and isolating myself in the guys' locker room seemed to be the only place of solace I could find in this damned school.

Normally, I enjoyed the challenge a Fire Fae like Ignis would bring, maybe even indulge her with a round or two before I moved on, but I'd fallen into a temporary funk that I couldn't explain.

I leaned back against the lockers and let my head *thump* against the unforgiving steel. It was the only place on the premises that wasn't covered in nature and shit. I needed metal and grounding. I needed to focus. Closing my eyes, I focused on the flames licking at my insides and threatening to burst out of me. The air around me wavered, and I knew I risked melting school property if I didn't get my shit under control.

"You okay, man?" River asked, wiping both the sweat and conjured water from his face with a towel.

As a Water Fae, he was the only guy who'd dare approach me in an enclosed locker room. That was predominantly why the shy fae and I had become friends over the past year. In some ways, I seemed to be even more isolated than him. A side effect of being the Powerless Champion—winner of the ring where fighting to the death was common and the use of powers meant execution in the most fantastical manner.

One rule: no powers—hence the title the "Powerless Champion."

It took a certain kind of mental state for me to win in that kind of fighting ring, but that had been me for quite a few years. That was before the accident. Before the Academy. Before a friend like River.

Another spasm rushed through my body that left me feeling nauseous. I felt as if I were being pulled somewhere off campus, like my whole body wanted to run. I never ran from my problems, no matter how big or irritating they were.

Rubbing the back of my neck, I suppressed a groan. Everything hurt as if I'd been back in the fighting ring for weeks, but the days of bashing skulls were behind me. I was trying to turn over a new leaf and control my powers instead of pretending they didn't exist—which had gotten half of my family killed when they finally demanded acknowledgment.

Fuck if that was going as planned.

"I must be sick," I replied to River. I showed him my palm. Instead of veins, embers writhed under my skin like possessed snakes. After so many years of denying myself my powers, they were coming through with merciless greed— or something was calling them to the surface.

Instead of fear, River looked amused. "Must be the curse," he said as he flicked his wrist and sent water splashing onto my skin. Steam hissed immediately and fogged the air, but it felt good.

Waving away the mist, I glowered at him. "Don't tell me you believe in that bullshit, too."

He cocked his brow and strapped the towel around the back of his neck. "So you heard about her?"

Of course I'd heard about her. News of the Halfling was spreading faster than any wildfire I could create. Maybe it was the anxiety surrounding her arrival that set me on edge.

"I have no interest in humans," I said flatly, although the surge of heat in my core suggested otherwise, as if she were somehow the source of all my power trying to burst out of me. Ignoring it, I popped open the locker and snatched my fireproof shirt, stretching the fibers before pulling it over my head. "Why don't you go take a shower?"

It was a poor attempt at tricking River into leaving me alone. The Water Fae didn't need a proper shower, not with his powers fully under control.

Showing off, River spritzed himself with a splash of water and stepped closer to me to evaporate the excess. He grinned before pulling his shirt over his head.

"You know the Halfling is a female… right?" River waggled his brows, no doubt hoping to entice me to go check her out for ourselves. He would be far too shy to approach her, but he was always fascinated by humans. He took every elective and training session he could get his hands on to study the short-lived race.

I rolled my eyes. "I don't care what she is. I don't want to see another girl right now."

Just when I was about to lean back onto the lockers again, River took me by the wrist and yanked hard. He flushed his grip with water that sent fresh steam into the air and protected him against my burning skin. "Stop pouting," he said. "We both know Ignis is waiting right outside, and you've been avoiding her. It's time to confront her and get the bullshit out of the way. Then we can go sniff out the Halfling and see if she's put a curse on you," he added with a smirk.

I narrowed my eyes but allowed River to drag me out of the locker room. He was right. The sooner I faced Ignis and told her to fuck off, the sooner I'd feel better. Something was wrong with me, and I didn't need to be stressing about her right now.

Sunlight made me wince when we stepped out into the cool exterior of the gym. It wasn't like my pad back in the Fire Kingdom, with iron and walls that blocked out the elements. The Academy encouraged all elements to play freely, meaning an exercise and training building would be open for all. Enormous windows spanned the ceiling, allowing wind and light to slip through to caress the great oaks and vines that acted as climbing walls with shifting footholds. I let my eyesight adjust, and three female fae came into focus.

Ignis glowered at me, tall and furious. Her red hair curled around her cheeks in a way that could have made her look innocent if it hadn't been for the tiny flames that licked across her fingertips.

I groaned when I saw that she'd brought reinforcements. The Water Fae, Sickle, and the Air Fae, Aerie, stood on either side of her with hatred blazing in their eyes.

"Thank you, River," Ignis said curtly and waved him away as if she'd ordered him to retrieve me, which she likely had.

River ducked his head and let go of my wrist, but I spotted the mischievous glint in his eyes as he glanced up at me through the shaggy hair covering his face. The bastard thought this was immensely entertaining. "I'll catch up with you at the entrance," he muttered, stuffing his hands into his pockets and shuffling out of sight.

I sighed. "Look, Ignis—"

She stormed up to me and slammed a crooked finger into my chest. Any other fae would have gotten burned by an act like that, but her fire seemed to have grown overnight—after she'd tricked me into sleeping with her.

Damn it.

I was a moron.

"Why have you been avoiding me?" she snapped. "You're mine now, Titus. You and I fucked, which is a binding contract between Fire Fae for at least a month's time."

Well, she wasn't going to beat around the bush about it, was she?

She grinned, no doubt thinking she had me right where she wanted me. I was going to be her trophy for a month? No fucking way was that going to happen.

I matched the fire in her eyes with my own. Maybe if we'd been back in the Fire Kingdom, I'd have to indulge her—no matter if she'd poisoned me with seduction magic or not—but not here, not in the Academy, where freedom was encouraged and elemental customs wavered.

That didn't make my predicament much better. She would fight for this particular custom to be enforced if only to imprison me to her side and add to the growing reputation as a Fire Fae not to be messed with. Taming the Powerless Champion no doubt was on the top of her list of recent achievements and would reduce my pride to the most withering of embers when she was done with me.

The most logical prevention would have been to not sleep with her, and of course I knew better than to stick my

LEXI C. FOSS & J.R. THORN

dick in this crazy bitch. Just because I had a playboy reputation didn't mean I always acted on it. No one would believe me if I told them that she'd tricked me into sleeping with her.

Seduction magic was a black-market commodity and not permitted on Academy premises, but I still had the sour aftertaste of its recognizable compulsion in my mouth. The bitch had stoked flames that weren't intended for her, which was likely what had left me feeling so off right now. She might have gotten a taste, but never again.

Growling, I gripped her fingers and forced her arm to bend backward. Like most fae, she was graceful and lean, but she was still of the fire element. With the amount of power coursing through her right now, I suspected she might even be a suitable match if we really went head-to-head. I'd already gotten dinged for fighting this year and couldn't afford another mark.

"I'm not interested in entertaining your fantasies, Ignis. You might have tricked me into your bed, but in the light of day, I see you for what you really are." I leaned in, enunciating my words carefully. "Not. My. Type." I let go of her arm. "I'll watch my drinks with a closer eye from now on. Don't think you can trick me again."

Ignis stumbled, overacting the motion as if I'd hurt her. Her eyes brimmed with crocodile tears, and her friends rushed to her side. "You would accuse me of spiking your drink?" she shrieked.

"You brute!" Sickle snapped at me, her voice grating against my ears with the icy edge of her power, making me wince. "How could you treat a kindred fae like Ignis so poorly? What a horrid accusation!"

I narrowed my eyes and crossed my arms over my chest, which was more of a motion to try to keep the growing inferno contained than anything else. "When she acts like a kindred fae, perhaps I'll treat her in the manner worthy of her station."

Ignoring them, I flared my heat, allowing enough of it to

singe the air until the fae instinctually backed off, allowing me through.

Normally, I would have been flattered that a powerful Fire Fae would have thought me untouchable enough to have to spike my drink to procure a night with me, but now I just felt angry, manipulated, my pride bruised. Seduction magic might not be permitted on campus, but it wasn't entirely illegal generally because it couldn't force someone into bed unless an ember of desire existed in the first place. It grew passions; it didn't create them.

But I didn't even *like* Ignis, let alone find the devilish female attractive.

No, something felt wrong. My powers were stirring restlessly inside of me, as if on the brink of chaos. And it had started late last night.

Which, from what I had heard, was when the Halfling had arrived in our realm.

Whispers reached my ears, all of the other fae talking about her.

"I heard she's killed already. Should she really be here?"

"Is she bound?"

"Who is her mentor?"

"I heard she's hot!"

Growling, I found River leaning against the entrance and brushed past him. "Since when do you play lapdog to Ignis?"

He shrugged, a little sheepish. "She's a little scary, if you haven't noticed."

"Oh, I've noticed." Damn female had bitten me last night, too. Leaving her claim proudly on my neck. "She's—"

"You," Exos interrupted, his sapphire eyes trained on me. From the state of his shredded clothes, he'd been in a battle or two—on the losing end, for sure.

My eyes widened. The Royal Prince of Spirit Fae was a legend, his connection to Spirit magic the strongest anyone had ever seen, his affinity for fire besting several of my brethren. "Yes?" I asked him, unsure if I should bow or refer to him formally. "Uh, Your Highness?" *What are you doing here?* I wanted to ask.

Then it struck me.

He's here because of the Halfling.

Exos leveled me with a powerful gaze. "I need you to come with me."

I didn't ask questions. When a Royal Fae issued a demand, everyone adhered to it. Especially when that Royal Fae was a legendary Fae Warrior. Like Exos.

He led us—me and River, who had insisted on tagging along—deep into the forest surrounding the Academy, having already shown us the destruction at Chancellor Elana's home just off campus. In a quick debrief, Exos had informed us that he'd been put in charge of the Halfling's protection, and lost her.

Which was why he needed me.

The girl's affinity for fire had left a string of smoky notes in the air, too faint for him to catch. And I was the strongest Fire Fae within immediate reach.

"Keep up. I need your proximity to sense her," Exos said, his feet moving quickly over the exposed roots and fallen leaves.

Great, giant boughs seemed to sway away from Exos as we followed the faint scent of the most powerful fire magic I'd ever felt—and that was saying something. "You're sure she only just came into her powers?" I ventured, struggling to keep myself from sprinting past the fae. Not only was I strong, but I was fast, too, and now that I had her trail, I wanted to follow it.

"Yes, and so far, I sense multiple elements from her. Spirit and Fire, of course, but also Air and Water." He glanced back at River, who trailed behind us. "Is he going to be up to the task? The Halfling is powerful."

I nodded, confident in River's ability. When his head was on straight, he was strong—stronger than even he realized. "He'll be able to help."

Exos gave a curt nod before reaching out a hand to stop us. "Good, because she seems to enjoy playing with fire." He sounded disgruntled over that, which explained some of his singed attire.

"Hold on," I said, my nostrils flaring as I picked up the tendrils of her smoky power. "She's near."

"Lead us" was Exos's reply, his vigilant gaze sweeping the grounds.

My eyes darted across the clearing we'd stepped into. It presented a calm facade, an oasis that now descended into dusk with the softness of purple butterflies lazily lingering over the sleepy meadow. But I sensed the Halfling, her exquisite aura of molten iron mixed with a tornado of power that dared me to take a single step closer.

Exos eyed me warily as I followed the tug that seemed to grow straight from my chest toward a heap of flowers with the shadow of a curled form hidden beneath the colorful earth. Was that her?

I inched closer, studying the sleeping Halfling lying on a makeshift bed of roses. Her skin glowed with inner embers that seemed to react to my presence, making me suck in a breath at her beauty.

Fuck.

I'd never seen a creature quite like this. Soft blonde strands draped over a delicate face marred by little brown spots that gave me the peculiar urge to stoop down for a closer look. Fae didn't have flaws, but humans did. It made her endearing, gorgeous, and exotic.

Without thinking, I crouched beside her and trailed my fingers up her arm, smoothing over the volcanic heat that called to me. She shifted in her sleep, her eyebrows knitting with a surge of discomfort before she quieted again, seeming to accept me. My touch went up to her rounded ears, so different from my own.

Then her eyes opened and the most alluring blue irises trapped me in a piece of heaven.

"Hi there, beautiful," I whispered, smiling.

41

Her pupils shrank like I'd given her a shot of adrenaline, and the ground rumbled.

She screamed in utter terror and surprised me with a gust of wind, sending me flat on my ass. Exos and River shouted something, but I lifted a hand to stop them.

Just in time, too.

A ring of fire erupted around us as the Halfling shot to her feet. Her chest heaved like a bird trapped in a cage, and she flung her face left and right, trying to gather her bearings. "Fuck, I just woke up, so either this is one of those trick dreams or..."

"Not a dream!" Exos shouted unhelpfully from the other side of the flames.

Sighing, I examined the flames the Halfling had sprung into existence. Powerful, yes, but manageable. Sensing the ignition she'd established, I snapped my fingers and sent the fires fizzling into ash.

She startled, blinked at me, then took a step back. "Did you just...?"

"Exterminate your little fire frenzy? Yeah, sweetheart." I grinned. "You're not the only one who likes to play with fire."

"We need to get her back to the estate," Exos growled.

Again, not helpful.

The Halfling seemed stressed by his voice, and energies hummed around her, threatening to explode again. If she called on one of her other elements, I'd be useless.

"Hey," I said softly, lowering myself to one knee. I knew I could be intimidating at my full height, but I wouldn't wish any harm to come to this creature. "We're not here to hurt you, sweetheart."

"Yeah? Tell that to *him*." She pointed at Exos, causing me to fight back a smile.

"I'm not him," I told her, offering her a conspiratorial glance. "I barely know him, actually. But I can see the lack of appeal." Dangerous words to say about a Royal Fae, but I'd deal with the consequences later.

She blinked, startled. "What?"

I cocked my head to the side, allowing my lips to tilt in a way I knew charmed most of the female fae at the Academy. "He demanded I help find you. I'm Titus."

Another blink, this one slower. "Titus?"

"That's me."

She swallowed, looking at Exos and River, then took in her surroundings again. "Where the hell am I?"

"The enchanted boundaries," I informed her, still on my knee, staring up at her. It left me in a far more vulnerable position that seemed to be easing her nerves at least a little.

"I don't know what that means." She shook her head. "I don't know what any of this means."

Exos hadn't given me a lot of insight into what she knew, just that she was a powerful Halfling and her name was Claire, but her knowledge of our world seemed to be very little. "They're the protective borders around the Academy. It's the only area in the Fae Realm where all the elements are allowed to play together, and we learn how to coexist." A load of shit, really. It was all a political game to force the different elements to get along, to live in harmony.

"Fae Realm," she repeated on a breath, her shoulders beginning to shake. "It's all real."

"For fuck's sake," Exos said, his fingers combing through his ash-blond hair.

The pixie of a woman took a step backward, her gaze snapping to his, then to mine, then to his again. "I-I didn't mean to... to..."

"Blow me into a wall? *Again*?" he asked.

Tears gathered in her eyes, her lower lip trembling. "This can't... I don't..."

"How did you blow him into a wall?" I asked, genuinely curious. "Can you do it again? Maybe into a tree?"

"Wh-what?" she asked, her big blue eyes refocusing on me.

"Sorry, it just sounds amusing as hell. Can you do it again?" I didn't really want her to, but I did want to distract her. "Not many fae can take on someone as famous as Exos, so you've intrigued me."

"Exos?" she repeated, her brow furrowing.

"Dude, you didn't even tell her your name?" I asked, shocked and dismayed. "No wonder she kicked your ass."

"I brought you here to help, kid. Not to be a pain in my ass."

"Kid?" I repeated, raising my brows. "I'm twenty-two, *Your Highness.*"

He gave me a look that said he couldn't care less. "Fine. *Man.*"

"Better," I agreed, shifting my attention back to the girl who was observing us with a furrowed brow. Much better than the terrified-little-mouse expression. "Seriously, can you blow him into a tree for me? All I can do is light him on fire, and he'll just extinguish the flames." Not exactly true. I could burn him if I tried hard enough.

"Fire," she whispered, her expression pained.

"Yes," I said slowly, confused. "I'm a Fire Fae."

"She's thinking about the bar." Exos folded his arms. "Which I already told her wasn't her fault."

She crumpled to the ground, her knees giving out beneath her, tears tracking down her face. "A bar?" I asked, inching toward her. "What about it?"

"R-rick," she breathed, her palm covering her heart.

"Her friend," Exos translated. "He... He didn't make it."

The woman let loose an agonized scream, flames singeing the air and igniting my soul. I caught the embers before they could cause any damage, blanketing her in my essence and forcing her fiery abilities to behave as she broke down before my eyes.

"What the hell?" River asked, taking the words right out of my mouth. "What friend? What bar?"

Exos blew out a breath. "Short version: Her powers exploded in the Human Realm. She burned down a building—with her friend inside."

And he couldn't have told us that *before* we found her?

"Fuck," I breathed, rubbing my hand down my face. *"Fuck."*

CHAPTER FIVE
CLAIRE

I COULDN'T SEE.

Couldn't breathe.

Couldn't think.

Rick's dark eyes flashed before me, his sexy-as-sin grin, his ridiculously spiky hair. I cradled my chest, the burn radiating throughout my body intense. I wanted to scream. To cry. To run. But my limbs refused to move, some invisible weight holding me captive in my cocoon of flowers.

Oh God, I'm covered in... in pollen!

None of this made any sense. The surroundings. The colors. The endless forest. The too-orange sun illuminating the field. The male crouching a few feet away...

His dark green eyes reminded me of the trees framing

his muscular form.

I shuddered, curling in on myself, wishing that this would all just go away. That my world would return to normal. That this was all just a drunken nightmare.

Maybe I died in the fire?

I startled at the thought. Was this heaven? That would explain the magic, the odd scents, my bizarre connection to the elements.

"Claire," the one closest to me murmured, his voice deep and soothing and sending a shiver down my spine.

Titus, he'd called himself.

What kind of name is Titus?

"Everyone will tell you it wasn't your fault," he murmured, lying down on his side and bringing our heads to the same level, about five feet of flowers separating us. "But I know those words don't help. I used to hear them all the time. It made me so angry because no one understood. The guilt is suffocating. The agony of loss soul-destroying. And you feel so lonely, so incredibly alone."

Sadness tinged his handsome features, pulling down his brow and his full lips. Dark memories tainted his green gaze, his history etched into the rigid lines of his long, lean body. His elbow drew up to pillow his head of thick, auburn locks, his presence somehow soothing rather than terrifying.

I didn't know him at all.

Yet I felt that strange draw to him, just like I had with the other one. An inkling to trust, to fold myself against him, to escape in the heat of his skin.

"I'm losing my mind," I whispered. "Completely losing my fucking mind."

Titus chuckled. "Yeah? Me, too, sweetheart. Me, too."

I couldn't help the laugh that escaped me. Here this man was, an utter stranger, lying on the ground with me, commiserating over our fall into the land of insanity.

"That's a lovely sound," he murmured. "If a little broken."

"This is crazy." I shook my head, rolling to my back to

stare blankly up at the cloudless sky. "I… I don't…" No other words came to me, my mind completely shutting down. I had nothing. No comeback. No comment. Probably about a million questions I had no energy to voice. Just… *nothing*.

"I can't even begin to imagine how alarming this must be for you, to have no idea you're part fae while growing up in the Human Realm. Honestly, I don't know much about it, having spent my whole life ingrained in fae society. I mean, I didn't even want to attend the Academy. The Council forced me, which, it seems, they're going to do to you, too. So, I guess I understand a little bit, but to be raised as a human and stolen to this land, I don't blame you at all for thinking it's crazy."

His tenor, soft and calming, lulled me into a strange sense of comfort. I looked at him again. *Really* looked at him.

He resembled a model sprawled out for a photo shoot, apart from the slight downward curve of his mouth. But he truly resembled perfection in an almost inhuman way. There was a powerful air around him, a humming energy that seemed to sizzle between us as I held his darkening gaze.

Then I noticed his ears.

Not round like mine, but slightly pointed.

My brow furrowed. "Why do you look like an elf?"

His eyes widened. "An elf?" A laugh bubbled out of him, deep and humorous and beautiful. Hmm, yes, I did like the way he sounded, both his voice and his chuckles. "I'm a fae, sweetheart. Not an elf."

"Do you all have pointy ears?"

"We do."

"I don't."

"Because you're a Halfling," he said, smiling. "Your mum was a fae. Your da a human."

The way he said *mum* and *da* had my lips twitching again. *Now he sort of sounds like a leprechaun.* But he was missing the trademark red beard.

"What's funny?" he asked, a smile in his voice.

I shook my head. "Nothing." I couldn't call him a leprechaun. He'd just find me even more nuts. Which, of course, I was, considering my surroundings and the fact that I was starting to believe all this nonsense.

Ugh. What choice did I have? Clearly, I wasn't going to wake up. And I couldn't deny the strange sensations coursing through my veins or the slight memory of the bar flickering in my thoughts.

I burned it down.

I killed Rick.

My gaze fell, my shoulders rounding as another spike of pain splintered my chest.

"Hey," Titus said softly. "Stay with me, sweetheart. We'll get through this."

That sensation to laugh again hit me in the gut, my eyes filling with tears. "I don't even know you. You don't know me. I don't know anything or anyone or what the hell is…" I trailed off, tired of repeating the same words over and over. They did nothing to improve my situation, just leaving me to wallow in the same endless cycle of pity and despair.

"I think you'll find you know me quite well," Titus murmured. "Perhaps not about me, or who I am, but your Fire recognizes mine."

"What?" That didn't make any sense. "What Fire?"

"Your inner flame, Claire." He held out his hand, a flicker of light dancing over the tips. "You're strong. Much stronger than you should be."

"I don't understand."

His smile was sad. "I know, sweetheart. But you will." The flames flickered out, his hand falling to the ground. "We want to help you. To teach you."

"Why?"

"Because you're fae. We take care of our own."

"But I burned down the bar…"

"Which wouldn't have happened if you'd been properly trained," he whispered. "I know what it's like to come into your power too early, to not be prepared. It's terrifying. It's consuming. It kills."

"Yes," I agreed, my voice equally quiet.

"I can help you." He reached for me again, his hand so close but not near enough to touch. "Let me show you."

"How?"

"Lift your hand toward mine," he encouraged me. "You'll see."

Somehow I doubted that but found my arm lifting of its own accord, my sense of curiosity piqued. What did he intend to do? Grab me? He could have done that already. It was three against one. I stood no chance here, even with my bizarre… *gifts*.

"Here." He wiggled his fingers, the tips brushing mine as I rolled closer to him. They were warm. Welcoming. Oddly familiar.

Electricity sizzled between us, sending a zap up my arm that had me pulling back.

"Come on, Claire," he urged, amusement flirting with his mouth. "Let me show you."

"That wasn't it?"

He chuckled. "No. That was mutual attraction, not fire."

My eyebrows shot up. "What?" He couldn't mean that we found each other attractive, right? We didn't *know* each other. I mean, sure, he was good-looking. Actually, no, he was *hot*. But… No. I was not attracted to anything or anyone right now, least of all a pointy-eared man with a too-sexy grin.

"It's a fae thing," he said, a pair of adorable dimples flashing. "Our elements sing to each other when we find a potential mate. That's what you felt. Now come on, don't hide." He held out his hand again, but I was too busy gaping at him to move.

Potential mate? What in the fuck? No. Hell no. "Mate?"

"Elements bond for power," he explained. "No more stalling, sweetheart. Let me show you what I really mean."

"You want to be my… *mate*?"

He sighed. "No. I don't want to be anyone's mate. It's just a part of society. You'll feel it with others, especially since you're multi-elemental. It's about matching power to power. And right now, all I want to do is show you how our essences are linked to one another. Please?"

The way he said that final word, the slight dip in his tone, had me feeling warm all over. None of this made any sense, but somehow, for some peculiar reason, I wanted to trust him. To let him show me whatever it was he desired to show me.

Because I found him likable.

Not in a *mate* kind of way—that sounded too permanent and weird and not at all appropriate for a girl my age.

But in a potential date kind of way. Well, apart from the whole Fae Realm, stolen from my home and life, nonsense.

Okay, so maybe not a *date*.

Just stop thinking, I told myself, exhausted. *See what he wants to do.*

What could it hurt?

Nibbling my lip, I extended my arm, laying my hand palm up in the flower bed. His smile reached his gorgeous eyes as he shifted a little closer to link his fingers over mine. More of that electric energy sizzled up my arm, shocking my system and sending a bolt of heat directly to my lower abdomen.

Okay, he's not kidding about the mutual attraction thing. Because wow.

A totally inappropriate and inexplicable reaction.

Just like I had to that guy at the bar.

My gaze darted across the clearing to the leather-clad bad boy, the one Titus had called Exos. He observed us with no expression, his arms crossed as he leaned against a tree along the edge of the field. Another boy stood beside him, his gaze wide with curiosity.

"Why are they watching us?" I asked, my insides tingling with nerves.

"They're watching you," Titus whispered, his fingers

lightly tracing mine. "Your power is a marvel, Claire. It's considered a miracle that Spirit Fae—like Exos—can access two elements."

"Okay." I swallowed, refocusing on his alluring features. "I have fire and air?" A guess because I couldn't remember everything Exos had told me, our time together an emotionally laden blur of moments.

"No." Titus drew a line of fire across my skin, the heat causing me to flinch and gape at the same time.

"That... It doesn't hurt."

He chuckled. "Because your fire responds to mine."

"But you just said I don't have Fire."

"Oh, you have Fire." His irises lifted to mine. "An incredible amount of it, too." He shifted even closer, leaving maybe a foot between our prone forms. He continued his path up my arm, the flame dancing upward, heating me in the most amazing way.

"I like that," I admitted.

"I know." He smiled, continuing his touch over my clothed shoulder to my neck, branding my pulse. "Do you feel the connection between us, Claire? The way my fire flirts with yours? Taunting it to the surface? Warming the air around us?"

I swallowed, my lungs feeling a bit tight. "Y-yes."

"That's your power." His voice dropped to a husky tone that caused my heart to skip a beat.

"What about Air?" I asked.

"Hmm, I'm not an Air Fae." He slid an ember across my jaw and upward into my hairline where he pulled the flower from behind my ear—the flower Exos had put there. "I'm not a Spirit Fae, either." He brought the petals to his nose and inhaled. "But you're both."

"That's three elements."

"Yes," he agreed. "You asked why they're staring at you?"

I nodded, my heart thudding roughly in my chest.

"It's because you don't have access to just two elements,

Claire." He palmed my cheek, his gaze kind. "You have access to all five."

My eyebrows shot upward. "All five?"

His lips twitched. "Trust me, I'm just as shocked as you are, but I can feel it in your essence. You manipulated this field, bringing all these flowers to life to provide you with a bed to rest upon. The air sings your name. My fire is drawn to your fire, just as Exos's spirit is drawn to your spirit, and I can feel the layer of humidity—water—softening your skin. You're very special, indeed."

"But why?"

"I don't know." He drew his thumb across my cheekbone, his caress warm and far too welcome. "But I can help you. That's all we want to do."

"Help me how?"

"By teaching you." His fingers slid into my hair, threading through my tangling blonde strands and drawing them down to my shoulder. "Control is the only way to live with all that power inside of you. I realize you have no reason to trust me, or any of us, but I'm speaking from experience. If you don't allow anyone to train you, those gifts will consume you beyond reason."

I'd always been one to listen to my instincts, and they told me now that he was speaking the truth. Still, something nagged at me. Not about him, or Exos, or even the other boy, but about this place. This *realm*.

It felt as if I didn't belong. Which was likely related to having been brought here without my permission.

But it went beyond that.

Something about this place seemed *dangerous*.

"What are you thinking?" he asked, his tone genuine and curious. "What caused this frown to form?" He pressed his thumb to the edge of my mouth, his comfort with touching me a little unsettling even while feeling right.

We don't know each other.

But I sort of want to know him.

I shook the thoughts from my head, confused by all the

sensations and sounds and *sparks*. "This is all, uh, overwhelming." Not a lie. I just left out the sense-of-danger part. How could I confide that in an essential stranger? In this strange land?

"How about dinner," he suggested.

"Dinner?" I repeated, dubious.

"When's the last time you ate?"

"Uh..." I blinked several times. "I... I don't know."

"Then I'd say dinner is a must." His dimples appeared again, but rather than turn his features boyish, they only seemed to solidify his incredible beauty. "Then maybe we can tour campus together. It'll be quiet, most of the students in their dorms. Maybe you'll see that it isn't too bad here and decide to stay."

Campus? Dorms? Where am I? "Do I even have a choice?" I wondered out loud, referring to dinner and the aforementioned *tour*.

He chuckled. "Depends on your definition of the word. How about we reach that bridge when we're ready to cross it and just take this one step at a time? Dinner first. And I'll answer any and every question you throw at me."

I nibbled my lower lip, considering his proposal. He was right about the *choice*. Did I truly have one when there were no other options?

"Can I, uh, change first?" I asked, noting my soiled state. A long shower sounded appealing. And then maybe some coffee followed by a decent meal.

"Exos can help us arrange that," he said, smiling.

"Exos," I repeated, glancing at the still-emotionless male across the clearing. "Uh, will he be going to dinner, too?"

The man cocked a brow at that, clearly having heard me even from a distance. Which meant he'd heard everything. "Would you prefer I not join you?" he asked, sounding slightly offended.

"Depends on whether or not you're going to be an ass," I said, feeling oddly defensive. He hadn't exactly broken all these details to me in the politest manner, and it was *his* fault

I ended up here. And while I was on that path, I could also lay some of the blame for the bar at his feet because he'd been the one to entice me into that kiss.

No, that wasn't fair.

I couldn't blame him for everything. Only a coward would deny all culpability.

But that didn't mean I had to like him.

He snorted as if hearing my thoughts, or perhaps reading them on my face. "Whatever you want, princess," he said. "Just don't fucking blow me into a wall again."

I winced a little at that, feeling bad again. It wasn't like I meant to shove him with my power; it just sort of happened.

"Can we go now?" he asked, his gaze going to Titus. "Because I've had the day from hell and would love a shower."

And I didn't feel bad anymore. "Ass," I muttered.

Titus chuckled beside me. "You know, Exos, I'm starting to see why all this happened. Your bedside manner sucks."

"Do you speak to all Royal Fae in this manner, or am I a special case?"

Titus paled a little. "I... I'm..."

"Yeah, that's what I thought," Exos said, turning away from the field. "Let's go."

Titus cursed softly, his hand falling from my skin and leaving me cold without him. "We, uh, need to follow him."

"Why?" I asked, not understanding the power play here.

"Because Exos says it's time to go." He stood and held out a hand for me.

"And we have to do what he says?" I asked as I accepted his help up from the ground—mostly because I wanted to touch him again.

"Yes." He linked his fingers through mine, something that seemed a little unconscious on his part. His focus was on the third male, with the floppy hair, waiting for us near the tree line.

"Why?" I pressed as we started forward. "Why do we

have to do what he says?" Because a part of me *really* wanted to disobey him.

"He's a Royal Fae," Titus replied.

"Okay?" That meant little to me.

He glanced at me. "He's the Royal Prince of the Spirit Fae, Claire."

I nearly tripped over the flowers beneath my feet. "Wh-what?" Was that like... like a European prince or something?

"Technically, he's King of the Spirit Fae," the other man mumbled, his cheeks flushing pink. "He, uh, renounced his throne to his brother, preferring the warrior life. But, well, Exos and Cyrus are the last of the royal line. At least until Cyrus finds a mate, which isn't likely since, uh, yeah, you know, most of the Spirit Fae are dead." He didn't look at me the entire time he spoke, his gaze on my bare feet.

"This is River," Titus said, grinning. "He's a Water Fae."

"Hi." He waved, his focus still on the ground.

"Hi," I replied, concerned that I'd offended him somehow. Or maybe he was just shy? "I'm Claire," I hedged, trying to see him through his mop of dark curls.

"I know." He peeked up at me, his eyes widening when he realized I was staring directly at him. He stumbled backward, almost falling, except Titus caught his wrist and yanked him upright.

"She's not going to bite you, dude."

"I-I know," he repeated. "It's j-just that, well, she's... she's *human*."

Titus sighed. "River has an obsession," he told me, glancing sideways.

"And I need a fucking shower," Exos snapped, appearing again on the path. "Can we please go back to Elana's now?"

Titus straightened, his gaze narrowing. "This woman has been through hell, Exos. Cut her some slack."

"Yeah? She's also put me through hell. What a coincidence." He didn't pay me a glance as he turned to lead the way—again.

"I don't want him to go to dinner," I decided.

"Something tells me he won't be giving us much choice," Titus muttered. "He's been assigned as your protector."

"My protector?" I frowned. "Why?"

Titus just shook his head. "Let's just follow him. We can talk about more over dinner, okay? I promise." His words sent a tingle down my spine as if his vow held power and purpose. Maybe it did.

"Dinner," I repeated. A meal. Followed by a tour. And more information. "Okay. Yeah, I can do that."

Because, again, what other option did I have? Hide here in the meadow forever? Hope for some miracle to take me back to Earth?

An idea nagged at me.

Actually... Maybe I could use this all to my advantage to find a way back home. Play along for a while, learn more about these so-called fae, this realm, my supposed gifts, and perhaps escape.

Assuming that was what I wanted.

I frowned. Oh, hell, I had no idea *what* I wanted anymore.

But I did like the sound of a shower and food.

So, yeah. Going with Titus made sense. At least for now.

"I can sense your indecision," he whispered, his lips against my ear. "Just give me the evening, sweetheart. You'll see." A soft flame warmed our clasped hands. "And if you want, I'll show you how to create fireballs. Maybe you can accidentally throw one at Exos."

A snort from the forest ahead said he'd heard that. He must have just disappeared from view but was clearly still waiting on us to follow.

"A fireball," I mused, pondering the possibilities. "Yeah, I think I like that idea."

"Just try not to burn down any more buildings" was his dark reply.

My amusement died.

Yeah.

Okay.

Maybe no fireballs.

Titus sighed beside me. "Spoilsport," he muttered. "I'll show you how to control it, Claire. You have my word."

I nodded mutely, unable to say anything else.

A shower.

Some clothes.

Food.

Hopefully, one of those things would help me feel human again.

Except I wasn't human, not according to these men.

I'm part fae.

Whatever the hell that really means.

I was too exhausted to dwell on it, my limbs aching, my heart shattered. Titus squeezed my hand again, a jolt of heat sliding up my arm to dispel the ice coating my veins. No words, just a touch, one that seemed to thaw some of the pain. He pulled me close, the warmth from his body a comforting blanket over my skin. I leaned into him, absorbing his essence, his kindness, his strength, and allowing it to fuel my steps.

Maybe I really had lost my mind.

Because some foreign part of me trusted him despite our brief acquaintance. Possibly because he felt like the only friend I might have in this strange land.

Or perhaps something more powerful was at play...

CHAPTER SIX
TITUS

CLAIRE CLUTCHED MY HAND TIGHTLY, her body rigid beside mine. Exos had led us back to Elana's estate and disappeared after showing us to one of the guest suites.

"I... I d-don't understand," Claire stammered. "I blew out that wall."

Ah, that explained the elemental essences lurking in this room. I'd felt it all over the property when we arrived, but it grew stronger as we moved upstairs. "Chancellor Elana must have repaired it."

"Chancellor Elana?" Claire repeated, glancing up at me. "How?"

"She's a very powerful fae and the leader of the Academy." I gave her a small smile. "This is her home." And actually quite rare for a student to visit. In fact, this was my first time entering these famous walls.

Claire frowned. "But I destroyed that wall."

"And I fixed it," a voice murmured from down the hallway. Elana appeared with her light hair wrapped up in a bun atop her head and threaded with flowers. She was a gorgeous woman, the awe of many men, and completely unattainable due to her high status. Rumors said she never mated because she didn't want to share her powers. But it was not for a lack of trying by the male fae.

I bowed my head in reverence. "Chancellor Elana."

"Titus," she returned. "Thank you for helping Exos today."

"It was my pleasure." Not a lie. I rather enjoyed lying in that field with Claire. Wrong, yes, but being near her intrigued me. The power brewing under her skin called to my own, marking her as a potential mate. She wasn't the first to call to my inner gifts, but she was the first to excite me by the prospect. "I was just helping Claire change for dinner."

"Ah yes, it is that time, isn't it?" She stopped in front of us, her slender hands clasped before her. "Why don't you and River stay for dinner? I think it may help Claire feel more comfortable."

Oh. I'd meant to take Claire somewhere on the fire campus and give her a tour as well, but if the Chancellor wanted us to join her here, then we didn't have much choice.

The death grip on my hand suggested Elana's words regarding comfort were true. It seemed I'd become Claire's anchor. "We'll stay," I said, the words meant for both of them.

"Excellent." Elana's smile crinkled the edges of her silver-flecked eyes. "I look forward to getting to know you better, Claire. Once upon a time, your mother was one of my favorite students." Sadness filtered through her softening expression. "Well, we'll catch up over dinner. Oh, and I left you something suitable to wear." She tilted her lips again before floating down the hallway in her long, elegant gown.

"Who is that?" Claire whispered, her eyes rounded.

"Chancellor Elana."

"No, I got that part." She shook my head. "I meant… I… I don't know what I meant. She's beautiful."

"Yes. And very powerful." I'd already said that, but it was worth repeating. "She's a Spirit Fae, like you."

"And she knew my mother?"

"Yes. She was your mother's mentor." A very famous history, considering everything that had transpired after the Academy. But now wasn't the time to discuss all that. "Do you need any help? Or do you want to meet me downstairs?"

"I…" She nibbled her lip and glanced at the dress lying on the bed and then at the doorway beyond that led to the en-suite bathroom. "I, uh, should be all right. But you promise to stay?"

Warmth touched my chest at her show of trust. We hardly knew each other, but her inner flame recognized mine already whether she realized it or not. I drew a line of fire across her cheek with my index finger and smiled. "Yes. I'll be here."

Her shoulders seemed to fall on a sigh, her relief palpable. "Okay," she whispered. "I'll meet you downstairs."

I lifted her hand to my lips and kissed her wrist. "See you then, Claire."

Her lips parted in wonder as I released her. I took a few steps backward, wanting to give her space before I did something stupid like follow her into that bedroom. Her essence was so strong, almost intoxicatingly so. It fucked with my head.

"Titus?" she called after me, concern in her voice.

I faced her at the top of the stairs. "Yes, Claire?"

"Uh, how will I find the dining room?"

I almost told her I'd wait at the bottom for her, but a

LEXI C. FOSS & J.R. THORN

better idea came to me. A way to test if she felt this connection the way I did. "Follow the heat."

"The heat?" she asked, her brow puckering.

Embers danced over my fingertips as I lifted my hand. "Yes. I'll leave you some hints in the air, and you'll find me." I was sure of it, even if she looked completely baffled by the idea. "You'll see, sweetheart."

I left her gaping after me in the hallway, a smile on my face the whole way down the stairs.

River waited for me at the bottom, his eyebrow raised knowingly.

"Just the lingering effects from Ignis," I said, blaming my peculiar behavior on the seduction magic even if it had worn off long ago. Maybe I was more susceptible to it, or Ignis had given me a double dose. Wouldn't have put it past the bitch. "Where's Exos?" I had a few things I wanted to say to him about his treatment of Claire.

"Changing," River replied. "We're supposed to meet him in the dining room."

"So you know about our dinner plans?"

"You mean the dining edict? Yes." River's voice was soft so as to not be overheard. "I'm not dressed for this." He gestured to his casual attire. "Not for dining with the Chancellor."

"I think her focus is more on Claire more than our jeans," I said, following the aroma of food while leaving a subtle trail of my essence behind for Claire to follow. Sensing that, coupled with the finer scents in the air, she should find us without any problem.

"Um, aren't you worried the human might run again?" River whispered.

"No." I didn't even need to consider it. My instincts seemed to be tied to hers after that little flirtation in the field. I'd sense it if she wanted to run, and that wasn't the vibe I received from her at all. "She's too intrigued to—"

I froze on the threshold of the dining area.

The room was buzzing with *pixies*.

Even though pixies and fairies were myths, elder Spirit Fae like Elana had enough magic to conjure their very own army of servants in whatever form they chose. But to choose a swarm of mythical creatures as house servants sent a message, one I was keen to listen to. Elana was powerful, and she wanted everyone to know it.

A pixie hurried past me, its tiny wings brushing my cheek and leaving behind a kiss of humidity, betraying the water magic that mingled with Elana's powers. The tiny creatures chittered at each other like squirrels while they set the table with gleaming silverware, and several of them teamed up to supply bowls of soup, trays of delicacies, and finely cut slabs of meat that made my mouth water.

"Uh…" A horde of pixies tugged on one of the massive chairs until it was far enough away from the table for me. "Thank you." I glanced back at River as I took my seat, all the while hoping I didn't squash any of the poor things.

River sat beside me, his mystified gaze likely rivaling my own. "I've, erm, never eaten with an elder before," he mumbled, anxiety creeping into his voice. Being in Elana's esteemed presence had me on edge as well, so I could only imagine what River was feeling right now.

I cleared my throat and accepted a glass of golden, sparkling liquid from a trio of pixies. "You're the one who insisted on tagging along," I reminded him. I took a long sip, my eyelids fluttering as sweetness and heat slipped down my throat. Fire water—literally liquid infused with the elements of air and fire—made me feel at home.

Until I remembered my surroundings.

We were about to dine with an elder and a royal. Who knew what sort of edicts would follow? Not to mention this strange connection I felt to Claire. I shivered, the memory of her touch embedded in my skin. It had felt right—*too* right.

A shift in the air had me glancing at the doorway just as Exos made his entrance, his white-blond hair draped across his forehead in an absurdly regal manner. The pompous style matched his all-black suit.

Definitely a prince.

"Glad you're comfortable," Exos said smoothly as he sat directly across from me. He didn't seem the type to often smile, but the way he looked at me now said he was about to drop some serious bullshit in my lap. "I have some things to discuss with you before Claire joins us."

Great.

"Of course," I replied, keeping my voice controlled and respectful. Part of me still wanted to shake some sense into him for his behavior back in the field with Claire, but I knew better. He didn't seem to understand that she needed a tender hand, not a harsh one.

Exos eyed the delicacies as a pixie settled a glass of fire water in front of him, but he only stared at it. "The Halfling needs more boundaries than I'm able to impose," he said, folding his hands and getting straight to the point. "She's stronger than any of us realized."

He held my gaze, his ocean-blue eyes so deep that I could almost sense the power that rested underneath the surface. If the Halfling bested this guy, then I knew I didn't stand a chance if I ever lost her trust.

I rested my elbows on the table, leaning forward, and opted for a different approach. "If you don't mind me saying, Your Highness, I think you're treating her too harshly. She's not one of your warriors that you can just bark orders and expect to be obeyed. She grew up in the Human Realm without knowledge of our practices and policies. Obedience won't come as naturally to her as it would to others." There. That was politically correct enough, right?

River nodded beside me in agreement, seeming to find his confidence. "Humans are notorious when it comes to equality and free will, especially in certain regions."

Exos sighed, relaxing in his chair. "Yes, she adopts not only the strong personality of a Spirit Fae but human traits as well. However, she is still *fae*. She will learn to obey her betters."

I agreed with him until that final sentence.

Betters.

All my life I'd been told that had I been born with royal blood, I might have possessed the strength to control my unruly fire. But I wasn't royal-born. I wasn't even high-born. My lineage came from a long line of fae who fought for sport and worked in the hot mines of the Fire Kingdom.

Embers crawled through my veins and singed the tablecloth, demonstrating my frustration. Exos raised a brow in response, noticing my inability to hide the annoyance bubbling within me.

I drew in a deep breath before speaking. "She holds elements you can't control," I reminded him. "Forcing her into obedience won't end well."

He nodded. "That's why I can't train her alone. I need help." He paused, his lips twitching. "Starting with you."

I raised a brow at him. "I've already agreed to help her with dinner. I'm here, right?"

"You are," Exos agreed, finally taking the fine flute of his glass and swirling it, activating the embers lingering in the liquid. "But that's not what I meant. I already spoke with Elana, and she agrees. You're being assigned as one of Claire's bodyguards, and you will mentor her on fire."

Not a request.

An order.

No subtlety to see if I would be up for the task or if I had other plans for my time at the Academy. Just a straight edict that Exos expected me to follow. And apparently, Elana did as well.

My blood boiled with the arrogance of his *demand*, and more so, the power behind his blood that allowed him to lord over me.

"It makes sense with you being the most powerful Fire Fae at the Academy, not to mention your uncanny ability to encourage her cooperation." He glanced at me over his glass. "It's also a unique opportunity to appease the Council. You could consider it an internship of sorts."

"And if I don't want an internship?" I couldn't help the growl in my voice. This prick thought to own me, to force me into a position of his own choosing without any regard for what *I* wanted.

"We both know what you want," Exos replied, his gaze knowing. "You won't say no, Titus."

To putting my reputation on the line for a Halfling? To having to protect her from what had to be an army of fae who wanted to kill her? To training her how to use her fire?

Well, that last bit appealed to me. But the other parts? I started to shake my head, but a buzzing of excitement caused all of us to glance at the doorway.

"Ah, here we are." Elana clapped as she entered the room, drawing the pixies to her in a flourish of a grand greeting. "The dining area is lovely, thank you." The pixies chirped in happiness, leading her to the head of the table beside Exos's seat.

"Have you discussed our plans?" she asked, her focus on Exos.

"Yes." He set his flute down. "Titus was just accepting."

Accepting, my ass.

"Excellent," Elana replied, her kind eyes lifting my way. "After observing your interaction upstairs, I do think this is best. Claire clearly likes you, and she needs someone she can trust and rely on at her side. You're a good match for her fire as well." The knowing way she said that last bit had a chill running up my spine.

Spirit Fae were powerful beings. They could sense and control all aspects of the life cycle. And she'd clearly noticed the mating potential between me and Claire. Which meant Exos had as well.

I cleared my throat. "If that's—"

A shriek from the other room had me on my feet in a second, the explosion of fire a seduction to my inner flame.

Claire.

I ran into the foyer to find her curled in a ball, the walls around her ablaze with light. River extinguished the inferno with a mist of power while I clamped down on her gifts with my own, calming them on instinct.

She trembled, a cry escaping her throat as a pixie squeezed out of her grasp with an angry chirp. Another wave of fiery power spiked across the room in response, Claire quivering violently on the ground. "This isn't real," she whispered on repeat. "This isn't real. Fairies don't exist."

Exos snorted. "Oh, for fuck's sake." He gestured to her as if to say, *This. I can't deal with this.* And returned to the dining room.

I sighed. His lack of patience made him a shitty mentor. No wonder he needed me.

Crouching beside her, I murmured, "They're not real, Claire. Elana conjured them to help with dinner."

"Wh-what?" Glassy blue eyes met mine. "C-conjured?"

I smiled. "Yes, fae magic." I held out my hand for her. "Come on, I'll show you."

She swallowed. "I… I don't…"

"They're harmless," I promised. "Just little pixies. You'll see."

"Sh-she tried t-to pull my dress, and I… I…"

"You reacted," I finished for her. "But everything's fine." I gestured around the foyer. "Not even a charred mark." Thanks to River's hasty reaction. And likely Elana's, too. "Come on, sweetheart. I think you'll like the little fairies once you see them in action."

"Exos s-said f-fairies weren't real."

"Because they're not," he called from the other room.

Her eyes widened. "But it *touched* me."

"Yes, I told you. Elana's powerful." I waggled my fingers. "Will you come to the dining area with me?"

She slowly lifted her palm to mine, allowing me to help her up from the floor. The pretty purple dress she wore fluttered around her knees, her hair damp and combed over one shoulder. I tucked a stray strand behind her ear and caught the fiery ember drifting up her neck in response.

The power inside her seemed ready to explode.

"Hey, do me a favor," I whispered.

Her beautiful blue eyes held mine, her lashes thick as she blinked. "Wh-what?"

"Put your hands up like this." I held mine in front of me, palms outward to face her.

She copied the motion with a frown. "Okay."

"Now I want you to think about everything that's bothering you, all the pain, the anger, the frustration and confusion. And I want you to channel it into your hands like you want to hit someone." At her incredulous look, I smiled. "Trust me. Just pull all that energy into your arms and let it fly through your palms. Like you're gearing up to punch someone in a fight."

"I don't fight," she mumbled.

"But you're angry, right?" I pressed. "Upset? Confused?"

"Of course I am."

"And wouldn't it feel really good to just hit someone?"

"Yes." No hesitation. "But not you. I'd rather hit Exos."

I couldn't help my chuckle. "Well, we'd all enjoy that. But I want you to try to hit me. Pretend I'm him."

She shook her head. "You're not. You're actually nice to me."

Exos entered the foyer, his hands in his pockets. "Then hit me," he said, coming to stand beside me. He must have figured out what I wanted to do, or perhaps realized he deserved her annoyance. "Come on, princess. Let me have it."

Her gaze narrowed. "*You*." Energy hummed inside her. "You made me destroy the bar."

"You're the one who approached me," he reminded her, an edge to his voice. "*You* destroyed the bar. I *saved* people."

Her hands balled into fists, her gaze narrowing to slits. "You could have stopped me!"

Exos shrugged. "I had no idea you were going to light the damn place on fire, Claire."

"Rick's dead," she continued, not hearing him. "He's *dead!*"

"Yes." Exos didn't flinch, just continued to stare her down. "Come on, princess. Hit me."

"I *hate* you," she said, tears glistening in her eyes. She opened her palms, unleashing an impressive stream of fire that I caught and absorbed before it could hit Exos. Another blast left her hands, weaker than the first one, followed by a third and a fourth until her knees gave out beneath her on a cry. I grabbed her before she could fall, catching her against my torso and holding her tight.

Exos met my gaze, his expression unreadable. "Welcome to the team, Titus."

CHAPTER SEVEN
TITUS

"YOU'LL FIT RIGHT IN AT THE ACADEMY," Elana said, smiling from the entryway. "Shall we eat? The food is getting cold." She gestured for us to follow her, but Claire seemed unable to move.

"In a minute," I replied, running my fingers through her hair.

Elana's eyes grinned as she nodded and disappeared.

"What just happened?" Claire whispered, shaking against me.

"You expunged some built-up power." My lips brushed her forehead, something that seemed to happen without my permission but felt right. "And I absorbed it."

She gasped, pulling back to look me over, her gaze wild. "D-did I hurt you? Exos?"

"We're fine." I cupped her cheek. "I just wanted to show you how to channel your emotions into your gifts, to control it better."

She shook, more tears glistening in her eyes. "I don't understand what's happening to me." She swallowed, clearing her throat and letting out a sad little laugh. "God, I've never felt so emotional in my life. You must think I'm a wreck."

"No, I think you were stolen from your world and placed in a land you never knew existed. Pretty sure I'd feel the same if someone put me in the Human Realm." I chuckled at the thought and shook my head. "I'd destroy, like, everything."

She blinked. "You would?"

"Oh yeah. My power is barely contained here. Around mortals? I'd be like a firestorm."

Her lips twitched, a funny look gleaming in her eyes.

"What?" I asked.

"Nothing." But that look didn't go away. If anything, it intensified.

"Tell me," I encouraged her, curious as hell.

"You... You sound like a superhero from one of those movies." She giggled, her palm lifting to cover her lips, but a laugh escaped between her fingers. "*Firestorm.*" Her eyes crinkled, her shoulders shaking. "Oh God." A burst of sound came from her, something I enjoyed much more than her shrieking and crying. And I couldn't help joining her even though I didn't quite grasp the joke. I just really, really liked that sound.

"Sorry," she said, wiping the tears from her eyes. "God, I feel insane. All of this. I just don't even know what to do, how to react... anything."

"Well, I vote we start by trying to eat dinner," I suggested, gesturing to the dining area. "Unless you'd prefer fighting more pixies?"

"Pixies?" she repeated.

"The fairies that tried to guide you to the dining room."

"Oh." She scrunched her forehead. "Is that what you meant about a path to follow?"

I shook my head. "No, I meant for you to trace my essence of fire." I trailed a line of fire along her forearm to her hand, causing her lips to part on a big *O*. "But it seems the pixies were eager for you to join us. They don't want the food to get cold."

"Right," she whispered. "Okay."

"Okay, you want to eat? Or okay, you understand?"

"B-both," she stammered. "I'm... hungry."

I looked her over with a smile. "Yeah, me, too." I held up my palm one more time. "Shall we, Claire?"

She pressed her palm to mine, nodding. "A room of fairies and food. Sure."

I chuckled. "You'll get used to it."

"Yeah. That's what I'm afraid of," she said so softly that I barely heard her. The poor girl clearly thought she was going mad, but after a few days in this realm, she'd realize the reality of her situation. Hopefully.

The seating arrangements in the room had changed with River joining Exos on the opposite side of the table, Elana still at the head, leaving two open seats for me and Claire—beside each other. I pulled out her chair, causing her to smile shyly as she sat, and joined her quickly, my hand finding hers beneath the table to give it a squeeze.

She tightened her hold as the pixies fluttered in to begin delivering food. It seemed they'd replaced the soup with fresh bowls, likely because the old had grown cold. They continued swapping out the dishes until a blend of fresh aromas wafted off the table, the array of foods causing my stomach to grumble in want and my heart to beat in admiration.

Elana was controlling all of this, her power an almost magnetic energy that called to my inner fae and required submission. Because not many could boast such a feast in their homes, especially after repairing the walls.

Claire didn't appear nearly as enthused.

"It's a bit much, huh?" I teased, eyeing the magic sprinkling across the room.

She relaxed, then gave me a small smile of her own. Fuck, she was beautiful. I wanted to make her smile every moment of every day.

Exos remained stoic, his focus shifting to Elana as he asked her something about Claire's schedule. This caused the woman at my side to glance between them, her brow furrowing as they discussed her life without her input.

"Eat, dear," Elana said when she noticed Claire staring at her.

My companion didn't reach out for the food but eyed it hungrily. When she refused to pick her own course, I released her hand to pick up her dish and then plucked a little bit of everything for her to try before setting it in front of her.

"I recommend that one first," I told her, gesturing to the dried pieces of meat. "I love those." I punctuated the statement by heaping several spoonfuls onto my own plate, as well as a few nibbles from other dishes.

When Claire still didn't touch her food, I took a bite of mine to demonstrate that it wasn't poisonous. And then I made an exaggerated moan of approval that caused her lips to twitch.

"Try it," I encouraged her. "It's really, really good."

She shifted in her seat, her mouth pinching to the side. Then she took one of the dried pieces of meat I suggested and nibbled on it, her eyes going wide. She took a larger bite.

I chuckled. "Told you."

She didn't reply, too lost in the flavors of the foods.

"Yes," Elana said quietly. "I think that's best. One day at each campus, and I'll work with the professors tomorrow on her schedule. We should start her in the Fire Quad."

Exos nodded. "I agree. Are her quarters ready?"

"No, you'll stay here tonight. I didn't have enough energy to finish rebuilding the Spirit Dorm."

"You're putting her on the Spirit Quad?" I asked, setting

my fork down. River cleared his throat, but I ignored him. He must not have liked my tone, but this was a horrible idea and I wanted them to know it. "It's empty and void of life."

"And therefore safe," Exos added.

"For who? Her or the others?" I shook my head. "If you want her to attend the Academy, you need to have her around other fae. That's how you introduce her to our world. By showing her what the Fae Realm is like and introducing her to fae her own age."

Claire had stopped eating, her eyes dancing between us. "You keep mentioning the Academy and a campus, but what is it? Like a college?" she whispered.

"The Elemental Fae Academy, dear," Elana said, her voice warm. "And yes, it's similar to your university life, but for fae. Everyone in this realm attends from age nineteen to twenty-three, unless there are extenuating circumstances. Like Titus, for example."

"Titus?" Claire glanced at me, frowning. "I don't understand."

"She means I started the Academy late. I'm twenty-two but didn't begin until this year."

"Why?" she asked.

"Because I was born and raised to fight in the Powerless Champion circuit." I shrugged. "I retired and now I'm here."

"After winning," River put in, pride in his voice. "He's the Powerless Champion."

"Like... boxing?" she guessed.

"Nah, that's a boring human sport. Fae fight to the death. And Titus has killed, like, well, everyone who challenged him. His numbers are—"

Exos cleared his throat, cutting off the Water Fae. "What River is trying to say is that Titus started the Academy a little later because of an extenuating circumstance. Just as you will start a little later because of your, well, circumstances."

"You mean my kidnapping?" Claire asked. "Because that's what this is, right? I mean, you *kidnapped* me from my home."

"This is your home," Exos replied. "Your true home. And the Academy is your future."

"And I have no say in this?" Claire pressed. "Because where I come from, that's kidnapping and forcing someone to do something against her will."

"And where I come from, it's rude to argue with your betters."

Her eyebrows lifted. "Betters? Like what? My parents? Because you're not even ten years older than me. And neither is she." She gestured to Elana. "Which is totally irrelevant, by the way, because I will argue with whoever I damn well please." The fire in her had my lips twitching. I much preferred this to the weeping girl I found in the field earlier.

"Exos is royalty," Elana explained softly. "And I'm Chancellor of the Academy. Therefore, in our society, we are considered your betters."

"Because you were promoted at the ripe young age of, what, thirty? That makes you better than me?" Claire snorted. "Yeah, no. That's not happening. Not least of all because you kidnapped me. And now you want me to attend an academy against my will? Yeah, hard pass."

River choked on his food while I held back a grin.

"You seem to think there's a choice here." The calmness in Exos's voice sent a chill of foreboding down my spine. "Of which, I suppose, there is. Would you like me to explain it to you, Claire?"

"Exos," Elana warned.

"No, no." Exos waved her off, his status coming out in that small gesture. Elana might be the Chancellor, but he was heir to the Spirit Kingdom, making him *her* better in our fucked-up political system. "She wants to hear her choices. Don't you, Claire?"

"I do," she agreed. "Since it's my life, it's my decision. Not that you've given me much of one by forcing me to come here."

He smiled, but it lacked humor. "Yes, well, that's because you can no longer live in the Human Realm without being a threat to everyone around you. The bar proves that."

Her face paled, causing me to curse internally. He had to go there, didn't he? This was clearly a tense subject for her, not that the Spirit Prince seemed to give a fuck.

"I-I didn't mean to do that," she whispered. "I don't even know if it's true."

"If you care for proof, I'll provide it," Exos replied, his voice flat. "But the fact remains that you cannot reside in the Human Realm. You're too powerful, so much so that we can hardly contain you here. Which brings me to your choices, Claire. Are you listening?"

She nodded, her lip between her teeth, her shoulders hunched. "Yes."

"You can attend the Academy and learn how to control your abilities, at which point you may be permitted visitor rights back to the Human Realm. Or, you will be banished to the Spirit Kingdom—the same kingdom your mother single-handedly destroyed in her battle with Mortus. It's void of life and essence, leaving it impossible for you to hurt anyone with your lack of control." He dabbed his mouth with his napkin in a casual gesture as he shrugged. "The third option, of course, is death. Because we can't have a powerful rogue fae wandering the realm. Especially one who lacks training and understanding of our ways."

Claire's mouth opened and closed, her eyes wide, no words coming from her lips.

But of course, what the hell could she say after that calmly delivered edict?

Fucking royal blood, not thinking at all about the consequences of his words. Just uttering them as if he were speaking to a fellow warrior, not a female who had clearly been through hell over the last day or two.

"So what would you choose, Claire? Because I thought the Academy route to be the most humane and practical of options, but if you prefer I drop you in the Spirit Kingdom, we can leave tonight."

"How about we provide Claire with a tour tomorrow of the Academy and let her see what life here would be like before you force her to choose," I suggested, my teeth grating over every word. "And maybe give her a chance to understand the Fae Realm as well while you're at it."

Exos met my gaze, his blue eyes simmering. "Just because I've tagged you for her team does not mean you may speak out of line."

"My job is to protect her. Consider that my current goal." I narrowed my eyes. "Unless you think threatening her life is something I should be overlooking?"

His lips actually twitched. "You are to protect her from others, not from me."

"Maybe she needs protection from you the most," I countered, flames inching beneath my skin.

Elana coughed, dispelling the mood with a wave of her hand. "I think a tour is a great idea. Claire can remain here tonight, then Titus can provide a tour in the morning of Fire Quad. And we'll work out dorm arrangements afterward."

Meaning she wanted to see Claire's reaction to the world before she assigned her sleeping quarters.

"Assuming that is okay with you, dear?" Elana asked, her benevolent gaze finding Claire. The woman was the peacekeeper of our race for a reason, and it showed as she smiled. "Would you like to see the Academy? I think you might find it enlightening. And Titus could take you to the game this weekend, to see the competition of elements. Assuming he's up for it."

I hadn't planned to go, but if it was something Claire wanted to see, I'd take her. "Sure."

Claire glanced sideways at me, her hands clasped tightly in her lap. "Y-you're a student." Not a question, but a statement.

Still, I nodded. "First year, yep."

"A-and I would be near you on the tour?" she asked, her throat working over each word. I rather enjoyed the hopeful glint in her eyes.

"I'll happily show you around campus." I reached over for her hand. "It's really beautiful. You'll love it. Lots of trees and flowers and nature."

She nibbled her lip. "Fairies?"

I chuckled. "No. Those are just here."

"Anything else magical?"

"All sorts of elemental magic, sweetheart." I squeezed her hand. "We're fae. We live and breathe our powers. But the purpose of the Academy is control, so you won't have to fear anyone or anything. Everyone is learning."

"Like a university," she said, repeating Elana's sentiments.

"Yeah, except we learn how to hone our gifts for the betterment of society, while you attended college for, like, a job. And half of the crap you all study is worthless." River's cheeks pinkened as Claire met his gaze. "Sorry, I've studied some of the Human Realm. It's, uh, fun to me."

"What kind of fae are you?" she asked, eyeing him with curiosity. "I can't sense your energy like I do Exos's and Titus's."

Her words had my gaze snapping up to Exos, who merely smirked. Those words, so innocent on her lips, meant far more than she realized. If she sensed Exos the way she did me, it meant he was a potential mate for her as well.

And the slight curve of Elana's lips confirmed she knew it all along.

As did the startled expression River wore.

Fae mated once, for life. But only with one person and always of their element.

That Claire had found a potential connection with two fae, of different elements, was unique. No, it was unheard of.

Maybe she meant she felt Exos's aura the way I felt other Fire Fae who were a potential match to my own magic?

"I, uh, control water," River said, swallowing. "I'm a

Water Fae."

"Oh," Claire murmured. "So would you be on the tour?"

He snorted. "Not of the Fire Fae Quad, no. We keep our own quadrants. Too many complications when you mingle the elements."

Her brow furrowed. "But... but I have some?" She looked to Exos. "R-right?"

"You have all five," he confirmed, not meeting her gaze yet somehow knowing she'd leaned on him for the detail. "Which is why I suggested the Spirit Quad." Now he raised his gaze to mine. "Because it would be too dangerous to assign her another place to stay."

"Let's see how the tour goes," Elana interjected, playing peacekeeper yet again. "Then we can decide where she might want to reside. And for tonight, Claire will remain here. Is that all right, dear?"

Claire blinked. "I, uh, okay." She glanced at me. "Are you staying, too?"

"Uh." I glanced at Exos, who nodded. "Yes. I can stay."

"The two of you can work on control," he added. "Might as well start now. I would hate for Claire to blow up a building on campus the way she did earlier." He pushed away from the table. "I need to phone an update to my brother, so if you all will excuse me."

"Is he always this abrupt?" Claire asked as the Spirit Fae left the room.

"I don't know. I hardly know him," I admitted.

"You're not friends?"

I snorted. "He's a royal. He doesn't *befriend* fae like me."

She frowned. "What do you mean?"

"It'd be like the Queen of England befriending a peasant," River interjected helpfully. "That'd be rare, right?"

"I, well, yes." She frowned. "So he's, like, important?"

"He's the most powerful Spirit Fae in existence," I confirmed. "And heir to the Spirit Kingdom."

"He's, like, thirty," she replied.

"Appearances can be deceiving," Elana chimed in,

reminding me that she still sat with us. "Well, I'll leave you to your sleeping arrangements. River, you're welcome to stay as well, if your curiosity continues to get the best of you." She winked as she stood. "I require a bit of sleep after all the festivities of today." She paused on the threshold, her eyes going to Claire. "It is lovely to have you with us, dear. I hope you enjoy your tour tomorrow."

CHAPTER EIGHT
CLAIRE

RIVER STOOD, shuffling from foot to foot while nibbling his lip. "I, uh…"

"You don't have to stay," Titus told him, a smile in his voice. "You can go back to your dorm."

Relief flooded the Water Fae's gaze. "Are you sure?"

"Yeah, man. I'll catch up with you tomorrow."

"Thank you." He started away from the table, then paused to glance back at me. "It, uh, was good to meet you, Claire." He immediately dropped his focus to the ground and shuffled some more.

"You, too," I replied, confused by his bashfulness.

He gave a little wave and practically ran out of the room.

I frowned after him. "Is he afraid of me?" I asked, a little hurt. It wasn't like I meant to keep setting shit on fire.

Titus chuckled. "No. It's being in the Chancellor's place. It's, uh, sort of a big deal. She might not be royalty like Exos, but she's very important in our society. And her affinity for water is probably teasing his a bit, you know, since he's a Water Fae."

"Wait, so she has two elements?" Didn't they just say it wasn't normal to mingle elements? Or did I misunderstand what that meant?

"All Spirit Fae do," he replied. "Exos has spirit and fire, Elana has water and spirit. You, it seems, have access to all the elements."

"And that's not normal." It was a guess—an educated one based on the last twenty-four hours or however long I'd been here.

"No. It's, uh, unique."

"How unique?"

He palmed the back of his neck. "You, uh, are the first and only fae to control more than two elements."

"More than two?" I squeaked, repeating his words.

"Yeah, as I said, Spirit Fae have two. That's the most there's ever been."

And I had five. I blinked. *Five.* "I... What does that mean?"

He shook his head. "I don't actually know," he admitted softly. "But what I can tell you is that the Academy is your best course. They'll teach you how to control the gifts, Claire. And it sounds like you'll be rotating between campuses throughout the week."

I sat back in my chair, flinching as a horde of those colorful insects fluttered into the room. My instinct to kill one earlier, like one would a fly, had overwhelmed me in the lobby. And then I'd screamed when the thing started *yelling* at me.

That kind of shit did not happen in, well, reality.

Except I'd given up considering any of this to be a dream. It was far too fucked up for even me to fathom.

Especially the bits about my mom.

"What, uh, did Exos mean when he said my mother destroyed the Spirit Kingdom?" I asked. He'd mentioned her a few times today, but I hadn't been in the right frame of mind to hear him, let alone understand him.

"You don't know?" Titus asked, sounding surprised.

I gave him a look. "In case it's not clear, I was celebrating my twenty-first birthday at a college bar just... whenever ago. And I knew nothing about fae or fairies or pixies or elemental magic. Until, like, whenever I fell here." My English professor would be appalled by the way I just explained all that, but who could expect any sort of clarity after throwing me into this insanity?

Titus nodded. "Right, yeah. Okay. Are you done eating?"

I eyed my partially finished plate. "Uh, yeah." I couldn't eat any more even if I tried. Not with the gymnastics going on inside my belly. "But that doesn't answer my question."

"I know," he said. "I was just trying to figure out if we should have that conversation here or, uh, elsewhere."

"Like upstairs?" I suggested, liking the idea of being somewhere less out in the open and away from those sparkly, chattering bugs.

"If that's where you want to go." He rubbed the back of his neck. "I don't know where else to go, actually."

"You mean you don't know where else I'm allowed to go," I translated. "I'm not going to run again." At least not yet. Not until I knew more about this place. Otherwise, it was a waste of effort, and Exos's ultimatum about my *options* didn't leave me all that enthusiastic to act out again. Because I didn't doubt for a second that he meant his threat. He very clearly did not like me, and the feeling was mutual.

Well, mostly mutual.

Aside from the fact that I still sometimes wanted to kiss him.

I shook my head. "Let's go upstairs," I said, standing. Because, unlike Exos, I actually *liked* Titus. And also found him hot as hell.

A Titus and Exos sandwich would be, well, amazing. Two

powerful bodies thrusting, tongues dancing, hands roaming…

And, oh my God, I needed to stop that line of thought.

Wow.

No.

Not happening.

Ever.

And, Jesus Christ, what was wrong with me to even begin to imagine that? Very clearly losing—

"Claire?" Titus asked, his brow furrowed. He'd stood with me and seemed to be waiting for me to lead.

"Right." I turned and started toward the stairs. To lead him to my room. Which, after that last thought, probably wasn't the brightest of ideas, but it wasn't like Exos would be joining us. Although, I wouldn't exactly complain if he did.

No, wait, yes, I would.

I didn't like Exos.

He was a dick. A dick who just happened to be one of the sexiest men I'd ever seen. As well as Titus, but in entirely different ways.

I groaned, frustrated by the onslaught of images abrading my mind, each of them more graphic than the next.

"Are you okay, Claire?" Titus asked, sounding concerned.

No. "Yes. Just, uh, confused." Not exactly a lie.

His hand caught mine at the top of the stairs, pulling me back to him as his other palm went to cup my face. Eyes the color of an evergreen gazed down at me.

"It's going to be all right," he whispered, his thumb tracing my cheekbone. "I know it's all overwhelming right now, that you feel completely off-kilter in this realm, but I think you'll like it here. Minus maybe the pixies." He tried for a smile that I felt resonate inside of me.

Titus had completely misunderstood my awkwardness, yet his words were exactly what I needed to hear. "Thank you," I said, pressing my hand over his.

"You're welcome." His gaze dropped to my lips, heat flaring between us. It felt different from earlier, his comfort evolving into something more intense. Energy purred beneath his skin, lifting to stroke my own, inflaming a need inside me I didn't understand. It pulled me toward him, hypnotized me, excited me, made me fly. "Fuck, you're beautiful," he whispered, his awe rivaling my own.

I swallowed, tilting my head back—

The clearing of a throat had us jumping apart, my feet causing me to trip right into Exos's hard chest. He caught me with a hand on my hip, steadying me between them.

And what do you know—I'd suddenly become the center of an Exos and Titus sandwich.

My cheeks warmed at the thought, my throat going dry.

"I, uh, I mean, *we* were just going to my room, to, well…" Realizing how bad that all sounded, I stopped talking and gulped at Exos's arched brow.

"Talk," Titus said. "She wants to know about her mother, something apparently you haven't told her yet."

"When I tried, she blew me into a wall." Exos tilted his head at me. "Twice."

Flames seemed to lick across my skin. Perhaps literally. I couldn't tell because I couldn't seem to stop staring into Exos's ocean-blue eyes. That magnetic pull held me in place, paralyzing me before him. Then Titus grabbed my other hip, his chest hot against my back.

Oh, fuck…

I leaned against him, then swayed forward, and back again, unable to decide whom I wanted to touch more.

What is happening to me?

"Are you finally up for listening, princess?" Exos murmured. "Or will you use that impressive wind power of yours on me again?"

"Impressive?" I repeated.

"Very," he admitted, his gaze softening the slightest bit. His thumb swept over my lower lip, his opposite hand tightening on my hip. "So much power." He released me

85

from his gaze as he lifted his eyes to Titus. "Where do you want to sleep?"

"I have no idea," he said, his warm voice tickling my hair. "We were only heading up here to talk about her mother."

"Yes, I heard that the first time." His thumb continued to caress my lip, as if memorizing the feel. "I was asking if you plan to sleep in her room."

"We hadn't gotten that far in terms of arrangements," Titus replied.

"Hmm. Well, I'll be down the hall. If you need a room, the one beside my guest suite is open." His gaze dropped to mine, his mouth curling into a beautiful grin. "And, Titus?"

"Yes?"

"Be careful with this one." His thumb pressed between my lips, lightly catching my tongue before withdrawing and letting his hand fall to his side. "Claire has a penchant for kissing strangers. Don't you, sweetheart?"

My face went up in flames, or at least it felt that way. A vivid memory of the bar pierced my thoughts, taking me back to his first words. *Do you often kiss men you hardly know?*

Exos smiled. "Night, princess."

"N-night," I stammered, my hip tingling as he released me. He didn't turn around as he sauntered down the hallway, his suit clinging to his muscular form and leaving me salivating for the body beneath.

This is seriously fucked up.

I shouldn't be lusting after him. I shouldn't be lusting after anyone. I should be focused on finding a way home.

"You, uh, kissed Exos?" Titus asked, his palm sliding away from me as he moved around to face me, his expression unreadable.

"Um." I cleared my throat. "Sort of. It was a dare."

"A dare?" he asked, raising a brow.

"Like in truth or dare."

He frowned. "I don't understand."

"It's a game. You've never played?"

He slowly shook his head, causing me to smile.

"It's dumb. You're not missing much. But essentially, it's played with a group of friends, and you pick a truth or a dare. A truth might be, like, what's the craziest place you've had sex? And you have to answer honestly. A dare could be something like, go kiss that guy at the bar. That was my dare—to kiss Exos. Rick can be..." I trailed off, the thought of my friend sending a jolt through my heart.

I didn't even get to say goodbye.

Just whisked away to this other realm, without a thought of my past.

Would my friends miss me? Would they come looking for me? My grandparents died last year, leaving me enough money to make it through school. But I had no other family.

Titus cupped my cheek, his forest-green eyes full of emotion. "I'm sorry about your friend."

"Me, too," I whispered, clearing my throat again. "C-can you tell me about my mom?" I asked, needing the distraction. "Tell me why I'm here? *How* I'm here?"

His throat bobbed as he nodded. "Yeah. Of course." He glanced at the corridor of doors before us. "Uh, in your room?"

"Yes, please." I didn't want to be out in the open any longer. I led the way with him trailing behind me, his hands tucked into his jeans as if he were trying not to touch me again. Probably because of Exos's little reveal. The kiss hardly counted, but yeah, I'd been pretty inappropriate that night. Then again, so had he, since he let me kiss him.

I pushed the memory from my head, focusing on the present.

Titus followed me into the room, his demeanor reserved as I closed the door.

He glanced around the flowery space, eyeing the tree in the center of the room and the vines climbing over the walls. "It's definitely Spirity in here."

"What's your place like?" I wondered.

"Black." He smirked. "I like to burn things."

"Apparently, so do I," I grumbled, lowering my gaze.

How much damage had I caused without meaning to? Not that I could entirely blame myself. It wasn't like someone had trained me on how to be a... a... *fae*.

Fuck, I really do believe this, don't I?

I shivered, not wanting to admit to the logic flowing through my mind. This sort of shit was impossible. Or it should be. Yet, I couldn't deny all the magic flowing around me, the fact that flames literally shot out of my hands, that I'd destroyed a wall of, uh, vines? I shook my head, trying to clear it.

Titus caught my chin, tilting my head back to stare warmly down at me. "You'll learn to control it, Claire."

"Will I?" I countered. "I didn't even know any of this was real until today, or yesterday, or whenever it was that Exos kidnapped me." It felt like a lifetime ago, my existence forever changed by this new world. "I don't even understand why these powers, or whatever they are, didn't manifest until recently. Or how to begin controlling them."

"It's rumored your mother hexed you," he replied, his fingers gliding along my jaw and down my neck before dropping down to his side. "Exos would be much better at dictating the history, as he sits on the Council of Fae, but I can tell you what I know." There was an edge to his voice when he spoke of Exos, but it didn't reflect in the kindness of his features.

"I'd rather you tell me," I admitted. Something told me Exos would be blunt, and perhaps purposely harsh. And I couldn't handle that right now. I needed someone who would break me into this gently. Someone like Titus.

He palmed the back of his neck and let out a breath. "What all do you know?"

I sat on the bed, which was admirably soft considering the base was made of a tree trunk. "Uh, well..."

I considered the minimal information my grandmother gave me, while toying with the charm dangling from the chain around my neck. An old habit whenever I thought of her, as it'd been one of the last gifts she'd given me before she died.

Pinching my lips to the side, I shrugged. "Honestly, not much. I don't remember her at all. My grandmother said she left when I was a baby and never came home. Then claimed my father died of a broken heart."

He grimaced and leaned against the tree trunk across from me. "Right, we'll need to go back to the beginning, then." He crossed one ankle over the other, his hands tucking into his jean pockets. "So your mother—Ophelia Snow—was a Spirit Fae. Very powerful, as is the case with most female Spirit Fae of a certain birthright. Mortus, another Spirit Fae, was her chosen mate. They never completed the vows because she met your father soon after and created you."

He looked extremely uncomfortable when he finished, but I had to ask: "Chosen mate? Like my mother cheated on this Morty guy?" That didn't sound good.

"Mortus," he corrected. "And basically, yes. When fae mate, we mate for life. There's a power exchange that essentially binds the essences together, and she'd begun that process with Mortus before she met your, uh, father. The rumors say she ventured into the Human Realm on some sort of assignment, then refused to come home after meeting your father. Mortus, being her intended mate, issued an edict that she return and atone for her crimes. So she did, and then she fought him."

A chill shivered down my spine. "And...?" I prompted, my voice barely a whisper.

Titus ran his fingers through his auburn strands and sighed. "When fae agree to a power binding, it's irreversible. To do so causes a disruption in the balance. That's why he called her home, to finish the bond because the elements were already fracturing due to their unresolved vows. Of course, this is all hearsay. I wasn't there when it all happened. But my familiarity with the rituals suggests the truth behind this."

"Rituals?" I repeated. "I don't understand the *bond* part."

He seemed thoughtful, as if searching for the words. Then he pushed off the tree to stand before me, holding out his hand. "Touch me."

I wasn't sure what this had to do with anything, but I pressed my palm to his, curious. "O-okay."

Titus slid to his knees, his gaze kind as he stared up at me. "Close your eyes and just describe the sensations rolling over your skin."

Swallowing, I allowed my lids to fall, confused as to why he'd derailed our conversation. But he clearly had a point to make about something.

"What do you feel, Claire?" he asked, his voice soft. "Tell me what you sense."

"I…" I licked my lips, focusing on the heat spiraling up my arm, the caress oddly familiar after only a few hours of knowing him. "Hot," I whispered. "And…" I bit my cheek, fighting the urge to lean into him, to seek comfort from his known intimacy. Some foreign part of me trusted him despite my mind rebelling against the notion.

I don't really know him.

But I want to.

I like him.

"It feels… natural… to touch you." My cheeks warmed from the admission. It also felt natural to touch Exos.

"Because you feel the connection blossoming between your essence and mine," he whispered, his opposite hand cupping my cheek. "Fae are essence-based. We rely on our links to the elements to guide us, and when we find someone we are compatible with, we gravitate toward that person. My Fire calls to yours, and vice versa. Just as it seems your Spirit is intrigued by Exos. Definitely not common, but nothing about you is ordinary."

"O-oh," I breathed, unable to say more. While his words made sense, they also didn't. He'd essentially just implied that I was attracted to two men.

Two men I hardly knew.

Two men who couldn't be any more different.

Two men who turned me on like no other.

This realm is fucking with my mind, and apparently my libido.

Titus tilted his head to the side, his hands still on me. "Ophelia, your mother, had allowed her affinity to bind itself to Mortus through a series of rituals that the fae undergo when solidifying a mating. But she didn't finish it. Instead, she went to Earth, created you, and only returned when Mortus threatened to go after her. And then she fought him. I don't know the specifics, but I know the outcome."

I gazed into his eyes, waiting for him to continue. When he didn't, I said, "Tell me."

His expression fell, his touch turning cool against my skin. "Ninety percent of the Spirit Fae died of unknown causes that day, destroying the kingdom. Your mother died with them. Mortus lived. And it seems to have awoken a curse, or that's the myth, anyway."

"A curse?" I repeated, my gaze darting back and forth across his face. "What curse?"

"No Spirit Fae has been able to procreate since that day. It's said your mother's betrayal cursed the Spirit Fae, sentencing their species to death."

I gasped. "What?"

"There's more." He looked away, staring at the vines on the wall beside us. "Spirit Fae are life and death, the balance between all the elements. Without them..." He paused, clearing his throat and finally glancing back at me. "Without them, we're expected to die."

CHAPTER NINE
CLAIRE

I STARED AT THE VINES ABOVE ME, Titus's words repeating over and over in my mind.

My mother cheated on her betrothed with my dad and created me.

Then fought her betrothed to the death.

And created a curse that would apparently kill fae kind.

I blinked. Numb. Cold. Alone. How did one just accept all that information? It wasn't as if I cared much for my mother, having been abandoned by her at birth. But holy shit, what kind of person did this to other people? Er, fae, or whatever. It didn't matter.

My mother had caused a pandemic. On purpose? By accident? I didn't know. But that sort of legacy painted my mom in a horrid light.

It made her sound evil.

"Claire?" Titus murmured, having moved to sit beside me on the bed.

"Still processing," I replied.

"Maybe we should talk about it more tomorrow?" he suggested.

I nodded mutely, not sure I could handle any more tonight. Hell, I couldn't handle any more, period. "You must hate my mother," I realized. "Oh God, everyone will hate me, too." My chest ached at the sudden understanding. I would be condemned with her as the result of her infidelity, not just to Mortus, but to fae kind.

"Depends on their opinion of the prophecy," Titus muttered, blowing out a breath. "But yeah, I think sleep is probably a good idea."

"What prophecy?" I asked, ignoring his idea despite knowing I was at my limit for information.

"It's a tale, Claire. A myth. It's not true. Honestly, I think the whole curse thing is bullshit, too."

"Then what is it?" I pushed. "Why would it impact someone's opinion of me?"

"Because the prophecy says a fae with access to all the elements will break the curse," he replied flatly. "Or doom us all."

"Oh." I started nodding. "Yeah, that's brilliant. So I'm the daughter of a woman who destroyed the Spirit Fae, and possibly all fae. And I have access to all the elements, which could either rectify the situation or kill you all." I gave a hysterical laugh that bubbled into a sob as I curled into myself. "This is just too much."

I'd never experienced an easy life, having lost my parents before I could walk and being raised by two aloof grandparents who saw me as more of a burden than a gift. But this definitely took the cake.

"And you all want me to go to an Academy tomorrow? With a bunch of people who will clearly hate or fear me?" Another chuckle burst out of me. "Yeah, that's going to go well." Fuck. "*Fuck.*" I wanted to scream. To rant. To run. To fly. To *something.*

"Claire," Titus murmured, his hand on my shoulder.

I brushed him off, but he gripped me harder, tugging me to him.

"*Claire.*"

I ignored him, too busy shaking my head back and forth as I laugh-cried at the insanity of this entire situation. It was as if I'd fallen into a wonderland of crazy people with stories and expectations that made no sense. And this bizarre *energy* that I couldn't control. It swam around me, urging me to use it, to destroy, to create, to *burn.*

"Claire!" Titus yelled, his arms wrapping around me. "*Stop.*"

"Stop what?" I asked on a giggle that sounded maniacal to my ears. The entire world was crashing around me, and he wanted me to, what, relax? Breathe? Focus? Were those the words he was saying? No. It sounded like Exos. In my head. No, my ear. Whatever. I just wanted to hide, to never come out, and ignore everything around me. To disappear.

To leave.

A punch to my gut had me cringing, the power strong and encompassing, yanking me out of my state and back into the present to stare into two glowering blue eyes. Bright with power. Consuming me. Forcing me to yield. To submit. I didn't understand it, tried to fight it, but the magnetic pull was too great, overwhelming every part of my mind and grounding me in the present. His hands were on my cheeks, bands of muscular steel were around my waist, a hot body pressed to my back.

I blinked several times, confused. When did Exos get here? And why was Titus holding me so tightly?

"That's it," Exos breathed, his mouth dangerously close to mine. "Most fae come into their power slowly, but the hex your mo—" He cleared his throat. "You have twenty-one years of pent-up elements slamming into you at once. That you're even conscious is a miracle. It shows a strength very few possess, a strength I admire. But I need you to use that strength to control yourself, Claire. This volatile behavior is what the Council is afraid of, why they don't want you to attend the Academy. But I pushed for you to be allowed, have volunteered to train and guard you myself. And I will not fail. Do you understand me?"

Glittering waves. That was what his gaze reminded me of, so intense, so powerful, so alluring. I fell into him as one would an ocean, allowing the tide to pull me under with a force that stole my breath, and found peace beneath the roaring wake. Blissful and dark and mine.

Another strength came from behind in the form of an inferno, jerking me backward as my soul seemed to fight for control over them both.

Exos had asked if I understood.

But I didn't.

None of this made sense, my mind and body overwhelmed by the dueling sensations and my heart ripping in two. How could I desire two men? Now? Here? In this foreign place?

"She needs sleep," the fiery one said.

"I know," Spirit replied. "Guard her?"

"With my life." A hot vow spoken into my hair.

"I'll be nearby," Spirit whispered, warm lips brushing my forehead. "Try to rest, Claire. We have a lot to discuss tomorrow."

Someone mumbled. Maybe me. I didn't know, couldn't grasp the silky strands of reality floating around me. But oh, my ocean was leaving. That peace. I reached for him, hitting air instead, but a breath into my mind put me at ease.

Still there.

Still with me.

Still easing my pain.

My Spirit.

My other half.

The flames dancing inside me cooled, soothed by the presence of yet another, the one who called to the embers of my soul. I stopped trying to decipher the meaning and gave in to the sensation, trusting those around me to keep me afloat, to never let me drown.

"Good night, Claire," the voice behind me whispered, arms holding me tight. Somewhere in my mind, I noted the lack of clothing, my dress singed into ash around me. But I was too exhausted to verify, too consumed with the need to rest to validate my modesty.

Sleep sounded nice.

Maybe when I awoke, it would be to reality.

Yet somehow I knew this was my life now. My present and future. A fae teetering on the brink of disaster while trying to master elements I couldn't possibly understand.

I might die here.

But I also might live.

* * *

Ugh. Someone had left the heat on too high again. It felt as if I were wrapped up in a scorching blanket, singeing my hairs and leaving a trail of sweat in its wake. This was why I preferred a fan at night, a subtle breeze to help shift the hot air.

Ah, there it was, subtly brushing over my sweltering skin. *More,* I urged, craving the icy chill to cool the flames inching around me, consuming the room.

Wait... I flew upward, my mouth gaping wide at the swirl of power overwhelming the suite.

In the fae world.

Where I now resided.

Surrounded by chaos.

"Titus!" I shrieked, slamming my palm into his bare chest. His eyes flew open, his body going on alert as fast as mine.

He frowned at the maelstrom of elements. "Well, that's, um, different."

"Different?" I repeated on a squeak.

"Yeah, I've never seen anything like that." He shook his head, then grabbed my hand. "Okay, crash course. I need you to concentrate on pulling the elements to you. Think of it like the hop game where you catch the flurries."

I gaped at him. "What?" *Flurries? Hop game?*

"Er, right." He winced. "Uh, do you have an activity where you try to grab things with your mind?" At my blank stare, he sighed. "Okay, focus on the core of the fire, that blue flicker in the middle, and call it to you."

"Call it to me," I repeated. "Right."

"Come on, sweetheart. Trust me and try." His dimples flickered. "Please?"

I must still be dreaming, I decided, giving in to the lunacy of the moment. "All right." I focused on the bright blue of the flame, as he suggested, and bit my lip. *Now what?* Titus had said to call the fire. Okay. But how? Like, was I supposed to talk to it?

Pinching my mouth to the side, I shrugged. *Come here.* Nothing.

Well, of course nothing. Why would it listen to me?

Except I felt a flicker of something in response. An odd sort of heated string, invisible to my eye but tangible against my finger.

Weird.

I tugged on it, my eyebrows lifting as the flame danced a little in response.

No way...

I tried again, my jaw dropping as the inferno definitely responded. With a twirl of my finger, the blazing colors rotated into a sphere, shrinking as I willed it to resemble the size of a baseball, and landed in the palm of my hand.

"Excellent," Titus praised. "Now use that mist over there to put it out."

Mist?

Oh.

There was a shower happening in the corner of the room, watering what appeared to be a bed of flowers that reminded me of the ones I'd lain on in the field. Coincidence? Maybe.

Another strand tugged at my being as I willed the water to condense and blow toward my hand. My palm sizzled as the elements met, a deep-seated peace overwhelming my senses as all three elements—air, water, and fire—mingled together over my skin.

"Beautiful," Titus breathed, running a finger through the aftermath of my miracle. "I think the flowers can stay."

I gazed at the patch in question, frowning. "Are you saying I did that?"

"You did," he replied, grinning. "Earth and spirit, mingled as one. Not only did you create them, but you also used the soil to help the flowers grow and water to make them bloom."

"And the fire?" I prompted.

"A natural defense. You protected us in your sleep, the air keeping it from burning us or the walls. I'm actually really impressed." He tucked a strand of unruly hair behind my ear. "Exos was right. You're very powerful." He studied my face, as if memorizing my features, his awe a palpable emotion floating between us. "So gorgeous."

"Me or the flowers?" It came out huskier than I intended, my body alight with a different awareness now that the panic had subsided. The intimacy of what I'd just done, with his coaching, stirred something inside me. A dark yearning, utterly inappropriate and yet satisfyingly right.

"You," he whispered, his green irises lowering to my mouth. "You're gorgeous." His gaze continued downward, his pupils enlarging, his lips parting in awe.

It took me a moment to realize why.

My dress had definitely disappeared last night, leaving me naked beside him. And while that should have alarmed me, it didn't. Somehow I trusted him not to act on it, perhaps because he'd held me for the last however many hours without harm. Or maybe because I *wanted* him to see me.

"Titus," I breathed, my fingers running up his bare, muscular arms to his shoulders.

"Claire," he replied, my name a husky melody that seemed to center between my thighs.

"Is this pull normal?" I asked, threading my fingers through his auburn strands. "This instant connection that makes me want to kiss you?"

"It's the fire," he explained, his emerald gaze smoldering as it lifted to mine. "Your element is calling to mine."

"To mate?"

"To test the potential for mating." His palm slid to the back of my neck, branding my skin and causing me to lean closer to him. "It's a call to play, to explore the boundaries and the potential between us."

"What happens if we give in?" I whispered, my lips angling toward his.

"We're bound for a month, where your power tastes mine and vice versa." The words were warm against my mouth, a flicker of fire dancing between us and kissing the air with unspoken promise.

"A month?" I repeated, deciding I liked the sound of that.

"A trial period, yes."

"Like dating?" I surmised.

"Yes, I believe that's what you call it in the Human Realm. A courtship period where we're exclusive to one another."

I frowned. "Just from a kiss?"

He nodded, his free hand going to my exposed hip, holding me. "You would not be able to touch another Fire Fae until our courtship wore off."

"That sounds…"

"Binding," he murmured. "Yes. That's what you've done to Exos."

His words startled me from the stupor overwhelming my mind. "What?"

"You kissed him, thereby initiating the trial." He

swallowed, his grip tightening. "And because you are made of various elements, you can entertain more than one courtship at a time."

"Oh," I whispered, my eyes widening. "Is that normal?"

"No." He pressed his forehead to mine. "Not at all."

"Oh," I repeated, my voice hoarse. "Is that why I want you both?"

His deep chuckle vibrated the sensual atmosphere around us, scattering goose bumps along my limbs. "Your elemental gifts crave us both, yes."

"And a kiss binds us?"

"Temporarily, yes. If it's desired and agreed upon by both parties."

Meaning Exos wanted the bond, too. Or had he only yearned to kiss me? I pushed away the thought, preferring to focus on the now, on the way Titus's hands felt against my skin. His breath, a fiery intoxication warming my lips, urging me to close the gap between us, to take what I desired and more. To bind us. To explore him. To taste him. To *feel* him.

I slid onto his lap, my legs straddling his own, my arms wrapping around his neck. "Kiss me, Titus," I whispered, my mouth brushing the words against his. "Please kiss me."

He smiled, his fingers threading through my hair, taking control by angling my head to his liking. "Try not to light the room on fire, sweetheart."

"No promises," I mouthed, the embers already coiling in my stomach. The erection seated firmly between my thighs didn't help, nor did the way his chest burned mine as he tugged me closer, his arm a brand around my lower back.

He led with his tongue, not bothering to ease me into our embrace. It wasn't needed. One touch unleashed the passion between us in an explosion of sensation and lust. My nails dug into his shoulders, anchoring me to him as he dominated my mouth in a way no other man had. It left me breathless, needy, and moaning for more, his experience in this arena detonating all my expectations and laying a new foundation in his path.

Hungers only he could satiate.

A passion only he could cool.

Such fire.

A blaze that trembled over my skin, lighting up every fiber of my being.

"Titus," I moaned, his body owning mine in that moment. He could do whatever he wanted, however he desired, and I would let him. I'd never felt more alive, more energized in my entire life. It was as if he'd introduced me to a new level of existence, one aflame with endless heat and fiery sensations.

And all he'd done was kiss me.

Deeply.

Devouring me to my very soul.

"More," I urged. "Please."

He groaned, the arm around my lower back pulling me closer. "You're killing me, Claire." He tugged my lower lip into his mouth, sucking hard, the hand in my hair tightening. "We need to take this slow."

"Why?" I shifted to press my heated center to his cock, loving the way he felt between my legs. So right. So perfect. So *mine*.

The possessive urge to claim him swept over me, sending a jolt to my system and causing my eyes to widen. I never did this with men I wasn't dating steadily, let alone one I just met. A kiss, yes.

But I required monogamy before sex.

I needed to know the man.

Which was why I'd only been with two—my high school boyfriend and Tucker from last year. And I'd made both of them wait almost six months.

Not six hours, or however long it'd been.

Titus pressed his mouth to mine, slower, less demanding than before. "It's overwhelming," he whispered, his lips touching mine with each word. "You have to ease into it, or the elements will take over. They're very much a part of us,

101

of who we are, of the decisions we make. And nature doesn't always listen to reason. We rely on our minds for that."

Another kiss, softer, coaxing, his tongue gently tracing mine.

I fell into the sensation, my body igniting from within and sending another wave of warmth through my belly.

Fuck, I wanted him.

But I didn't know him.

It was all so confusing, so consuming, so empowering. I shook beneath the onslaught of emotions, my grip on him tightening, my breathing quickening in my chest.

"Titus…"

"It's okay, Claire," he whispered, shifting us so I lay on my back, his lower body settling between my thighs.

His lips remained firm, his tongue a dominant presence in my mouth. Embers seemed to dance over our skin, his palm trailing a fiery path down my side before grabbing my hip to still my movements. I hadn't even realized I was lifting myself against him until he stopped me, his touch a welcome claim.

"You feel like heaven beneath me," he murmured, his lips tasting my cheek before moving to my neck. "Fuck, Claire." He nibbled my racing pulse, sliding down to my collarbone and then back up to my mouth. "We need to sleep, sweetheart."

"I'm not tired," I replied, arching into him on a luscious sigh.

He chuckled, his lips brushing mine. "Trust me, I wish that were true. But we both know you're exhausted, and pushing this any further wouldn't be right."

"It feels right." The words were a soft exhale, my body melting beneath his. "It feels amazing."

"It does," he agreed, his voice husky and hot. "Too damn right." His tongue slid into my mouth again, the taste of him searing me from the inside out. I couldn't think beneath his onslaught, the sensations too great, the fire brewing inside us a combustible element awaiting our permission to erupt.

I whimpered and writhed beneath him, a wanton woman unleashed beneath a passion I didn't fully understand. His name fell from my lips, a chant and a plea, my nipples chafing against his hot, hard chest. I needed more. I needed him. I needed *this*.

"Enough," a deep voice said, reverberating the walls around us, yanking me from the chains of desire. Dark blue pools met mine as I glanced upward into a face so beautiful my heart threatened to combust.

Exos.

"I told you to train her, not fuck her," he growled, his words dousing me in a wave of cold water. "She doesn't understand our rules, our world, or the bonds that bind. Think with your head, Titus, not your dick."

Titus cursed, his face falling to my neck as Exos stormed out of the room, slamming the door behind him. "*Fuck*."

I suddenly felt cold despite the blanket of heat on top of me and shivered as he rolled away, his palms digging into his eyes.

"I'm sorry, Claire," he whispered. "I… I… I wasn't thinking."

Neither was I, I wanted to say back to him, but couldn't, too flabbergasted by what just happened. I'd almost begged him to take me. Had wanted him to more than anything in the world. It'd been a temporary escape from the craziness of this realm, of this new life, and he'd almost given it to me.

Except Exos had interrupted.

I didn't know if I wanted to thank him or punch him.

Confused and overwhelmed, and slightly embarrassed, I curled into a ball, tucking my knees to my chest and fighting for the heat of seconds ago to flicker through my veins.

Titus responded by pulling the blankets up around me, his silence a burden at my back.

I didn't know what to say to him. Did he want an

apology as well? A compliment? A request for that to happen again?

I had no idea because I didn't *know* him.

Yet I'd been about to let him inside me in the most intimate way.

All to escape a reality I wasn't ready to face.

And because it had felt all too right.

He pressed a kiss to my spine, right between my shoulder blades, then higher against the back of my neck, and slowly slid his arm around my waist. "Is this okay?" he asked softly, a hint of wariness in his tone. "Or do you prefer not to be touched?"

I swallowed, considering his words, another shudder rattling my limbs. How had I gone from feeling so hot to so cold?

Because he took away his heat, I realized.

He began to remove his arm again, taking with him the last vestiges of warmth around me, and I dug my fingernails into his forearm, desperate to keep him close. Needy, yes. But I couldn't stand the thought of being frozen and alone.

Titus provided a comfort that felt familiar while also serving as a new experience. And I craved both.

"Stay," I whispered. "Please."

He guided me into his body, his arm folding around me in a protective manner as his heated chest enveloped my bare back.

A temporary heaven.

Or maybe it qualified as hell.

I neither knew nor cared, too comforted by his touch to debate any further.

"Sweet dreams, Claire," he whispered.

Dreams, I thought. *Do those even exist anymore?*

My eyes fell closed, the nightmares of my existence sprouting to life behind my eyes in the vision of my mother. A cruel woman destined to destroy the fae.

Except, when I looked her in the eyes, all I saw was a vision of myself.

No, there were no dreams here.
Not for me.
Only delusions of fate.
My fate.

CHAPTER TEN
TITUS

I'M AN ASSHOLE.

Tightening my grip on Claire's hip while she slept, I tried to think of any angle in this situation where I wasn't a bastard, but came up with ashes. Exos had done the right thing by stopping me before I went too far. Claire didn't know me—didn't know this world. I didn't mean to take advantage of her, but damn, the pull between us was so strong.

She destroyed our clothes. That shouldn't have been possible. My wardrobe was customized for Fire Fae. Yet she'd demolished the fibers with the ease of a millennia-old fae. And fuck if that hadn't turned me on even more.

Her power was an aphrodisiac, seducing my fire and exciting a need I could hardly control. Not an excuse or even an explanation, just a fact. But I needed to do better.

She deserved better.

Embers flickered where my skin touched Claire's, reacting to our newly established bond—a bond that would awaken the deepest fiery passions innate to the carnal Fire Fae. Claire wasn't my first courting, but it felt different with her. Almost like I couldn't keep my thoughts straight and our dancing elements went straight to my dick.

Fuck it. Exos was right. I couldn't trust myself to be this close to her. We needed to get up, anyway.

I eased away from Claire and grimaced when she curled into herself and whimpered in her sleep.

"So cold," she mumbled.

"Shh," I whispered, drawing a finger down her cheek and sending more of my fire into her. "Today's a big day. We can't cocoon in our element all morning."

She groaned but didn't open her eyes, as if fighting the urge to wake up. She clutched the charred blanket closer to her chin and turned her face into the pillow.

Holding her through the night had been a selfish pleasure for me. I'd tried to be strong and give her the space she needed, but she'd demanded my touch. Perhaps I'd been weak to oblige her, or maybe I needed her, too.

I wasn't going to fool myself into thinking I meant more to her than what I was: an ally in a world of strangers. Maybe our connection would only make things more difficult for her, or maybe it was the anchor she needed right now.

Or a distraction.

I shoved that thought aside and forced myself out of bed. Elana's guest room of vines and mist and foreign elements seeped into me. I shivered, missing the warm embrace of the Fire Dorms.

Looking down, I smirked as ash fell from my naked body. So much power in the fireball that was Claire. *How did you do it?* I wondered again.

A soft touch across my shoulder blade made me stiffen.

Damn, I hadn't even heard her move.

"Where, uh, are your clothes?" she asked softly, as if reading my mind.

Her fingers continued to explore my back, running over the long scars I'd earned during my time in the ring. Fighting without powers didn't protect me from the harsh edge of a blade.

"You burned them off, sweetheart," I said with a grin, making sure not to turn around. She didn't need to see all of me. Yet. "I don't suppose Elana keeps extra pairs of pants around here?" It was more of a rhetorical question since I doubted Claire knew.

She drew in a soft gasp, and then I realized she was laughing. "Are you going to have to walk out of here naked?"

I finally turned enough to peer over my shoulder and raised a brow. "You sound far too pleased by that idea."

Her gaze dipped, and I knew she wanted to see what I'd been keeping from her last night, but that was our intimate link pushing her—or her grief. I wouldn't take advantage of her again, even if I thought for just a moment that I could help her forget everything.

That maybe she could help *me* forget everything.

Clearing my throat, I forced myself to bring up the one topic that would dispel the moment, to remind her of our predicament.

"Exos might have some clothes I can borrow." The words hurt, but they had to be said. This was the connection between us driving her emotions and reactions. She was too inexperienced as a fae to understand that. Taking advantage of that would be wrong.

She hesitated before her touch retreated, leaving me cold. The impulse to lean back into her overwhelmed me for just a moment before I doused the growing flames in my chest.

"Exos." She repeated the name as if she'd just remembered last night. "I... I'm connected to him, too."

The raw emotion in her voice had me glancing back to

find her cheeks flushing pink. Her blue eyes snapped up to find mine, reminding me that she was a Spirit Fae, better suited to one of her own kind.

No.

The very thought of leaving her to fend for herself against Exos—one of the only potential mates left among the Spirit Fae—made me cringe. She may have linked with him, but she needed me to keep him in line.

Gods, I didn't care if she bonded with a fae of every element, as long as I could stand by her side. We shared fire. That was the hottest of all the matings, one no fae could share with her, apart from me.

Taking her hand in mine, tiny flames sparked between us, causing her eyes to widen. "Yes, you've created a connection with him. But *our* bond is strong, even for a courtship," I admitted.

She smiled, making something inside me flip a switch. "Stronger than my bond with Exos?"

She meant it as a tease, but I sensed the tension beneath her words. Even though she couldn't possibly know what it really meant, she clearly felt some guilt at having bound both of us at the same time. Her eyes searched mine, pleading for my approval and assurance.

"Not stronger," I said, drawing the words out slowly as I ran my fingers up the soft curve of her elbow. "Just different."

Her gaze dropped. Not the answer she wanted to hear. "He barged in last night. How did he...?"

I lightly traced her shoulder before cupping her cheek. Her eyelids fluttered closed as she leaned into my touch. She wasn't going to like my response, but Claire deserved the truth. She needed to know what it meant to be bonded.

"He sensed your desire," I said softly. "Whenever you are, well, *aroused*, he'll know. As will I."

She flinched away. "Well, that's embarrassing."

Chuckling, I wrapped a blanket around my waist. I was so busy trying to cover myself to prevent tempting her that

I forgot she was completely naked as well. She allowed the charred fabric to pull away from her, revealing lush, sensual skin that glowed with the heat of our connection. She watched me, waiting to see what I would do.

It took every ember of willpower to look away from her. If I indulged myself even for a moment, I'd toss away all my reservations and take her right now.

She's grieving.
She's scared.
She needs you to be strong.
She doesn't understand the bond.

I reminded myself of all the things the Halfling was likely going through right now. Today was going to be rough for her. She needed to see the Academy, and more so, she needed to understand how important it was for her to be here. The alternatives weren't choices at all.

Isolation…

Death…

The sooner she faced the Academy and fae society, the sooner she would be equipped to deal with her new life. My needs were nothing compared to hers.

Before I could look at Claire again and spiral into the depths of our newfound bond, Exos blundered into the bedroom.

Claire snatched her knees to her chest and cried out. "Exos!"

I would have offered her the blanket to cover herself, but there was something in Exos's eyes that said our nakedness was the least of his problems right now. "You two. Get dressed." His gaze flickered to the doorway, and I sensed the low boom of the ground I'd missed a moment before. "Now."

* * *

"News has spread that the Halfling is here." Elana folded her hands in front of her dress and let out a long sigh. Vines

110

budding with blue flowers wound through her hair, a living ornament that made her look ethereal and regal.

I frowned and bit my tongue—hard. The rumor was already on campus. River had been the one to tell me about the Halfling, but the fact that a bunch of unruly students were causing a scene right outside Elana's estate? That didn't just happen. Someone had told them Claire was here.

Not River, because I knew him and he would never do that, but *someone* had.

"What do they want?" Claire asked, her voice taut as her fingers clenched around mine. I shouldn't be indulging her need to touch me, or my need to touch her, but somehow our hands kept finding one another without my permission.

Elana stared at Claire, her expression soft and wise. "Forgive my bluntness, but they're protesting."

"Protesting?" she squeaked and dug her fingernails into my skin.

I tugged at my borrowed clothes with my free hand. They were far too tight around my biceps and chest, and the agonizing frills ruffling around my elbows made me feel like a complete moron. Which, I supposed, was Exos's goal when he gave me this pompous outfit.

His wry smile confirmed it. "Don't worry, Claire. Everyone will be so taken aback by Titus in royal garb that you'll be yesterday's news."

I suppressed a retort for the jackass, but Exos was right. This would help take some of the attention off of Claire, which was the least I could do considering her situation.

However, even my comical attire couldn't win Claire's attention. Her gaze was locked on the hall that glittered with motes that had drifted in with the morning sunlight. Low chanting sounded outside the door in our old language, which Claire wouldn't understand, the words making my teeth clench.

Dooms-bringer.
Finish what your mother started.
Fae killer.

"What are they saying?" Claire asked as she tilted her head to the side.

Exos plucked Claire's hand from mine and gave her knuckles a kiss, startling all of us out of our unease. "Nothing of importance, princess." His eyes held hers for a beat before he bowed, releasing her as quickly as he'd grabbed her. "I, uh, need to ready our future accommodations." He refocused on me. "I trust you'll be able to give Claire a proper tour and bring her to the Fire Quad?"

"No one will touch her," I vowed, not because Exos had ordered me to play guardian, but because my blood boiled knowing how many fae wanted Claire dead. Maybe it was just the courtship bond, but instinct told me to shred apart anyone who dared to whisper a threat within her vicinity.

Which was apparently half the entire fucking Academy, if the chants outside were anything to go by.

Exos leaned in, dropping his voice to a whisper. "Don't kill anyone. Just show her around campus. Keep your head on your shoulders." He gave me a once-over. "And your dick in your pants."

That last part was totally unnecessary.

Okay, maybe a little bit necessary after last night.

But for fuck's sake, the jackass really needed to cool it with all the damn orders.

"Come on, Claire," I said, unable to muster anything more respectable than a slight bowing of my head to Exos. "We've been given our *instructions* for the day."

She swallowed hard, but I felt the heat of her trust where her skin touched mine, our hands instinctively finding each other again. It told me that as long as I was with her, perhaps she could face anything, even a protesting crowd of fae.

Elana waved her hand, causing the bangles on her wrist to jingle. The wide doors of her estate opened with low groans, reminding me of ancient trees bowing in the wind.

Sunlight poured into the foyer and illuminated the golden spirals around Claire's face. I wanted to reach out and run my fingers through her silky strands, gather her hair in my fist, and kiss her.

Again.

Fuck. This uncontrollable need to take her was going to be the death of me if I didn't learn how to tamper it. A tour would help. Assuming we could make it through the masses.

"Now or never," I said, more to myself than to Claire.

"I'd rather get the shit show over with now," Claire replied, surprising me with the vigor of her words. She shrugged. "Beats staying in this, uh, forest of a house. Show me your fae world, Titus." She squeezed my hand, her gaze warm and trusting.

A smile twitched at my lips as we stepped out onto the dried leaves in front of the estate. The chanting near the front gates ceased, students' eyes going wide. "Here we go," I said, pulling Claire along at my side.

"There's a lot of them," she whispered.

I snorted. "Yeah. I'm not concerned." I created a fireball in my hand and threw it up in the air, before catching it. Many of the fae at the gates took several steps back, some even going as far as to leave. They all knew me, understood my gifts and how powerful I could be in a full rage.

Begrudgingly, I also had to admit that borrowing Exos's royal attire helped matters. Because they would see *his* symbol on my clothing, which boldly announced my actions to be official orders. And fucking with those orders was a good way to end up in the fire pits.

I tossed a ball at the gates for fun, smirking as several more fae dispersed.

Another flame appeared along the periphery, the signature belonging to Exos, who stood behind us in the doorway wearing a stoic mask.

That caused almost the entire crowd to die, the students not wanting to mess with me or the notorious Spirit Royal.

"Yeah, you'll be fine," I told Claire, winking.

She gaped back and forth between me and Exos. "Did he just…?"

"Yep." I glanced back at him with a nod that he returned before disappearing into the house. "He's just throwing his weight behind mine, not that it's needed with this ridiculous outfit."

Claire giggled, her cheeks pinkening. "You look…"

"Handsome?" I prompted, waggling my brows. "Hot? Sexy as fuck?"

Her laugh was music to my ears, even as she shook her head. "You look hideous."

I covered my heart, feigning a wounded expression. "Claire… How could you? You know my ego is fragile."

She snorted. "Somehow I doubt that."

I slung my arm around her shoulders, tugging her into my side. "You're right. I'm pretty sure even I make this outfit look good."

She patted my abdomen. "Pretty sure you don't."

"Yeah, yeah. You want this tour or not?" I teased. The majority of the onlookers were gone, leaving Claire much more at ease beside me.

"Yeah, I do." She gave me a small smile. "I'm actually a little curious."

"Just a little?"

She ducked her head shyly, her blue eyes sparkling with power. "Scared, too. But mostly curious."

"You have nothing to fear, sweetheart. I've got you." I kissed her forehead, the action so natural, as if we'd been doing this for years, not hours. Not wanting to dig too deeply into that realization, I released her shoulders and held out my hand. "Let's go."

"Okay," she whispered, placing her palm in mine.

The beautiful day unfolded around us as we moved, trees seeming to bow to Claire in her wake. She had no idea what kind of power she exuded in this world, how palpable her essence was to the kingdom surrounding us. Yet, she seemed quite taken with the atmosphere, her free hand curling into the air with each step, her eyes dancing with wonder.

"It's so enchanting," she breathed.

"And you've not even seen the Academy yet," I replied, smiling.

"How far is—" Her mouth fell open as the famous iron gates came into view down the flower-laden hill. "Holy shit, we are not in Kansas anymore."

I blinked. "What?"

"You know, the…" She trailed off and shook her head. "Never mind. It's a line from a well-known movie."

"Oh, human cinema." I smiled. "We don't really have that here, preferring to spend our time outdoors and whatnot." Or at the gym. Or in a fighting ring. "Although, I guess they kind of televise some of our sporting events, but it's not the same. It's all carried by elemental magic, sort of unfolding in replays. And yeah, I'm boring you. Let's head that way."

I pointed to the main entrance, charmed by four of the elements dancing around it. Beyond it were the renowned stone structures of the school, all laced with greenery and adorned in flowers. At least, the main buildings were. Each quad catered to the various elementals. I'd show her the charred towers of the Fire Quad first. It wouldn't be as lively as the Chancellor's home, but just as captivating.

"Are you, like, supposed to be in class right now?" she asked as we walked.

"Nah, you arrived at a good time. It's our downtime right now between courses. Everything starts back up tomorrow."

"Like a weekend," she surmised.

"Similar, yeah. But we do six days on, six days off. Helps keep up the creative flow and allows us to participate in the mandatory intramurals."

"Intramurals?" she repeated, her gaze on the water dancing with fire along the gate as we passed beneath it.

"Fae mingling." I smirked. "It's Elana's way of trying to make all the fae get along, by forcing us to engage in physical activities and other general education courses together. Like

Human Studies. We also have a morning or afternoon of obligatory gymnasium activities during our six days on— which, again, includes all the fae."

Her brow puckered. "You don't get along otherwise?"

I shrugged. "Some of us do. Some of us don't. There's a council that guides us, but each kingdom has its own governing structure."

"So... you're like different countries?"

"From what I understand of your world, it'd be more similar to continents." I took a right through a long woodsy corridor between two of the stone buildings. "This is the main campus, by the way. Where the intramural courses are that I mentioned. Then each quad caters to the specific fae, so I'll show you Fire Quad first since I'm most familiar with it."

We stepped into a courtyard where several fae were mingling, all of whom went silent upon spotting us.

Claire gave a little wave that had them all taking several steps backward, their eyes going wide and whispers in the ancient language taking over.

It's her.

I heard she caused the quake last night.

Evil.

Why would they allow her here?

She's going to kill us all.

Claire's cheeks pinkened, her inability to understand their words not mattering. Their tones said it all.

"Enough," I said, irritated.

"It's fine," Claire whispered. "I get it."

"It's not fine." I pulled her across the courtyard, only to find a row of fae waiting along the pathway that led to the Fire Quad.

Fuck.

A trio of fae approached us, their hips swaying and merciless eyes gleaming with mischief.

Ignis and her bratty friends.

"Well, I must say, the Halfling is not what I expected,"

Ignis said as she curled writhing fire around her fingertips in a blatant display of aggression. "She's so... *blonde*."

Claire narrowed her eyes, but she didn't seem intimidated. Her gaze dipped slightly to the flames, betraying her moment's hesitation that she'd noticed anything amiss.

"Ah, yeah. I know girls like you," she said, her voice low and full of foreboding. She raised her chin and peered down her nose at Ignis. "You think you have everyone wrapped around your little finger. Well, luckily, there are bitches in the Human Realm, too, and I don't have time for them." She tugged at my hand. "Come on, Titus. I'd much rather watch you play with fire."

Sickle sent a stream flooding in front of Claire, and I jerked her back before she could step into it and get caught in the trap. Aerie laughed, sending a breeze to splash the water onto Claire.

It sizzled on contact.

Good, Claire was pissed.

That meant she would focus on her fire abilities—abilities I could help her with.

Ignis chuckled and stepped close enough to reach me. "Oh, Titus, are you going to let her boss you around like that?" She moved to wrap her fingers around my bicep but hissed when the contact burned her. "Fuck, Titus!" Her eyes went wide, and she bounced her gaze between us, her wild auburn curls fanning out as heat spread across her face. She let out a rude laugh and covered her mouth. "Oh, seriously? You and I fuck, and then the next day, you initiate a courtship bond with a Halfling? Oh, this is too good."

Gods. I'd almost forgotten about the other night, with Claire being so close. Ignis had tried to force the bond, which, by fae custom, meant I owed it to her to try to reciprocate. But clearly, I broke that rule.

"*What?*" Sickle screeched, her voice like nails on a chalkboard. "That's a violation!"

I sighed. *Here we go.*

"Can't expect much from him," Aerie put in. "I mean, you knew he was a player before you let him lure you into bed, Ig."

"He said he loved me."

"Oh, for the love of the gods, cut that shit out," I demanded. "You know I didn't."

Her lower lip wobbled. "And now you deny it?" She shook her head, real live tears popping into her eyes. "Three times, Titus. We made love three times."

"I thought we fucked," I countered, livid. "Which is it, Ignis?"

"How can you be so cold?" She perfected the art of woman hurt. "Oh, because you went and tricked the Halfling into bonding with you. Is it some sort of bet?" Her eyes narrowed. "That's it, isn't it? You're in on the bet on who can fuck her first?"

"Oh, you know he is," Sickle said, confusing the hell out of me. "I heard the stakes are high, too. But initiating an elemental link is a bit of a cheat, if you ask me. The others will disqualify you for it."

"Bet?" Claire repeated, her voice far softer than it was a few minutes ago. Her hand felt like ice in my hand, her arm brittle.

"They're lying," I promised. "I don't even know what they're talking about."

Ignis snorted. "I bet you'll say the same about how you fucked me two days ago, but I have elemental proof." She lifted her shirt to reveal a red handprint on her abdomen. "What can I say? Things heated up."

Claire pulled away from me, her arms folding around herself.

"Aww, not so tough now?" Ignis continued, her tone frigid. "And here I thought you'd be as ballsy as your mum."

"That's enough, Ignis," I growled.

She shrugged. "I don't think she cares. Elements knows her mother didn't when she destroyed the fae race."

"Ignis!"

"What? She's a whore just like her mother, and you're going to stand there and defend her?" She scoffed, tossing her long red hair over one shoulder. "You deserve better, baby. You know you do." She tried to stroke my arm again, but flames erupted around us.

Not from me.

Not from Ignis.

But from Claire.

Tears shone bright in her eyes as flames poured from her hands, sending fae scattering down the pathway to avoid being caught in her emotional outburst.

"Claire," I murmured, reaching for her.

"*No*," she snapped. "Do not touch me."

I sighed. "Come on, sweetheart. Ignis is just being a bitch."

"Just being a bitch? One you slept with right before...?" She shook her head, unable to finish.

"It didn't mean anything," I vowed. "Not like with you."

Ignis laughed, the sound mean and cold. "Pretty sure you said the same thing to me about, who was it?" She snapped her fingers. "Mae?"

Fucking flames! "Would you just shut the fuck up?"

"What? Worried she might learn about your reputation, lover? A little late for that." She sounded so pleased with herself. If Claire hadn't looked ready to lose her shit, I might have considered teaching Ignis a lesson with my fire.

"Claire." I kept my voice soft. "Can—"

The entire wall went up in flames.

As did the path.

And the courtyard.

Fuck.

CHAPTER ELEVEN
CLAIRE

I HAD LET MY GUARD DOWN. Stupid. So fucking stupid. I knew better.

Titus tried to bond with me over a bet?

He fucked that bitch? Before me?

Everyone hates me.

What am I even doing here?

The fire raged around me, scalding my skin, so foreign and unfamiliar compared to the other flames I'd cast over the last few days. It actually burned me in places, singeing the dress Elana had given me to wear and searing my side.

I jumped away from it, confused.

Why is it hurting me?

Titus roared on the periphery, his body hidden behind the orange-and-yellow wall dancing before me. He seemed to be yelling at me to stop, but I couldn't. I didn't know how. The fire didn't feel right. I tried to call it to me the way he instructed, but all that did was cause it to flare upward toward the building.

Oh no…

People started screaming, the flames climbing and shifting, destroying the vines along the stone walls and creeping into open windows. It reminded me of a snake— lethal and fast.

And I had no control over it.

A hand on my shoulder yanked me backward. I screamed, only to realize I recognized the arm encircling my waist. "Focus for me, princess," Exos whispered, his lips against my ear. "Breathe."

"I-I'm trying."

"I know, and you're doing so good, Claire. I just need you to try a little more, okay?" The words were warm and soothing, causing my shoulders to relax back against him. He kept one arm around me while he used his opposite hand to grab my wrist and pull my hand upward. Then he yanked it back when the fire burned us both.

"It doesn't feel right," I said, shaking my head. "I don't even know what I'm saying." Or what any of it meant. It was pure instinct driving my senses and telling me that I didn't recognize the energy before us.

"Let's try to push against it." He cradled my hand in his, guiding it at an angle. "Right there, baby. I want you to call water and wind, and blast the focal point."

"How?" I asked, exasperated.

He shifted his grip around my waist to tap my heart. "It's right here, Claire. Inside you. Look for it, like you do your fire, and call it to you."

Tears pooled in my eyes, frustration taking over me. He made it sound so simple, but he wanted me to unlock a door I didn't possess the key to. "Exos, I can't."

"You can," he promised, his tone coaxing. Then he yanked my hand back as the flame reached out at us, the heat scorching our skin. Exos's grip tightened, his back hitting the wall behind us as the flames turned our way in a threatening sweep. He started muttering, his own flame glowing in his hand as he threw it at the approaching inferno.

But all that seemed to do was exasperate it.

The blaze yawned, blowing hot air toward us that slick sweat across my skin and caused Exos to shiver behind me.

"We need to find a way out," he said, his voice holding a sense of urgency. "Or that thing is going to destroy us."

I honestly couldn't believe we were even still standing. The fifty-foot tower of fire should have killed us just for being this close.

But something kept it at bay.

Something *protected* us.

I frowned, identifying the thin barrier with my mind while Exos spoke behind me. His statement went over my head, my attention on the odd film of mist that seemed to be pushing against the flames.

When I called to it, the essence responded.

That's mine, I realized, my lips parting. *What can I do with it?*

Exos said I needed air and water. To focus on that cavernous hole above, the source of the flames. I could see it now, the way it swirled dangerously like a whirlpool of lava.

There, I urged, shooting the water upward with a gust of wind, the power roaring out of me from someplace deep within my soul.

Exhilarating.

Powerful.

Lively.

I stole a deep breath, my lungs filling with fresh air, and blew the contents upward with the water, creating a twirl of my own—A breeze infused with cool springs that doused the flames—causing them to sizzle. I repeated the action, a sense of peace falling over me with each exhale, until the inferno fizzled into ash.

Ignis stood across from me, her eyes glowing red, her expression one of abject horror. "That bitch tried to kill me!" she accused while trying to grab Titus's arm. It must have shocked her again, because she flinched away from him, but it was Titus's expression that I couldn't stop staring at. He appeared just as horrified as Ignis.

Her friend with the bluish-blonde hair heaved a huge sigh, a sheet of ice melting beneath my water. "I thought we were gonna die. Not even playin'. Like, I'm fucking exhausted."

"You saved our lives, Sickle," the other girl said, her skirt indecently high as she collapsed against the wall. "Dear Elements..." She shuddered as she put her head on her knees.

"What are you all just standing here for? That bitch needs to be banished!" Ignis went on. "Or did you all just miss that fire tornado that tried to *kill me*! This is mutual ground, Your Highness. You know the rules."

"You provoked her, Ignis," Titus growled.

"I did not!"

"Yes, you did!" He threw up his hands. "You know she's volatile and you pushed all her buttons!"

I winced at his description. *Volatile.*

"She shouldn't even be here anyway! Or have you forgotten what her whore of a mother did? You wait until my daddy hears about this. He will not be happy." She folded her arms, her expression haughty as she stared down her nose at me. "Your days here are numbered, *Halfling*. Mark my words."

Exos's arm tightened around me. "Is that a threat, Fire Fae? Because as you already pointed out, violence on the Academy premises is frowned upon. I would hate to have to report your behavior to *your father,* who happens to sit on the Council. With me."

Her face paled. "He'll never believe you."

"I think you'll find that I am quite convincing," Exos

replied, all arrogance. His hold loosened, his hand falling to my hip. "Now, if you'll excuse us, I need to escort Claire to her sleeping quarters."

"Exos—"

"I think you've done enough for the day, Titus," he said, cutting him off. "I'll follow up with you later." His dismissive tone pissed me off before, but right now, it was what I needed. I wasn't ready to talk to Titus, not after everything Ignis had said.

He was with her right before he met me.

It wasn't fair to hold that against him, but I couldn't help it. The woman was an utter bitch, and he'd slept with her.

Right after someone named Mae.

Did he just sleep with all the females on campus?

Was I just a conquest to him? Something new?

No, a part of me whispered.

But what did I really even know about him? He'd almost fucked me last night. Exos was the one who stopped him. Clearly, Titus had a control problem when it came to sex.

Part of me knew the assessment was unfair.

The other part was too exhausted to care.

"Take me to the dorm," I said, voice low, my gaze falling to the ground. I didn't want to see Titus's expression, didn't want to know what he thought. I just wanted to lie down. Fighting those flames had taken a lot out of me. So had this entire morning, or day, or however long it'd been. Actually, no, this whole fucking week had exhausted me.

Exos pulled me with him, away from a sputtering Ignis and her two insipid friends.

Away from the warmth of Titus.

"I don't know what happened," I mumbled, Exos's palm a brand against my hip as he led me through yet another courtyard. *The fae really like being outside.* Except this one was vacant save for a few heads poking out of windows, all eyes on me. When I glanced at a few, they ducked. Afraid.

They all hate me.

"Your emotions created an inferno," Exos murmured.

"But you were able to contain it."

"Why did it burn me? It's never done that before." Sure, it singed my clothes to ash, but it didn't *hurt*.

"I don't know," he replied, taking me through a set of black gates lined in fire. The buildings took a drastic architectural turn, the landscape black and charred, all signs of flowers and trees gone. But it wasn't so much barren as it was intriguing, the fountains in the yard flowing fire instead of water. And little flickers that reminded me of lightning bugs buzzed about.

"Wow," I whispered, awed by the sight. "This is..." I had no words.

"Fire," he supplied. "I'm heeding Titus's point that you need to be near the students, and have procured you a dorm here. I'll be staying with you." I missed a step at his proclamation, but he caught me with ease, his lips curling. "Surprised, princess?"

"Y-you're staying with me?" I stuttered.

"Yes." He gave me a wry glance. "You need supervision. No more burned-down buildings. But hey, the Fire Quad is actually fire-retardant, so that's a plus." While he spoke the words in a teasing manner, they didn't lighten my feelings in the slightest.

Because he was right.

I kept hurting people and destroying everything around me.

Rick.

The bar.

Elana's house.

The path.

I really am volatile, just as Titus said.

"Hey," Exos murmured, gripping my chin and drawing us to a halt outside one of the buildings doors. "I wasn't trying to make you feel bad, Claire. I actually meant it as a positive thing—that we'll be safe here."

I swallowed, trying to look away from his too-blue eyes, but he held me in place, his pupils flaring. "I... I know you

125

didn't. But you're right." The last part was said on a whisper, my throat suddenly tight. "I don't mean to keep hurting people, Exos."

"Oh, darling, I know." He cupped my cheek, pulling me to him. "I can't begin to understand, Claire. Our upbringings are so different. But I can tell you one thing."

I clung to his suit jacket, allowing his comfort, seeking something, *anything*, to make the pain go away. "What?" I whispered.

"Watching you handle that fire was one of the most beautiful sights I've ever seen." The words were against my ear. "Whether you caused it or not remains to be seen. That you were able to dispel it, that's what counts, Claire. It means you're learning control, and far faster than anyone I've ever known." He shifted back to stare down at me. "You're going to be okay. I promise."

"I don't feel okay," I admitted.

"I know." He pressed his lips to my forehead. "But you will. Let's go up to the room. I'll make us something to eat, and maybe you can show me how you created that mist tunnel." He didn't wait for the answer but instead linked our fingers together and slowly led me inside.

Several students with pointy ears poked their heads into the hallway, their mouths gaping wide at seeing Exos. Then freezing as they spotted me behind him.

I didn't try to smile or wave this time. I learned my lesson in the quad.

No one wanted me here. That much was clear.

Well, I don't want to be here, either, I thought at them, my heart skipping a beat in my chest. *None of this was my choice.*

Not Exos.

Not Titus.

Not this entire damn world.

My mother did this to me. A warning would have been appreciated. Some sort of note that said, *Oh, by the way, you're part fae,* would have been great.

But I received nothing. Not even a warning call from the

Fae Realm. Just Exos showing up at the bar, kissing me, and stealing me into this world.

Now they wanted me to attend an academy where everyone hated me. Fan-fucking-tastic. Oh, and I had bound myself to two men. One of which was apparently a man-whore, and the other, a dick.

Well, he wasn't acting mean right now.

And Titus, I really didn't know. Maybe he had an excuse? He didn't know me when he slept with her.

Oh God. Of all the fae to sleep with, he chose *her?* What did that say about me? I was nothing like Ignis. Was that his usual type?

Why am I beating myself up over this? I hardly know him.

Yet, I almost slept with him.

"Here we are," Exos said, pushing through a door into a modern living area with all-black walls and furniture. Even the kitchen was painted in ebony shades. However, it maintained a clean feel, the marble beneath my feet reminding me of granite.

Exos closed the door behind me, pressing his thumb to some sort of high-tech lock that shifted beneath his touch. The shades in the room lifted to reveal a view of the forest lining the property, the leaves almost beckoning me out to play.

"Your bedroom is through there." He pointed to an open threshold that revealed a decent-sized bed and dresser. "I'll be in the one here." He gestured to the room across the hall. "I, uh, didn't know what clothes you wanted, so I ordered a selection. And of course your uniforms."

"Uniforms?" I repeated, frowning.

"Yeah, you know, traditional plaid skirt, sweater thing." He shrugged. "Guys wear slacks and button-downs. Pretty standard."

"For a private high school, maybe. But this is supposed to be like a university, right?"

He palmed the back of his neck, looking uncomfortable. "Elana thinks the uniforms help give the fae a united feel.

The less competition the better."

"Why?" I wondered.

"Because our elements can either exist peacefully or negatively." He dropped his hand and cocked his head toward the kitchen. "I'm going to fix us some sandwiches. Why don't you go check out your room?"

"Uh, sure," I said, staring at his back as he walked away, dismissing me.

Because he's Exos. A Royal Fae Prince.

And I'm just Claire, a volatile firecracker.

My lips curled down at the side. This whole pity thing wasn't me. I always fought through my hardships. My grandmother used to say I had a spine of steel.

But I didn't feel like that right now.

I felt more fluid. Bendy. Breakable.

And I hated it.

I wanted to fight yet didn't know what to fight against. Or how. Or even who.

Well, I knew one thing. Moping around in this state of hopelessness wasn't going to fix a damn thing. It wasn't me. I didn't just give up. I struggled until I won.

Stubborn to your very core, my grandmother used to say.

I am, I agreed, walking into the room Exos stated was mine. *I just need to accept what is and move forward.*

In this very strange bedroom...

My brow furrowed as I eyed the charcoaled furniture and black sheets. Not my usual style, but being immune to fire was certainly a plus. I brushed my fingertips across the quilt, finding it surprisingly soft. *What is this made of?* I marveled. It reminded me of silk.

I went through the drawers and then the closet. The uniform consisted of a plaid skirt and a sweater, just as Exos had described. But the pinks and purples were beautiful and unlike anything I'd ever seen. I plucked it off the hanger to hold it up to myself in the mirror, enjoying the way it popped against my skin and hair.

"The Fire Fae have special outfits that are flame-retardant for, well, obvious reasons." Exos stood just inside the walk-in closet, a mug in his hand, his shoulder braced against the door frame.

I'd not heard him approach, too lost in the mirror against the wall. "I, uh, okay." My cheeks pinkened to match the fabric in my reflection. "I was just seeing if it would fit."

He grinned. "It'll fit." He held out the mug. "I made you some hot chocolate, if you want it. The sandwiches are baking."

Baking? I pushed that thought away in favor of the item in his hand. "Hot chocolate?" My heart skipped a beat. "I... I would love some hot chocolate." I couldn't remember the last time I'd indulged in a hot chocolate. My grandmother used to make it for me as a child.

After hanging up the uniform, I accepted the warm gift and let the heat seep into my cool fingertips. "Thank you."

"You're welcome." He tucked a piece of my hair behind my ear and took a step backward into the bedroom. "Is this okay? The accommodations, I mean."

"Yeah, it's, well, different. But it's fine."

"Okay, good."

I followed him and sat on the bed with my back braced against the headboard, my dress flaring over my legs. My shoes were in the closet already, leaving my feet bare. I blew across the mug before allowing myself a sip and groaned at the flavors bursting on my tongue. This wasn't like any hot chocolate I'd ever tasted, the whipped goodness decadent and empowering.

He smirked and sat beside me on the bed, crossing his feet at the ankles to reveal a pair of dress socks that matched his elegant attire.

"Do you always wear suits?" I asked, trying for simple conversation.

He shrugged. "Depends on the situation."

"Yeah?" I eyed him sideways. "And when does the situation require you to wear that hideous royal garb you forced on Titus?"

Exos chuckled, shaking his head. "I can't believe he actually put that shit on. I had a pair of jeans and a shirt waiting for him in the other room."

"He was in a hurry after you told us to head downstairs."

"Not *that* much of a hurry," he said, laughing again. "It's a formal outfit that hasn't been worn in probably two or three hundred years. He's probably going to destroy it, which might disappoint Cyrus." He shrugged. "Was totally worth seeing Titus in it, though."

"You're mean," I accused, smiling. Who knew this man had a sense of humor?

He gave me a look. "You can't tell me you didn't enjoy seeing him in that atrocious outfit?"

I hid my amusement behind my mug. "Maybe a little."

"Uh-huh." He nudged me with his shoulder and reached over to press his palm against my mug. Heat flared against my fingertips as he used fire to keep the contents warm.

My lips parted in awe, my own fire igniting to do the same and bringing the liquid to a boil. "Wow," I whispered, staring down at the bubbling chocolate.

"Try stirring it," he murmured, releasing the mug.

"With what?" There was no spoon.

"Air." He studied the drink, his head tilting. "Perhaps water, too, as I added some to the mixture."

I considered his suggestion and exhaled over the top of the rim. It created a tiny ripple that I tugged on and swirled with my mind, the contents shifting with my mental command. "Oh…" It was working. The bubbles smoothed as I whirled the chocolate with another breath, the sweet aroma tickling my nose.

"It's all about control," Exos said softly, his blue eyes simmering as he observed.

"Why is fire so much easier?" I asked, calling for it again to heat my cup and infusing more air to twirl it through my drink.

"It seems to be tied to your emotions. Calling the flames is a natural defense. It's also the most passionate of the elements." Embers danced along his fingertips, jumping into my hot chocolate and joining my atmospheric storm.

I smiled as I absorbed his energy with mine, the feeling so incredibly natural. "Maybe I'm more Fire Fae?"

He shook his head. "No, you're very much a Spirit Fae."

"But I don't seem to be doing much with spirit."

"Because you don't know how to use it yet." His expression darkened a bit. "It's the most powerful element in existence and therefore the most important to understand before you access it. You literally hold the lives of those around you in your hands when you play with spirit."

I stopped playing with the hot chocolate, his words chilling me. "What do you mean?"

"When you have the power to create life, you can also take it. Or…" He met my gaze. "Or you can manipulate it."

"Like telling people what to do?"

He nodded. "But it's more than that. Spirit gives us access to the souls of every living, breathing thing, from the trees outside to the fae in this dorm. And the more powerful the Spirit Fae, the stronger the ability to take control. It's considered a very dark gift, Claire. Most of my kind only use it on a superficial level as a result."

"And you?" I asked.

His expression hardened. "I use it as required as the strongest Spirit Fae in the realm."

"By taking lives," I translated. "Or repurposing them."

"Only in very dire situations. But yes."

I swallowed, finally understanding his purpose here. "That's why you've been assigned to me. To rein me in, or kill me, as required."

"Yes." No hesitation or guilt or apology. "However, my goal is to help you thrive, Claire." He drew his finger across my cheek and down my neck as an alarm sounded in the other room. "Sandwiches." He gave me a small smile before sliding off the bed to leave me with the hot chocolate. It'd gone cold in my hands, my fingers turning it to ice at his words.

131

If Exos couldn't help me find control over these wayward powers, he would be forced to hurt me.

No, to kill me.

Or worse—possess me.

I shivered. *What if I can't master these abilities?*

Focusing again on my cup, I brought the drink to a boil and tried to access the water inside to stir the contents. When nothing happened, I blew again, re-creating the action from earlier. Then I tried something different by pulling the liquid up with my mind to create a funnel over the rim.

It resembled a tornado of molten chocolate.

I tried tasting it and found the flavor to be the same as it was before, but even more potent. *Magical.* And so, so delicious.

After a few more sips, I coaxed the liquid back into my cup and noticed Exos watching from the doorway with two plates, one in each hand. "I didn't want to interrupt you," he said, his voice huskier than before.

My cheeks heated as I set the mug aside. "I was playing."

"I know." He settled beside me again, handing me one of the dishes. "Your knack for air is growing. I don't have an advisor for you in that element yet, but I'll work on one. Elana mentioned a Vox; apparently, he's tutoring an Earth Fae already and doing a good job with him." He took a bite of the strange green thing in his hand and shrugged. "A task for tomorrow."

I was too busy staring at his food to really hear and comprehend his words. "What is that?" I had one on my plate as well. It reminded me of a lettuce wrap, except cooked. And the stuff inside was definitely not anything I'd seen before.

"Take a bite and find out," he taunted. "You'll see."

I poked the foresty globe on my plate. "Eh…"

"Live a little, princess." He winked and took another bite, then reached around me to grab my hot chocolate and took a swallow before returning it.

The act felt intimate somehow, as if we did this every day.

Yet this was the first time he'd ever been normal with me. Well, as normal as a fae could be, anyway. This sandwich didn't qualify. Neither did the elemental magic tricks.

He arched an eyebrow at me. "If you don't at least try it, I'm going to be offended, Claire. It's not as if I go about cooking for just anyone, you know."

Because he was a Prince. He probably had manservants. Or maybe more of those pixie things that Elana had used.

"Fine." I could at least taste it. The hot chocolate was one of the best I'd ever tasted. Maybe this *sandwich* would join the list? I eyed the globe and picked it up with my hands—like Exos had. The texture reminded me of a moist tortilla, only it was leafy like lettuce.

And so, so *green*.

I took a small bite, expecting the worst, and raised my eyebrows when the taste exploded in my mouth. Spicy but sweet, and delicious.

Yet, mushy.

And not at all what I would call a *sandwich.*

It was more like hummus mixed with crunchy vegetables and beans, heated into a spinach casing with a gooey texture.

Exos waited until I swallowed to ask, "Like it?"

"It's... different."

"It's a sandwich," he replied, acting as if I'd lost my marbles.

"This is not a sandwich," I assured him. "It's like a, uh, melted salad in brick form. There's not even meat on it. Or cheese."

He gave me the most offended look imaginable. "Why the hell would you put meat and cheese in a sandwich?"

I gaped at him.

And giggled.

"Meat and cheese in a sandwich." He shuddered. "Gross."

My giggle blossomed into a laugh that shook my shoulders, the goop on my plate forgotten as I keeled over in a humorous fit. He sounded so displeased by my comment, as if I'd made the most ridiculous suggestion. And hey, maybe to him, I had. Because he wasn't human.

He was a fae.

A fae meant to be my protector and executioner.

I couldn't stop laughing, the hilarity of the moment and situation unraveling inside me. I burned down a bar. *Me. Claire.* What were the chances? Oh, apparently good because I was a fae, too. I battled an inferno today—one I seemingly created. And I fought it with my *breath.*

My body vibrated with uncontrollable mirth. I couldn't stop, the burst of emotion requiring an escape. An outlet. *Something.*

Exos said something, but I couldn't hear him over the thoughts pelting my brain.

I'm a fae.

I control fire.

Wind. Er, air. Whatever.

Water.

Hot chocolate.

And I'm eating goo for lunch. Is it even lunch? Oh, who the hell knows?!

I lost it. Completely lost it. Tears sprouted in my eyes from laughing so hard, tears that turned to sobs. Sobs that *hurt.*

But I deserved it. Because I hurt people.

Rick.

Those girls outside. They may have provoked me, but that didn't warrant me burning them alive over some petty jealousy. Jealousy over a man I hardly knew, yet almost fucked last night.

Oh God... I couldn't stop crying. Couldn't stop laughing. Couldn't stop *being.*

So much for being strong and fighting through my shit, because all I wanted to do right now was curl into a ball and hide.

And I did just that, tucking my knees into my chest while burying my face against my forearms, and let it all out. Every ounce of fear, agony, and sadness, that I'd harbored for days, flew from me in a cacophony of sobs mingled with strangled laughs.

The plate clattered to the floor.

I didn't care.

Exos wrapped his arms around me, his chest to my back, his face in my hair.

I didn't care.

He whispered words of encouragement, his comfort an undeniable force behind me.

I didn't care.

The sun fell outside my window, the tears still flowing.

I didn't care.

I was broken.

Shattered.

Irreparably lost.

And...

I didn't care.

Except that was all a lie. I cared about every minute detail. Which was precisely the problem. I cared entirely too much.

That was what destroyed me.

My actual inability to let it all go, to just accept my fate. And maybe I would eventually. But not tonight.

Tonight, I mourned.

For Rick. For the bar and anyone else I hurt. For my friends that I would never see again. For Elana's house. For the girls I almost hurt outside hours ago.

And most importantly—I mourned for myself.

For Claire. For the woman I used to be. Because she didn't exist here.

It's only me.

CHAPTER TWELVE
EXOS

WATER.

Why am I in water?

I tried to shake off the strange dream, my nose catching in Claire's lavender-scented hair. My arms tightened around her reflexively, some ancient part of me pleased by her nearness—the part that called for our bond.

Falling asleep with her body pressed up against mine had felt natural. Almost *too* natural. But she needed comfort, and I wasn't strong enough to reject her. The spirit essence inside me recognized his mate, whether I liked it or not.

No other Spirit Fae had connected to me the way Claire had, and all through a meager kiss. She'd floored me, knocked me off-kilter, and ruined me for anyone else.

What made it worse was it seemed she required a mate

for each element. It wasn't necessarily unheard of for Spirit Fae to have two mates because of our ties to two elements, but most only bonded with one fae. However, on the occasion when a Spirit Fae took two mates, it was one for each element.

And Claire had access to five.

Fuck.

I never saw myself falling into the mating rites, having opted for a life of guardianship. My brother was the one meant to settle down with another and try to create more Spirit Fae.

If he saw me now, he'd laugh. *Cuddling.* An activity I never engaged in, even post-sex.

I almost laughed, then remembered how Claire had giggled over the sandwich and broke down in sobs. Her emotions were all over the map, making it very difficult to predict her reactions. Holding her as she slept was the only comfort I could offer her, and I worried it wasn't enough.

Nuzzling her hair, I sighed. She felt so incredibly right in my arms. I never wanted to let her go, or wake from this strange, warm cocoon. But something nagged at me. The reason I woke up.

I squinted into the darkness, her shutters closed for the night.

Everything seemed all right. So what caused me to stir? Had she moved? Was it a strange dream? I glanced around, searching for the culprit of our disturbance.

Then I *heard* it.

Water.

Had I left the faucet running in the kitchen? Damn. That was exactly what it sounded like.

Easing away from Claire, I made my way into the living room and frowned at the quiet sink. *Where is that noise com—*

The front door began to bow, trickles of water flowing in through the cracks.

"What the fuck?" I breathed, inching closer. Then my eyes widened at the crashing sound just outside. "Oh, shit!"

I ran back toward the bedroom, only to have the door slam into my back as a tidal wave swept into the room, throwing me to the ground and then up into a tornado of water.

Claire!

The room filled quickly, my access to air gone before I could utter a word or a warning. I swam toward her, my dress pants and shirt weighing me down. Kicking off my socks as I moved, I managed to meet her halfway, her eyes wild beneath the water.

I gestured at the window and blew a bubble.

She frowned.

Air, I mouthed. *Use your air!*

Because if she didn't burst the glass, we were both going to drown.

Unless I forced her… My spirit drove to the surface, my fight-or-flight responses kicking in, ready to dive into her and take hold of her powers. I hated doing this, the darkness of manipulating others not something that appealed to me, but this was life or—

Claire grabbed my hand and sent an explosion of air at the glass, shattering it. The water pushed us through the opening, sending us sprawling out across the charred ground outside with her on my chest, sputtering.

Several other students were already outside, soaking wet, most in little to no clothing due to the midnight hour. Many were crying. Others gulping in air, terror rendering them speechless.

Fire and water did not mingle well together given their opposite properties.

"Wh-what happened?" Claire asked, her soaked dress clinging to her curves.

"I don't know." I pushed her damp hair away from her face and pressed my lips to her forehead before guiding us both upright. The water seemed to have evaporated, several of the Fire Fae using their gifts against the tidal waves. But the damage was already done.

And from what I could sense, we'd lost at least one life

inside. Perhaps two.

"You!" A shriek came from across the yard, the bitchy female from earlier pointing her manicured nail at Claire. "You did this!"

Everyone turned to stare at us, several jaws dropping at the realization of just who had appeared outside.

"I... I didn't," Claire said, her voice soft, barely audible.

"First you try to fry me with my own essence, and now drown me?" the bitch continued, stalking toward us in a tiny pair of shorts and a completely translucent tank top, her fiery hair a mess over her shoulders. "If you want to duel, bitch, let's do it. Right now. Right here."

Gasps fluttered through the air, the challenge a lethal one.

"Sit down and shut the fuck up," I said, pushing to my feet to stand between her and Claire.

"No!" This girl—*Ignis*—clearly had an issue with authority, because she popped her hands on her hips and stared me down. "I'm not standing for this bullshit. That bitch tried to kill me today. *Twice.*"

"It's true," her blue-haired friend said, coming to stand at her side. "I recognize water when I feel it, and that essence came from her." She pointed a finger at a now-standing Claire, her gaze oozing malevolence.

"But I didn't," Claire whispered, her face falling. "I-I don't think I did, did I?"

Ignis snorted. "Oh, brilliant. She doesn't even know if she did it or not? Yeah, like I'm buying that shit."

The blue-haired Water Fae folded her arms and tapped her bare foot on the ground, her gaze narrowed. "You totally did. I can still feel the power rolling off you. So don't bother denying it."

I frowned. While I felt the power still swirling in the air, it didn't remind me of Claire. Just like with the fire earlier. Neither reminded me of her inner spirit, confusing my instincts.

Was she accessing power from a place I couldn't sense?

Was our bond not as deep as I thought?

"What the elements is going on out here?" a deep voice demanded.

Ah, fuck...

The crowd parted to allow Mortus entry, his silk robe cinched around his slender waist. A flicker of surprise entered his elegant features at spying Claire, then his gaze narrowed into tiny black slits. "What the fuck is she doing here?"

"Elana made arrangements for her to stay in the Fire Quad," I explained, my tone flat. I moved subtly in front of Claire, hiding her from Mortus's view. "I'll handle it."

"You'll handle it?" he repeated mockingly, glancing around the water-laden courtyard, the shattered glass windows, and the disheveled state of all the Fire Fae around us. "You're doing a great job of that, *Your Highness.*"

Ignis and her friend smirked, causing my eyes to narrow at them. "What are you even doing in the Fire Quad?" My query was meant for the Water Fae. I didn't know her name. She reminded me of a troll with her made-up eyes and wild blue hair.

"I don't think that's any of your business," she snipped. "But I was staying with Ignis after her traumatic experience earlier."

"Traumatic experience?" Mortus echoed.

"Yes. The Halfling tried to kill me," Ignis said, her tone breaking at the end and causing me to roll my eyes.

"Oh, cut the crap," someone snapped before I had a chance to speak. Titus appeared in a pair of pajama pants and slippers. He resided in one of the other dorms. Either the commotion awoke him, or Claire's distress. Likely the latter, as I felt it trickling through our bond like an alarming beacon. "You provoked her and she defended herself. And how do we know Sickle didn't cause the dorm flood?"

Sickle. That must be the Water Fae's name.

She looked positively affronted by the accusation. "Are you frigid kidding me? I was asleep, you jackass."

"So was Claire," I pointed out.

Sickle carried on with another ear-piercing squeal of an excuse while Ignis fed into the bullshit, and several others started speaking up on their behalves, siding with the mean-girl brigade. Mortus gave me a smug look as the tongue-lashing continued and calls for justice wrung out.

Claire's spirit diminished before me, her emotions turning dark, her shoulders hunched.

I ran my fingers through my hair, irritated as fuck. This had all gotten out of hand far too quickly. It would be a miracle to keep Claire at the Academy now after the two incidents today.

The fae were out for blood—*her* blood. Her innocence would matter little to them all.

"Enough!" Titus shouted, punctuating the command with a roar of fire that hummed over our heads and disappeared into smoke. "Go back to your fucking rooms, dry your shit, and go to bed."

Ignis smirked. "As if I will ever obey your command to go to bed. Again."

He took a step toward her, but I caught him by the arm and pulled him back. "You will do what he says. Now." I allowed her to see the power lurking in my gaze, the ability to force her to do just that, and smiled inside as the color drained from her perky little face. "I won't be repeating myself."

She took a step backward, tears gathering in her eyes.

"Don't even start," I snapped, tired of women crying today. "*Go.*" The word echoed across the quad, sending several fae running toward their dorms, including Ignis and her frigid bitch of a friend.

But Mortus stayed, his beady black eyes blazing with fury. "I told you this would happen. She shouldn't be here, Exos. This little experiment of yours is doomed to fail."

"Thank you for the input." I infused a hint of dismissal in my words, which, of course, infuriated him more.

"You're a pompous little prick, just like your father."

I raised my eyebrows. "You may be my senior in age, but make no mistake." I took a step toward him. "I am your superior in all ways. Now, fuck off before I make you fuck off." While I gave Ignis a glimpse of my power, I allowed this asshole to see it all. My gaze swirled with it, the aura of energy swimming between us and belittling his to ash.

He didn't bow, as one should, but instead stalked off, his shoulders stiff, in the direction of Elana's home rather than in the direction of the Fire Quad faculty quarters.

I sighed, glancing at a still-fuming Titus, who stood beside a shaking Claire. She wasn't crying—thank the gods—but her pale expression and curved shoulders indicated her to be on the verge of it. Or maybe shock.

"I-I didn't..." Her blue eyes flickered to mine, feeling my gaze upon her. "Exos, I-I'm sorry. I..."

I gathered her in my arms before she could finish, my lips in her hair and then pressing to her ear. "It's going to be okay, Claire."

She trembled against me, her head swaying back and forth. "B-but I almost killed you," she mumbled. "A-and I don't even r-remember doing it. Then the fire earlier, it was out of my control, and now this. And I can't do this, Exos. I'm so sorry. I'm making this all worse. Even when I try, I just hurt people. I hurt you." The last three words were a whisper, her broken voice fracturing my heart.

Something was happening here, something nefarious, because I would swear on my life that the flood had nothing to do with Claire. The signatures didn't match. Just like the flames. I *felt* her power in that bar. It didn't match what I sensed today.

Shaking my head, I cupped her cheeks, forcing her to meet my gaze. "We're going to figure this out, baby. I promise."

Her face crumpled. "I heard what they were saying, Exos. They hate me. Because of what my mother did, what I keep doing." She inhaled slowly, as if striving for control not to cry. "You shouldn't have to do any of this for me, not after, well, everything."

"Oh, Claire. I *want* to do this for you." I brushed my lips against hers, knowing like hell that I would regret this later and not giving a damn right now. "You're mine to protect, sweetheart."

"You barely know me," she replied so softly I almost missed the statement.

"You're thinking like a human, not a fae." I nuzzled her nose, smiling at our ridiculous situation. She had no idea what it meant to initiate the bonds, yet she'd fallen headfirst into our connection. While she might not think she knew me, her spirit did. And that was what I called to me now— her inner strength—the need to embolden her taking hold of my instincts. She needed to know I had her back, that I believed in her, that I knew she could do this.

Stop fighting it, I told myself. *Let her see.*

My mouth sealed over hers, my fingers sliding into her hair to tilt her head to the angle I desired. She grabbed my shirt, her surprise evident in the way she parted her lips. I slid my tongue inside, my grip tightening as I took control and truly kissed her. None of that truth-or-dare shit from the bar. This was a real embrace, the kind of lovers, not acquaintances.

I wanted her to know me, to have my taste in her mouth for the rest of the week, to truly experience our connection and yearn for more.

And most importantly, I wanted her to believe in herself the way I believed in her.

My comments about dropping her in the Spirit Realm were all empty threats, words meant to piss her off and embolden her. But that tactic had not worked as I wanted it to. So this was my new path, my way of showing my support and allowing her to know a piece of me I never revealed to anyone else.

Her spirit brushed mine, the energy warming between us and flourishing into the night. *Yes,* I urged. *Dance with me.*

Power erupted around us, our souls mingling on a wave

of existence only Spirit Fae could access. Wonder traveled through the bond, her surprise palpable and sweet and causing me to smile against her mouth.

"There's your spirit, baby," I whispered. Then I deepened our kiss before she could reply and showered her in adoration and encouragement in the only way I knew how—by allowing her access into my heart. It was where our bond originated and anchored, where the elements lived inside a fae. A private resource only mates could access and I granted her entrance into mine, providing her with the most intimate experience known to our kind.

But she needed this to ground her. She needed to *feel* my courage to bolster her own, to borrow some of my faith in her, to see how deep this connection could go if we allowed it.

You're going to be all right.
You can do this.
I'm here to help you.
Trust me.
Let me cherish you.

She couldn't hear my thoughts so much as sense them, the emotion behind them causing her to relax in my arms and return my embrace. So sweet and tentative, but addictive. If we weren't standing outside, drenched from head to toe, I'd take this a step further. But I could already feel the tug from Elana requesting my presence. Just a subtle nudge, one she could do as a Spirit Fae.

There would be another meeting.

And I needed to be there to protect Claire.

I pressed my forehead to hers, breathing deeply, my tongue already missing hers. We would pick this up later, after I assured her safety. "You're going to be all right," I vowed. "But I need to go handle Mortus."

"Why do I know that name?" she asked, her brow crumpling.

I cleared my throat. Titus must have provided her with the history. "Mortus is the fae your mother fought."

Her blue eyes flashed, her body going rigid all over again. "That's who…?" Her mouth dropped. "Oh God…"

I cupped her cheek again, pressing my lips to hers and then to her forehead. "Don't worry, sweetheart. I'll handle him."

"But he must hate me." Her gaze snagged mine. "I'm the product of her infidelity."

"Which isn't *your* fault," I said, wrapping my palm around the back of her neck. "You will not feel bad about actions and decisions that were out of your control. Do you understand?"

She swallowed, but nodded, her pupils dilating.

"Good." I kissed her temple before glancing at Titus. Fire blazed in his eyes, having witnessed the entire exchange between us.

Now you know how it feels, I told him with a look, understanding exactly how this appeared to him. Because I'd experienced the same pang of jealousy and annoyance when I found them naked in bed together. But unlike him, I already understood that Claire may need more than one mate to balance her power. That had happened to my mother, after all—hence Cyrus and I having different fathers.

Of course, that didn't mean I had to accept the same fate for myself.

Regardless, we didn't have time to waste on fighting over her. She needed our protection first and foremost, and right now, he was the only one I trusted who could help keep her safe.

"Can she stay with you for the rest of the night?" I asked.

He didn't hesitate, his response immediate. "Yes."

"This may take a while, which means you'll likely miss your classes today. Claire isn't ready to attend until we lay some ground rules for student interaction." Not to protect her classmates, but to protect *her*. The vicious things that were said to her over the last twenty-four hours were unacceptable and needed to be addressed.

Gods, I did not miss my time here. At all.

"Okay," Titus replied, his gaze falling to a frozen Claire. "I won't let anything happen to her."

"I know." And I did. Otherwise, I wouldn't be handing her over to him. But Claire seemed to need more convincing.

Oh, how the tides had turned.

I shook my head, amused.

And decided to throw Titus a bone.

"Ignis is a bitch, Claire." I tilted her chin upward, forcing her to focus on me. "She used an illegal potion to seduce him. I could smell it the second I found him yesterday. So try to take it easy on him. He's not a complete jackass." I winked to soften the insult.

She blinked. "A potion?"

"I'll let him explain." I pressed my mouth to hers once more—because I could, and wanted to—then finally released her. "Stay with Titus until I return, okay?"

She licked her lips, her gaze bright. "Uh, yeah. Okay."

I smirked, enjoying that dazed look on her face far more than I should. "Try to behave, princess. I'll be back soon."

Hopefully.

It all depended on the Council and how much begging I had to do. No one would believe me if I said it didn't feel like Claire. Which meant I needed a different approach.

Fortunately, I had one.

I just needed them all to accept it.

CHAPTER THIRTEEN
CLAIRE

MY LIPS TINGLED as I followed a silent Titus to his dorm.

Exos kissed me.

Like, well and truly kissed me.

And holy wow, was it good.

He'd awoken something inside me, something lively and buoyant—my spirit. I could feel it thriving through every step, the energy warm and familiar and strengthening my every breath. So much power. So much *life*.

It had shocked me at first, then floored me. He'd allowed me inside him in a way I didn't really comprehend, but I *saw* him. It felt as if I'd known him my entire life, my heart automatically trusting his to guide me.

For once in my life, I didn't overanalyze *why*. I just

allowed it. Embraced it. *Enjoyed* it. Perhaps not the right place or time, but what did it matter? It'd happened. It was done. And I didn't regret a second of it.

Except for a little bit now as I stared at Titus's broad back. Mostly because just seeing all that expanse of tanned skin reminded me that I'd spent the previous night in bed with him. Then kissed Exos tonight as if he were my only lover.

Yet, I'd been upset over Titus having fucked Ignis the night before we met?

Yeah, that makes me a hypocrite.

Shit. I needed to say that I was sorry. However, I couldn't find the words. Because I didn't feel bad about kissing Exos. It felt too right for me to belittle it with an apology.

This was all so damn confusing. Especially considering my still-brewing attraction to Titus, something that remained evident as I moved past him in the entryway while he held open the door. The bare skin of his abdomen practically burned my arm, the intense heat causing me to trip over my own feet.

He caught my elbow, steadying me, his touch a brand against my arm.

I just kissed Exos. Passionately. I should not want to lean back into Titus now.

Swallowing, I pulled away and waited for him to lead, unable to meet his gaze. Not because I was upset with him, but because I couldn't trust myself not to react.

He made an irritated noise and pushed past me. My elbow felt cold without him, yet my mouth continued to hum with electricity.

I can't have them both.

But I sort of want to have them both.

This is so damn confusing.

Just follow Titus!

I shook off the war waging in my head and trailed after him, my hands clasped tightly before me. We walked up two flights of stairs to the top floor and stopped at the second door.

He didn't say anything as he waved me inside.

Then I couldn't utter a word, too captivated by the view.

His room boasted floor-to-ceiling windows that overlooked a new part of campus, one I hadn't seen yet, all lit up by the moon and stars above. A majestic garden of sorts filled with glowing plants and flowers.

I padded over to the glass, staring down at the enchanted vines curling and growing at impossible speeds and then trimming to allow more flowers to bloom. Every second was a new evolution, the garden shifting and changing at impossible swiftness.

"This building backs up to the Earth Quad," he said, moving to my side. "The vast garden separates us, but there are pathways between. Of course, they're constantly moving to adapt to the greenery, so it's easy to get lost."

"Wow." I stroked the glass as if to touch one of the glowing flowers, entranced by the magic sprinkled throughout the immense field. I couldn't even see the dorms beyond. "This is…" *Amazing? Nothing like home?* I had no adequate words.

"Yeah, it's something," he replied, running his fingers through his hair and taking a step back. "Do you, uh, need something to wear?"

I glanced down at my soaked clothing, my cheeks pinkening at the realization of how revealing this dress had become. "Er, yes. Please."

He nodded and disappeared into a bedroom off the living area. The rest of his space reminded me of the dorm room Exos had taken me to—all modern appliances done in black, stone floors, charred walls, and fireproof furniture.

Titus returned carrying a pair of shorts and a T-shirt. "Here. Bathroom is through there." He pointed to his bedroom.

"No roommate?" I asked, noticing it was the only door.

"No. I don't play well with others." His flat tone had me

biting my lip and nodding.

"Right. I'll just go change." I walked quickly through his room, not wanting to invade his private space any more than I already had.

And found him waiting for me on his bed when I exited. His gaze ran over my shirt and shorts, his lips curling at the edges. "You look good in my clothes, Claire."

Oh. My face heated from the dark gleam in his green eyes. "I, uh, thank you?" The last word came out as a squeak, sending another wave of warmth over my skin.

I'm in so much trouble, I realized, my breath catching in my throat. *I really do want them both.* It was so wrong. I couldn't do this, couldn't be torn between them. But they each called to a different part of me. Parts I didn't understand. *My elements.*

Titus exhaled slowly, running his fingers through his thick, auburn hair. "Look, I know I fucked up. Well, sort of." He shook his head. "Look, Ignis is a bitch. She tried to force a bond on me with this seduction potion. And because her power is a reasonable match for mine, she managed to get me into bed. But I can't stand her. I'd never want to be with her, Claire."

I clasped my hands before me, unsure of what to say. It wouldn't be fair of me to judge him, not after my own behavior. Yet hearing his explanation put me slightly at ease. Until I remembered the rest of it. "What about the bet?"

His gaze narrowed. "You honestly think I'd be doing all this just to win some fucking bet?"

Did I? My lips twisted to the side as I considered, which had his face reddening.

"I realize you don't know me very well, but you should at least be able to discern my intentions. I mean, for fuck's sake, Claire. I willingly bonded with you. I'm a competitive man, but not *that* competitive." He pushed away from the bed to walk over to the windows, his shoulders tense as he shook his head. "I might kill Ignis."

For some reason, that last sentence made me smile. I

rather liked the idea of throttling her myself. "She's a bitch," I agreed, joining him by the glass.

A horde of violet flowers had formed, each of them releasing crystals into the air that danced around the ever-evolving vines.

We stood in silence for a while, something I hadn't realized I needed until right then. But it gave me a moment to ponder everything and sort through my thoughts. About Exos. About Titus. About this place. About *me*.

I called a flicker of fire to play over my fingertips, smiling at how different I felt—powerful and real.

Ever since I'd arrived, I'd been battling this new reality, fighting Exos, and wanting nothing more than to hide. I lost myself last night to misery. And woke to even more pain. But Exos had done something to me, had awoken some aspect of my being that I hadn't known.

And now everything felt right.

I watched the flame dance across my skin. This truly was a beautiful, unique world. I could be someone brand new here. Someone important. I had the opportunity to prove everyone wrong. The ultimate challenge. I just had to be strong enough to accept it. Fierce enough to master these elements. Wise enough to trust the right mentors.

Such as the male beside me. "I don't believe there even is a bet," I told him, speaking my thoughts out loud. "I think Ignis made it up."

He snorted. "I know she did. I tracked down over a dozen fae who are idiotic enough to consider such a ploy, and none of them had heard a word about it. She's full of shit."

"I'm not sure whether I should be offended by her tactics or flattered. She seems to be going out of her way to ruin me without knowing me."

"She's had it in her head for months that we're going to be a thing. Me and her, I mean. And it's never going to happen." He shivered, clearly repulsed by the idea. "I'm not a saint, Claire. I've dated a lot. But I'm not a cheater." He met my gaze. "I'm devoted to our courtship. Until you tell me otherwise, I mean."

My heart skipped a beat. *Oh God.* "But I kissed Exos." I winced, not meaning to just sputter the words out like that. "I mean, it's… Well, I…" I shook my head, irritated with my inability to form a sentence.

Titus chuckled. "He kissed you, sweetheart." He took a step closer, the heat from his body warming mine as he crowded me against the window. "I accepted that he initiated a connection with you already, Claire." His palm went to the glass beside my head, his opposite hand grabbing my hip. "Just as he's accepted my courtship."

I swallowed. "Oh." It was all I could say, the only word I seemed to know. First, Exos. Now, Titus. These men were going to send me into cardiac arrest if they kept up these seductive antics.

He grinned and leaned into my personal space, his irises capturing mine. "Did you think his kissing you thwarted my claim, Claire? Because I'll take you right now and prove how wrong you are. Your fire is all mine, sweetheart, and that's a part of you that I'm not sharing."

Goose bumps trailed down my arms, my mouth suddenly dry. "So, uh, you don't care that I kissed Exos?"

"Oh, I care." He inched closer. "What I'm saying is I understand and respect your need to date us both. Because what we have isn't comparable. We're fire, sweetheart. And fire is all passion." He licked my lower lip, a trail of flames following in his wake. "Do you forgive me, sweetheart? Or do you need me to grovel?"

Shouldn't I be the one begging for forgiveness here? For almost burning him and Ignis alive? For kissing Exos in front of him after our intimate night together?

"I'm so confused," I admitted.

"May I make a suggestion?" he countered, his hips leaning into mine.

"Y-yes." I swallowed. "Please." I'd do anything to solve the puzzle in my thoughts.

"Stop thinking," he whispered, embers flickering between our mouths. "Just feel." He pressed his lips to mine. So different from Exos's. Not that I should be comparing them, but it was hard considering the short time span that had passed from earlier to now.

Yet, as Titus slid his tongue inside, all my worries vanished. His skilled strokes consumed me, his heat absorbing mine and causing me to arch into him for more. He groaned, his grip on my hip tightening.

"Titus," I breathed, flames erupting over my skin.

He lifted me into the air, bracing my back against the glass as he wrapped my legs around his waist. Then his fist was in my hair, holding me to him as he devoured my mouth, stealing all the air from my lungs.

So hot.

But even as my fire brewed out of control, his tempered the inferno, creating an erotic dance of elements around us. He was right. No one could touch this part of us, not even Exos.

My fire belonged to Titus.

Just as my spirit belonged to Exos.

Acceptance washed over me, my mind too exhausted to fight the truth any longer. I wanted them both, and I would have them both, so long as they would have me. Titus was right. I needed to stop thinking and just live in the moment.

I wound my arms around his neck, my fingers threading through his auburn strands and giving them a tug. He growled against my mouth, deepening the kiss and stirring an inferno in my lower belly.

Exos had ignited a need in me.

Titus was stoking that need to a whole new level.

It left me feeling dizzy and so incredibly aroused. Both of these men touched me in entirely different ways, yet it was all so interconnected inside me in a complex web of elements. It left me craving an outlet, a way to expel some of my pent-up power in a safe environment. And Titus provided me with that, by calling out my fire and wrapping it up in his own. The entire room was alive with light—*our* light.

I felt safe here.

Protected.

Alive.

"More," I whispered, sliding my palms over the bare skin of his back. "I need more, Titus."

He smiled against my mouth. "You want to play with fire, sweetheart?"

I nodded. "Yes." He was my outlet and I needed him. "Please."

"Mmm." His hands fell to the hem of my shirt and pulled it over my head, causing my nipples to stiffen despite the warm air. He kissed me as he lowered my feet to the ground, his grip falling to the shorts at my waist. "Are you sure?"

I didn't know if we were still talking about playing with fire or if he wanted to know if stripping me was okay. Either way, my answer was "Yes."

Warmth caressed my legs as he tugged the fabric down, causing it to pool on the ground at my feet and leaving me naked before him. His gaze ran over me, his pupils dilating. "Oh, I'm going to enjoy this." He lifted me again before I could reply and laid me out over the bed.

My pulse thundered in my ears, my nipples tightening to painful points of anticipation. *What is he going to do now? What do I want him to do?*

I licked my lips, arching as need coursed through me, only to have him walk to the end of the bed to rest his palms on the quilt beside my ankles.

Not what I expected at all. "Titus?"

"Shh," he murmured, trailing his finger over the arch of my foot. "Just feel." A line of fire sizzled along my ankles, sending warmth into my veins and calling my own element out to play. "It's all about the dance." Molten sensation swirled over me, climbing up my legs, each kiss a sizzle against my skin.

"Oh…" I squirmed, my thighs clenching as the flames crept higher. "This is…"

"Fun?" he suggested, leaning over to lick the side of my knee. "Hot?" He knelt on the bed, his mouth trailing the embers up my thigh. "Arousing?" The warmth reached my center, sliding over my slick heat and cascading a series of tremors through my limbs.

This was so *new*. Most boys just fumbled around, touching me as they saw fit, but Titus's movements were deliberate. Skilled. Erotic as fuck.

And the use of our shared element only heightened the moment, eliciting a passion inside me that required release. His name left my mouth on a plea, a worship, a prayer for more. He intensified the pressure of his gift, creating an inferno that encased my body, inflaming the room and igniting my very soul.

"You look gorgeous like this, drenched in my power," he whispered, his lips against my hip and sliding across my lower belly. "I want to taste you, Claire. Can I taste you?"

I swallowed, my heart in my throat, my entire form literally alive with fire and energy. "Yes," I hissed. "Yes." The need to unravel tightened within me, my stomach a bundle of nerves with no outlet, and oh, fuck, was it hot. I could hardly breathe, could barely think.

Just Titus.

Just the feel of his heat caressing my skin, and his lips touching me *there*.

I bowed off the bed, his palm landing on my belly to hold me down with a growl. And all hell broke loose around us. So much fire. So much heat. So much *Titus*.

His tongue slid up and down my slick flesh, his mouth a miracle between my thighs. I wove my fingers into his hair, holding him there as embers drifted up my abdomen to my breasts. Some part of me registered how much this should hurt, but my elements pushed back, creating a sensation unlike anything I'd ever experienced.

Hot and cold.

Lava and ice.

Euphoria mingled with excitement, stirring a catastrophic force inside me that begged to be released. He caught my clit between his teeth, nibbling just hard enough to send a jolt through my limbs and force my gaze to his. The hunger reflected in his forest-green irises sent me flying, my orgasm ripping out of me on an animalistic scream that could likely be heard across the Fae Realm.

And I didn't care, too consumed by the rapture flooding my veins to focus on anything other than trying to remember how to breathe. Ashes seemed to coat my tongue, fire crawling down my throat, and then Titus's mouth was there, possessing me, teaching me how to exist beyond the elements. Helping me to overpower the inferno, to control it, to pull it all back inside and soothe it with a few calming strokes.

Out of this world did not begin to cover what just happened.

I blinked into the dark room, shocked. It felt as if a bomb had gone off inside me, rattling the foundations of the world. Yet, his room remained undisturbed, the garden still glowing outside the windows. "That was..." I cleared my throat, my voice hoarse from screaming. "That was..." Nope. Still didn't have the right word. "*Amazing* seems too dull a description."

He chuckled. "I'm taking that as a compliment." He gathered me into his arms and pressed a kiss to my forehead. "Let me know when you're ready to play again."

"Again?" I could barely feel my arms and legs. Oh, but I hadn't repaid the favor yet. That was what he meant. Rolling to my side, I pressed my palm to his hard abdomen, exploring the muscular dips down to the top of his pants. He caught my wrist in his hand and brought it up to his lips, giving me a kiss.

"When I mentioned playing again, I meant with you, sweetheart. And after you've gotten some sleep." He placed my hand on his chest, over his heart. "It's only three in the morning. I could use a little rest." He brushed his lips against my hair, easing me into contentment.

"Are you sure?" I asked, yawning.

He chuckled. "Yeah, sweetheart. I'm sure." He pulled the blankets up over us, his shoulder acting as my pillow as I snuggled into his side.

"'Kay. 'Cause sleep sounds good," I admitted.

"I know." Another kiss, his arm tightening around my upper back. "Good night, Claire."

"Good night, Titus," I whispered, my eyes drifting closed in a blissful state. I'd wake him later by repaying the favor. But for now, I'd take the reprieve and just... rest.

CHAPTER FOURTEEN
CLAIRE

SOMETHING SOFT DRIFTED OVER MY LIPS, causing me to stir from my cocoon of heat. Piercing blue eyes smiled down at me, causing me to grin in response. *Exos.*

He tilted his head, the motion endearing. "Morning," he whispered.

"Morning," I replied, stretching my legs.

Legs that were intertwined with Titus.

Who was asleep behind me with his chest pressed up against my naked back.

Oh, shit.

Exos knelt beside the bed, placing us at eye level. He brushed a curl away from my face before palming my cheek. "It's okay, Claire." His low murmur scattered a flurry of goose bumps down my arm. "But I am a little jealous that you sleep naked with him and fully clothed with me." His gaze dipped down to where Titus's arm was wrapped around my upper abdomen, my breasts completely revealed thanks to the fallen sheet.

I bit my lip, wincing. "I…" I wanted to apologize but didn't know how. Because I didn't feel remorse for spending the night with Titus, but I did feel bad about doing it so soon after kissing Exos. "I…" I cleared my throat, uncertain of how to proceed. "Sorry."

He leaned closer, his blue eyes smoldering as he refocused on my face. "There's nothing to forgive," he murmured, his mouth brushing mine. "You have five elements, Claire. Powerful elements. You need a balance."

I frowned. He couldn't possibly be implying that I needed five fae to help balance my elements. Right? Because that'd be insane. I could hardly handle the two of these men, let alone *five.*

He pressed his lips to mine once more, his kiss soft and coaxing, while Titus stirred behind me.

Uh-oh…

"How'd it go?" he asked, his voice deep with sleep and sounding sexy as sin against my ear.

"We've reached an agreement," Exos replied, the words fluttering over my lips. "The Council has granted my request to train Claire on Spirit Quad and prepare her powers for the Academy. If we can prove to them that she's stable, they'll allow her to attend classes." He kissed me softly before shifting to glance over my shoulder. "You've been excused from classes due to temporary reassignment."

"Good." Titus's arm lifted from my stomach, his hand shifting to my hip beneath the blankets. "I assume the three of us are relocating today?"

"Yes. The new quarters are being assembled right now." Exos cocked his head, his nose brushing mine as he gave me his undivided attention. "Spirit Quad is abandoned, but that gives us plenty of room to practice. Okay?"

I swallowed, a little hot and bothered by being

sandwiched between two incredibly good-looking men. And now they wanted me to live with both of them?

"I think you rendered her speechless, Your Highness," Titus murmured, his lips against my hair. "Perhaps you need to help her find her voice."

"Hmm, yes, I think she's feeling quite shy at my finding her naked in bed with you. Again." His gaze lowered to my chest, causing my nipples to harden in response, my body alight with wonder and sensation and confusion. "Any suggestions?"

"Several." Titus's palm slid across my lower belly, the touch a brand against my skin as he pulled me backward. "I introduced Claire to fire play."

"Did you?" Exos stood, his fingers playing over his dress shirt, popping open the buttons with nimble fingers.

This can't be happening.

It has to be a dream.

"You two don't even like each other," I blurted out, then winced at allowing my thoughts to grace my lips. *Are you trying to ruin this?*

Exos grinned. "Maybe not, but we both like you, Claire." The fabric parted around his torso, revealing the toned physique beneath. He was leaner than Titus, but just as muscularly defined, almost in a regal sort of way. Fitting, considering his title. "It's not common for a Spirit Fae to take two mates, but it's not unheard of. Sometimes our affinity for a secondary element is strong, requiring an outlet. Clearly, you have a lot of fire in you." He finished removing his shirt, folding it and setting it on the nightstand beside the bed.

"I'm willing to work with it if you both are," Titus added, his thumb drawing a hypnotic circle around my belly button.

I resisted the urge to pinch myself, certain this had to be my unconscious mind indulging in this inappropriate scenario. But as the mattress dipped beneath Exos's weight, his eyes darkened with desire on my breasts, I realized I'd never felt more alive.

"You have a lot of power in you, princess. This is one way to help expel some of your energy. We'll absorb it for you. If it's what you want." He lay down beside me and fondled a strand of my hair that had fallen across my cheek. "I felt you come undone through our bond, Claire. Now I want to see it with my own eyes."

My lips parted, my blood heating. "I'm really starting to think this is real," I whispered.

Titus and Exos chuckled, their collective warmth searing me from both sides. Titus's hand slid lower, exploring the apex between my thighs. "Definitely real, sweetheart," he said against my ear.

I shivered, licking my lips. Exos tracked the movement with his gaze before leaning in to trace the same path with his own tongue. *Oh, fuck...* It served as an invitation, one I was hopeless to turn down.

Tilting my head, I accepted his offer and moaned as Titus dipped his finger into my weeping sex. Exos took advantage of my groan, his tongue sneaking inside to begin a dance that set my body on fire. Not in the way Titus had last night, but in an entirely new way. This touch was underlined with spirit, energizing me in a way no one else could.

The combination of elements left me wired and hot and rejuvenated. I felt unstoppable, protected, adored.

How is this my life?

Oh, who the hell cares? Stop thinking!

I had no idea where that last voice came from, but I listened to it and indulged in the sensation flourishing between the three of us. I thread my fingers through Exos's thick, ash-blond hair, holding him to me as he devoured my mouth. My other hand went to lie over Titus's as he explored me intimately, his fingers knowing and sizzling against my flesh.

Fire and spirit dueled inside me, both tugging on different nerves and exciting a maelstrom of activity throughout my body. I shook beneath the onslaught, overwhelmed and consumed by both men and the gift of their touch.

Exos cupped my breast, his thumb brushing my nipple and sending a jolt of electricity through my bloodstream. Then he nipped my lower lip, his eyelids lifting to reveal a pair of glowing irises. "Your arousal is invigorating," he whispered. "I've never felt anything like it."

He kissed me again before I could reply, his fingers pinching my nipple. I arched back into Titus, gasping at the fierce contact. His lips went to my neck, kissing and nibbling, while his hand continued to work beneath mine, his fingers stroking a desperate need between my legs. "Are you going to show Exos how beautiful you are when you come, sweetheart?" he asked against my skin, his voice husky and dark. "I think he's jealous that I saw it first."

I shuddered, the flames inside dying to be released.

Then Exos shifted, his mouth leaving mine to kiss my jaw and then lower to my breast. His hand went to my thigh, lifting it to rest against his hip.

I gasped as his lips closed around my nipple, the heat of his tongue a brand against my skin.

Fuck.

I squirmed between them, the dual sensations sparking a volcano inside my core that throbbed for release. "Exos," I breathed, my grip tightening in his hair.

Titus nipped my neck, his finger driving deep and eliciting a scream from me that resembled his name. I panted both of their names in succession, confused and aroused and needy as hell. I didn't know whom to focus on—Exos at my breast or Titus's hand between my thighs. Both were so, so good. So perfect. So *mine*.

I gave in to that little voice that told me not to think, not to consider the complications of the moment. And I let go completely, enjoying the way they handled me, the way they encouraged my power to flourish between us.

Exos skimmed his teeth across my stiff peak, forcing my gaze to his. A knowing gleam blazed in his irises, his soul seducing mine into an intimate dance that forced me out of this plane of existence.

The tension building inside me unraveled, sending me spiraling into an oblivion of elements that thundered through the room. Incomprehensible words left my mouth, my limbs locking in pleasure, stars bursting before my eyes.

Intense.

Perfection.

Addictive.

I wanted more. I craved a deeper outlet, a more passionate understanding, a *mating*. The realization caused me to tremble, my heart skipping a beat. *What are they doing to me?*

"Balancing you," Exos whispered, licking a path back up to my lips. I must have spoken the words out loud. Or maybe he read them from my eyes. "We'll help you learn how to fly with steady wings, beautiful, when you're ready. But for now, we'll keep you grounded in the only ways we know how."

"I can feel the bond," I marveled, finally sensing it for the first time. "It makes me want more."

"I know." He kissed me softly while Titus slowly drew his hand from between my legs, the dampness of my arousal creating a wet path across my skin. It left me quivering, stirring a desire for another round. I felt insatiable, needy, and undeniably smitten.

"We'll take it slow," Titus spoke against my ear. "Teach you about our world, our customs, our powers. To make sure it's what you really want, Claire."

"Handling both of us won't be easy," Exos agreed, his lips moving against mine. "That's what the courtship is about—learning about the other and deciding if it's what both parties want. For that, you need a stronger comprehension of your abilities and this world. But we have time. And we'll start training immediately."

Titus kissed my shoulder. "He means after a shower."

Exos's lips twitched. "No, I meant now." He kissed me

again, his aura calling to mine on an intimate level that left me shaking against him. "Create something with me, princess."

"Like what?" I breathed, captivated by the swirling blue of his irises.

"Anything." He lifted his hand from my leg, holding it between us.

I pressed my palm to his and marveled at the stimulating connection. "More flowers?"

"If you want." An electrical charge caressed the air, causing Titus to shift at my back. He didn't leave but gave me space, allowing me to focus on the energy breathing life into my being.

The energy of Exos.

His spirit enticing mine.

"Think about something you want," he encouraged. "And show me with your hand."

"Anything?"

He grinned. "Within reason."

"Okay." I fell into the ocean of his gaze, drowning in all things Exos. Every inhale belonged to him. Every heartbeat. Every thought. He wanted me to create life. What would he enjoy? A pixie like Elana's?

Or maybe something from my home.

Like a butterfly.

I pictured a winged creature, giving it pink wings with my mind, and felt my heart warm at the idea as my fingertips tingled.

Exos smiled in approval as a butterfly fluttered above our joined hands.

"What is that?" he asked softly. "Your version of a fairy?"

"It's a butterfly." I urged it to fly around the room, its wings glistening with life. "It likes flowers."

"It's beautiful." He released me to tuck my hair behind my ears. "Just like you." He pressed his lips to mine once more, the kiss a possession and a promise wrapped up in one. "See how long you can keep it flying around. My record for a conjured spirit is three months, if you want a goal."

My lips parted. "Three months?"

He waggled his brows. "Consider it your first assignment, princess." He nuzzled my nose and glanced over my shoulder at Titus. "I think I might enjoy playing professor for a few weeks."

"We can teach her all sorts of things," Titus agreed, drawing a finger down my spine. "But I do want a shower first."

"You and me both," Exos said, some sort of understanding passing between them.

I gasped, understanding dawning. *They're still turned on.* "Wait, are you—"

Exos silenced me with his mouth, his tongue a familiar presence that scattered my thoughts. "Pleasuring you in the presence of another, I can handle. Watching you return that pleasure to a man who isn't me? Absolutely not."

"I agree," Titus said. "And I can't just leave the room, either."

Exos nodded. "We'll come up with a way to handle this. For now, I'll settle on a shower."

"There's only one here," I pointed out.

"Titus will go first while you show me what your butterfly can do. Then I'll shower."

"And me?" I asked, raising a brow. "When do I shower?"

Exos nodded. "You're right. You should shower first while we watch, then Titus can go after you, and I'll go last."

I slapped his shoulder. "That's not funny."

"I didn't say I was joking."

"For once, I actually like your demand," Titus added. "Up you go, Claire."

I scowled over my shoulder. "No."

"You can't turn down a royal," he said, smiling. "And he wants you to shower first."

"I thought you wanted a shower?" Exos gripped my chin

to pull me back to him, a smile in his eyes. "Or was that you being difficult?" He kissed me before I could retort, causing Titus to chuckle as he rolled out of the bed.

"I'll let you know when I'm done," he said on his way out of the room.

Exos ignored him and continued kissing me, the moment intensifying now that we were alone. He pushed me to my back, his hips settling between mine. "I'm going to kiss you until he returns, Claire."

"Okay," I whispered.

"And I'm going to make you come again." The dark promise sent my heart into overdrive. "With my tongue." He nipped my jaw on his way down, his gaze oozing sin as he looked up at me. "Consider it an introduction to the courtship bond, princess. And you have two of us vying for your attention."

Oh God...

I might not survive this.

Yet, I couldn't bring myself to worry, not with Exos drawing a hot path with his tongue through my slick folds.

This is my new life.

Best to just embrace it.

And I did.

Twice.

CHAPTER FIFTEEN
TITUS

TWO WEEKS.

Two... fucking... weeks... well, *not fucking*.

I was about to lose my damn mind.

Claire moved beyond the thin veil of the opaque windows as she dressed for our training session. I coveted our lessons together because it provided us with alone time—just us and our fire.

Watching her as she slipped the tight-fitting fireproof garments over her head made the embers in me burn hotter. A feat, considering they were constantly smoldering in her presence.

She glanced in my direction, likely feeling my eyes on her, memorizing every inch of her body. Then she disappeared from view, leaving my fingers curling into fists as the raw need in me demanded an outlet.

As if on cue, Exos appeared at the other window that overlooked the training courtyard just outside the Spirit Quad. He arched a brow as if to remind me that I wasn't the only one with a claim on Claire's body.

Yeah, yeah.

Neither of us could stand the idea of Claire fucking the other, so we'd come to a painful truce. Giving her pleasure took the bite out of our need, but it wasn't enough anymore. And I knew he felt it, too.

Exos's eyes narrowed as though he suspected I might take Claire right here in the courtyard—while he watched.

Not a bad idea, I thought darkly.

A part of me didn't care anymore, but I also knew it would cause a divide that would echo throughout all the kingdoms. I couldn't have Claire—not yet—not until we'd established an understanding of how to make this work.

Sex wasn't necessarily a trigger to deepening a bond, but something told me if either of us fucked Claire, it would deepen our connection to something far more permanent.

Which meant I couldn't touch her. Not like that. Not yet. Not until we all came to a mutual agreement, because it was very clear that Claire would require more than one mate. Perhaps up to five.

She entered the courtyard twirling a baton I'd given her last week. The way she handled it now showed her improvement. The tips bled with tiny flames as she gave me a seductive, mischievous grin.

"If you keep glaring up at Exos like that, he's going to jump down here and join our sparring session. And something tells me it'll be your face he uses for a physical demonstration." Her words were a bit too matter-of-fact for my liking.

I rolled my shoulders back and cracked my neck, making a show of it. "I'm not afraid of the scrawny royal."

I slipped my arm around her waist as she stepped within my reach, and brought her hips against mine so she could feel how hard she'd made me just by standing there showing off the fire that connected us.

Her eyes widened. "I thought you, uh, just took a shower."

As if a hand job could possibly reduce the excruciating need that screamed in me. I let my voice drop, and I didn't care if the demanding huskiness of my tone came off too rough. "I'm tired of showers. Of this place. Of Exos spying on our training." I shot him a look while I said it, which earned me a smirk in response. This was supposed to be my time with Claire, and the bastard knew it.

But he clearly didn't trust me not to take this to the next level. Which I couldn't truly blame him for, as I felt the same way about him.

Claire pouted, her adorable bottom lip plumping out. She thumped her baton against my leg, causing the flames to lick up my sides. "You don't really mean that, right?"

Ah, she didn't understand.

"I would never leave you, Claire. It's just... *hard*." I nuzzled into the groove of her neck.

"Oh," she said, breathless. She arched against me, pressing her breasts into my chest as my teeth grazed her pulse. Her resulting groan caused my cock to throb between us.

"Fuck, Claire," I whispered, my body on fire—literally.

She twisted in my grip to glance to where Exos tracked our every movement. "Exos is watching."

I know. I can feel his presence.

"You didn't seem to have a problem with that last night," I said instead, grinning when flames erupted around us. She sucked in a breath, the memory of her naked and crying out for more, painting her cheeks a delicious pink. That'd become our nightly routine. And sometimes a morning activity as well.

Claire dropped the baton and gripped my shoulders, her strength surprising me as she pushed me away. The echo of flames burned in her eyes, slowly overtaking the blue that marked her as a Spirit Fae.

Yes, give me your fire, sweetheart.

"I know what you're doing," she said as she narrowed her eyes. "You're trying to distract me, but I'm ready." She retrieved her baton and twirled it before crouching into the battle stance I'd taught her. "I'm going to prove to all the fae that I am not my mother."

A grin stretched across my face as I took a defensive position. Pride swelled in my chest. Yes, Claire was definitely ready to face the Academy.

But was I ready to let her face them without me by her side? Her first class would be on Air Quad—with Exos.

A fireball caught me on the chin, causing me to grunt before stumbling to my knee. I snapped my head back just in time to see Claire's baton coming straight for my face. She'd caught me off guard, but that was because I wasn't accustomed to elements being used against me in a fight. The one handicap of being a Powerless Champion was, well, real fae fought with their powers.

I caught the baton in my grip with ease and smiled at Claire's surprised expression. "Well done, sweetheart, but you'll have to do better than that to beat me."

I intended to yank Claire closer and seduce her some more, when she twisted from my grip in a maneuver I hadn't taught her. One glance up at a smug Exos told me I wasn't the only one who'd helped Claire grow.

My gaze dropped down to Claire, who held her palms together, her brows knitted with concentration as she summoned a new fireball—but it wasn't quite a fireball.

"Claire," I cautioned, hoping she wasn't attempting to combine her elements. She wasn't ready, even if Exos encouraged her. He didn't understand how raw and explosive her emotions were or how they impacted her powers.

Her jaw flexed as she worked on the ball of power. Its gleaming red flames licked around the edges of her fingertips before the other elements came into play in tufts of living color. A magical breeze kicked up and sent her hair flinging over her face, but she didn't move to push the strands away.

A sizzle of water fought against the flames, winning and morphing into something dangerous as an external, circular vortex crashed at her feet and wound circles up her body. It seemed to be climbing an invisible wall, threatening to cut her off from me. Permanently.

"Claire," I tried again, readying myself to intervene.

Except tight roots had bound my ankles to the spot.

Claire had used her spirit to create life, causing the ground to shift beneath us to secure her new creations.

"I'm okay," she said through gritted teeth, her voice distorted by the heavy magic weaving its way up her arms. "I can control it."

No. You can't.

I glowered up at Exos, who merely shrugged, clearly at ease with this display.

Jackass, I growled in my mind. Not that he could hear me. Not that he even mattered.

I refocused on Claire. I wanted to yell at her, strangle her, crash my mouth against hers and distract her from this nonsense, but I knew better. She possessed a fire that rivaled my own, and a passionate ambition that no one could take away from her. I would be a hypocrite to try.

My fingers curled into fists as she worked the fireball and tried to rein in the elements. A small smile played on her plump lips. "I think I'm doing it."

Exos joined us, his blue eyes glimmering in triumph. "That's beautiful, Claire."

Of course he approved.

"Yes, let's encourage her to work with elements we have no power over." Claire's fire might be mine, but the rest of her did not belong to me. If she lost control now, I would be useless to help her.

I did not like to feel useless.

"What's going on?" an approaching voice asked from

the edge of the courtyard.

Exos frowned, eyeing the monstrosity growing around Claire. "Prepare yourself, River. We may require your affinity for water in just a moment."

I glanced over my shoulder at a gaping River, having forgotten about Exos inviting him over today. Claire was steadily gaining control over her powers, and while River couldn't reach her elements the same way Exos and I could—thanks to our bonds—he could still help guide her when it came to water.

Good thing, too, because that was the first element to rip free from Claire's careful grasp.

Her smile faded as the churning water around her intensified, spiraling up into the sky like the ground had erupted in a geyser.

"Claire!" I shouted, straining against the vines, which only dug deeper into my skin in response. I winced as the prick of thorns threatened to make my imprisonment even worse.

Of course, I was a stubborn son of a bitch, so instead of obeying Claire's magic, I sent my fire writhing over the vines.

"Don't," Exos bit off.

A single word—a command, one that needed to be obeyed.

My teeth grated together in defiance, but I dispelled the flames only because Exos had an edge to his voice. One I wasn't used to hearing—panic.

Claire had stumbled backward, her body blurring behind a waterspout mingling with violent gusts of air that would soon turn into a full-fledged tornado if not brought under control.

"Now, River," Exos said.

River grunted as he thrust his arms out. An invisible force shifted, twisting the geyser the wrong way to make it lose momentum. A sound of pain came from inside the vortex, making me jerk against my restraints.

"Claire!"

The vortex thinned enough for us to finally see her, causing the blood to drain from my face. Her skin glowed with a silver hue while white flowers came to life and died over and over again at her feet in a panicked cycle of renewal.

Exos stepped inside, braving the whirlwind of power, and gently took hold of Claire's arms. I couldn't hear what he said to her, but her eyes flashed up to him, full of silver and blue power that swirled with distress. He calmed her, then she looked at me and the fireball still in her hand grew.

She let out a long breath before she set the vortex on fire. It was a terrifying sight as the very air around her burst into a swirling inferno, but I immediately understood what Exos had told her to do. By allowing fire—the power she maintained the most control over—to engulf the other elements, she could mingle everything together and draw the energy back into herself.

Clever.

I watched, both with pride and unease at her raw, barely trained strength as she closed her eyes and calmed the storm. The elements slowly drained away and drifted like ash to the ground, sprouting up more white flowers in their wake.

By the time she finished, the entire courtyard was covered in the beautiful blooms.

River let out a long breath. "By the Elements, I almost wasn't able to break through her vortex." He glanced at me, a shaky smile mixed with worry on his face. "I don't know if I'm cut out to be her water mentor, Titus. I'm not able to help her, not like you." His gaze returned to Claire, mesmerized with her just as all the fae should be. "Your bonds are strengthening her far more than I ever could."

Hmm, no, River was definitely not suited to mentor Claire. Nor did they possess a bond-mate compatibility like Claire had with me and Exos. Which, unfortunately, implied she would eventually need a water mate.

Exos already speculated she'd need one for each element.

I sort of hated that he was right.

Claire sank to her knees, her smile indicating it to be from exhaustion, not emotions. Her gaze danced with delight. "I did it. I brought it under control with minimal help."

Just barely. But yes, she did. "Please don't attempt that again, Claire. Not until we've found more mentors to help sharpen your elements."

"Hmm, yes, on this I agree with Titus. We need to find you an air mentor. Fortunately, I have someone in mind." Exos flicked a wrist at me, sending the vines binding my legs unwinding.

My eyes went wide. "Don't tell me you could have done that this whole time."

His resulting smirk said it all.

Royal bastard.

"River," Claire said, ignoring my banter with Exos. "I'm so sorry for losing control like that. Thank you for helping me."

He ducked his head as his face turned pink. "It was nothing, Claire. I'm sorry I wasn't able to do more." He glanced at me. "I'm not like your other mentors."

Her grin widened. "No, I suppose not."

"Yes, as I said, we need to find a suitable mentor for air." Exos glanced up at the sky that had been green and angry just moments ago. "We'll be meeting the candidate I have in mind tomorrow when we visit Air Quad. He's in your first class."

Claire blushed. "Just a mentor, right?"

Exos grinned and brushed his lips against her temple. "That's not up to me, princess."

She leaned into him, her comfort with his presence evident in their interaction. I waited for the spike of jealousy to come, but it didn't, surprising me. Over the last two weeks, I'd sort of learned to accept her bond with Exos.

Maybe because it was different, more subtle and mischievous. While with me, she burned with passion and need.

Intriguing.

Exos folded his hands behind his back and straightened, the Royal Fae returning for duty. "The candidate will be tested, of course." His gaze locked on Claire. "As will you. Do you feel truly prepared to face the fae and the Academy tomorrow?"

She smiled and slipped her arm through his, forcing him to buckle against her. "You'll be with me." Her gaze fluttered my way. "I just wish Titus could come, too."

"He has classes," Exos reminded her. "Don't you, Titus?"

I sighed. "I do."

As much as I wanted to be by Claire's side night and day, Exos was right. I had my own classes to attend now that I had permission to resume my academic schedule. So I buried my feelings and the need to protect her, finding the strength in myself to give my trust over to Exos to do that for me.

No matter what conflicts there were between Exos and me, he wouldn't let anything happen to her. Because his feelings for Claire rivaled my own.

He'd give his life to protect her.

Same as I would.

So, this new Air Fae had a lot to live up to. And, as Exos planned on testing him, all I could think was, *Good fucking luck, buddy.*

Chapter Sixteen
Vox

"YOU'RE THE ONE IN CHARGE HERE," I reminded myself, not caring if anyone heard me. Sometimes I needed a little pep talk before approaching Sol in the morning. The damn Earth Fae liked to forget that I was his mentor and he was only permitted in the guest room as a boon. He didn't get along with the Earth Fae—or any fae—but that was why I was his mentor. He needed me.

Right now, he was pissing me off.

Rolling my shoulders back, I inhaled a long, deep breath, held it, and then released it in a drawn-out gust that rattled his door.

Or, should have rattled it.

The damn Earth Fae had made a wall of stone around himself. I could feel it. A weight in the air made me want to sneeze, and my nostrils flared.

"Sol!" I shouted, then reduced myself to beating against the door with my fists. "You're going to make me late for class!" I couldn't just leave him in the Air Dorms unattended. He had to leave.

"Not going!" came the muffled reply of my earthy subordinate. "There's a wild Halfling on campus today!"

As if I didn't fucking know that. That was *precisely* why I needed to be bright and early for class.

I'd heard a rumor that she would be starting on Air Quad today, which meant I didn't have time for Sol's shit. No way was I going to miss this.

I stroked my short beard while I contemplated the best way to beat Sol at this idiotic game. He rarely walled me out like this, but when he did, it really drained my air magic to force him out. My powers needed to be at their height today.

Running my fingers to the back of my neck and securing the loop at my warrior's ponytail, I decided on a new tactic. "Are you telling me you're afraid of a girl?" I leaned in closer, knowing that Sol was right on the other side hanging on every word. "Or are you afraid of the royal?"

A hiss of sound, then a grating of stones as the wall shifted. I grinned.

"Not fucking afraid of that dirtbag!" was the reply.

I let out a low whistle, my powers over air sending the shrill notes vibrating through stone. "Oh really? Because it looks like you've spent the majority of your power making yourself a bunker in order to stay away from the royal. That's not the Sol I know."

I waited, then grinned when the stones shifted again and the slightest sliver of light came through the door. "Nice try, windbag. Not coming out."

I rolled my eyes. "Don't you have any more intelligent insults? Come on, Sol. The Air Quad is the last place you want to be today. They're saying the Halfling will be starting classes here, and if you want to be out of sight, then going back to the Earth Quad is your best bet to stay out of their path."

The wall crumbled, leaving the door to break off its hinges. I jumped back just in time for it to slam down on the place I'd been standing, leaving a very large and pissed-off Earth Fae on the other side. He wore his standard Earth Fae trousers that had gotten wrinkled from him sleeping in them, along with the loose tank around his broad shoulders. He intimidated most fae, but I knew Sol. He was all bark and no bite.

"You know why I can't go back there," he said, his words grating against the marble floors.

Not this again.

I threw my hands up and let them fall, releasing a gust of wind that blew away the dust from Sol's tantrum. Every time I indulged him and let him stay in the Air Quad, he thought he could just wall himself up here and not face the world.

Most fae would have kept their distance from Sol, but my powers made me fast and lithe, enough that I could move out of the way of his brutish strength as needed. Fighting an Earth Fae head-on was the mistake of many. I knew how to dodge, escape, and survive. It was what made me stronger than Sol in any match.

Moving to him, I rested a hand on his shoulder, only to brush aside the loose pebbles that had gathered in the crook of his collarbone. "Listen, Sol. Let's make a deal. I'll find out the Halfling's schedule and make sure you won't be anywhere near her or the royal guarding her, all right?" I gripped him and gave him a light shake. "Oh, also? Use what I have taught you. Don't wall yourself up when they come at you. Evade their attempts to rile you up. You can do it."

Sol set his jaw and looked like he was going to punch me. I angled my feet just in case he did, but then his face erupted in a wide grin and he crushed me to his chest in a hug. "You're right, Vox. You're right."

"Too... tight. Can't... breathe," I managed to squeak out of my crushed windpipe.

Sol laughed and released me, setting me back down. I was a tall fae, but Sol was a titan.

Coughing, I patted him on the arm again. "Okay, so, off with you."

I knew the Earth Fae didn't want to leave. The Chancellor had forced us into this collaboration, avid about multi-element partnerships, and Sol and I certainly had our ups and downs. I might be good for him, a little bit of air in his stubborn sails, but I was also a member of this Academy and needed some time on my own.

"Fine, Vox," Sol said reluctantly and marched past me, sending the walls shaking. He had so much trouble reining in his gifts. It was what made other Earth Fae afraid enough of him to bully him.

I could relate.

I had a history of my own, but I did better than most keeping that under tight wraps. It would take a tornado to reveal what had driven me to the Academy in the first place.

When blessed silence engulfed me after Sol's departure, I let out another long breath, wishing I could spend some time in meditation before starting the day. Today, however, there was no time for contemplation or reflection.

Excitement drifted through the air, palpable and enticing. Whatever energies this Halfling brought with her, it was realm-changing, and I wanted a front-row seat.

* * *

In spite of Sol's delay to my morning, I still arrived early to my conjuring class. This being a more advanced class, I didn't expect to see the Halfling. It made me want to wander outside and see if I could spot her.

"Did you hear we have a new student?" Aerie asked me, one of the Air Fae who often indulged in the latest gossip.

"Quit stirring up motes," I replied. Everyone on campus had heard about the new student. I didn't live under a rock.

"She's tried to kill Ignis twice now. First with her little

show of fire power. *Then* by trying to drown her and Sickle and several others in the Fire Dorms. If Sickle hadn't been there, she would have killed Ignis. I saw it all. Well, the first incident, anyway. The second one, I was in the Air Quad."

I resisted the urge to roll my eyes. "Sounds terrifying," I said, placating her. Last thing I wanted to do was goad a fae known to stir up trouble.

"It was!" She kept jabbering, but other students thankfully indulged her bullshit, giving me a chance to meander away.

Pretending to be engrossed in a piece of lint on my suit, I brushed it off before I took my seat, a floating pedestal three desks down that gave me a perfect view of the door. I liked to see who came in and out. Conjuring took place in an enclosed orb where anything summoned—intentionally or accidentally—couldn't escape. It left the doorway as the sole entrance and exit.

With the clock nearly at the late-morning dial, the students started to stream in. Dark hair and uniforms made all the Air Fae look almost the same, but I could spot the small traits that set them apart. They liked to keep their hair short, which was why I'd let mine grow out. The last thing I wanted to be was just another Air Fae.

Then, there she was. I'd been talking myself out of the possibility of seeing the Halfling up close, but she was actually here. A bright glimpse of sunlight and golden hair as she eased into the room with her hands clasped in front of her thighs. The standard Academy uniform clung to her curves, which were far more sensual than an Air Fae's and immediately made my eyes wander from her head to her toes. I could write a song about her grace, undoubtedly innate in the lithe movements of one who wielded the element of air, but there was so much more to her that had me mesmerized.

A flash of dangerous dark-blue eyes broke me from the spell. Exos, the notorious Royal Spirit Fae, instantly took note of me and glowered. "Eyes to yourself."

An order.

I wasn't used to those, but I knew better than to challenge the royal, especially after what he'd done to Sol. The Spirit Fae could manipulate one's very will, and I had no interest in testing the strength of this particular royal's ethical qualms about doing that inside the classroom.

The Halfling fidgeted while the Air Fae took their seats. I tried not to watch her, but it was damn near impossible. She was so utterly fascinating with her round ears and beautiful blonde hair.

Everyone took their assigned seats, leaving the usual circle of empty pedestals around me open. The Halfling took one of the chairs closest to me before glancing between Exos and me, murmuring something I couldn't hear—which was impressive, given that air currents normally obeyed me and I could hear any whispered secret within my vicinity.

"Yes. That's him." The royal nodded, his words soft as he sat behind her, providing him with a clear view of her back and the entryway.

"Hi," the Halfling said, startling me when I realized she was actually talking to me.

"Oh, uh, hi," I said, resisting the urge to glance at the powerful Spirit Fae that was just at the edge of my sight. I didn't care for his proximity, but based on the light tremors of power in the air, that was exactly what he wanted—for everyone to feel uneasy.

Definitely a warrior.

The Halfling smiled shyly, and it felt like sunlight was exploding all around me again. A warm breeze swirled around her that immediately called to my innate element, coaxing me to lean closer, so I did.

The royal cleared his throat. "Distance, Air Fae."

Before I could reply—and with what, I had no idea— the professor entered and tapped a staff against the ground, sending light bursts of air fluttering through the enclosed room.

Professor Helios, one of the more ancient Air Fae, was considered a master of conjuring. He wore his dark hair long, a customary style for one of his age. The thick strands swept around him on an invisible breeze, giving him the illusion of floating. Lengthy robes added to the effect, and he surveyed the class with his inky eyes. Most Air Fae had darker-hued eyes, but not dark enough to overtake the pupil. Professor Helios, however, was powerful—and *old*—so he had an eerie kind of gaze that made it difficult to look directly at him.

He wasted no time and conjured an air sprite to his side. The Halfling let out a soft gasp that made something in me unhinge, but I managed to keep myself in one piece.

The small creature immediately began chittering and buzzed around the Air Fae's head.

"Class, as you can see, we have a new student," Professor Helios said with a sweeping motion. Wind was normally invisible, but when scented with power, it could send color through a controlled breeze. Helios's power was dark, and a shadow swept over the Halfling, making her stiffen. The royal subtly reached out to stroke his fingers through her hair, whispering secret words that I couldn't hear.

Strange. Exos was a Spirit Fae with an affinity for fire, not air. I should be able to hear them.

Unless…

Oh.

Now I saw it. He and the Halfling had initiated a courtship bond. That was what allowed them to speak to one another beyond my intrusion. Fascinating.

An odd surge of jealousy burst through me, causing me to frown. I had no interest in starting a courtship bond with any fae, much less the fabled Halfling. But there was something about her air that called to me.

"Vox," Professor Helios barked, the slice to his words cutting across my ears and making me wince. "You will partner with the Halfling for today's exercise."

A collective gasp, both of shock and relief, swept through the rest of the class.

I hadn't realized I was staring, but the Halfling caught my gaze and offered me a slight smile. *Wait, does she know who I am already? That the professor had just assigned me to her?*

"Vox?" Professor Helios repeated, impatience coloring his tone. "Do you think you can bring our new student up to speed?"

"Yes," I said, clearing my throat as I undid the top button to my suit jacket, hoping I'd feel less suffocated. "Of course."

Professor Helios stabbed his staff into the ground twice, signaling that today's exercises were to begin. "We will pick up where we left off last time. Conjuring figments of our imaginations are great displays of power, and useful, but it all starts with a flicker of our element. Today you will conjure controlled spirals of air at your desk." The creature complained as it flitted around his staff. The professor ignored it. "Keep them controlled, or else this little figment of my imagination will punish you." The air sprite cheered its approval at being involved.

The Halfling's eyes went wide. "Punish?"

I smirked. "Don't mind him," I said, turning to face her as I tried my best to ignore the narrow-eyed royal behind her. "Professor Helios just likes to rule by fear. Thinks that's what'll motivate the students. If you mess up, the worst the air sprite can do is bite you."

She let out a soft gasp. "Bite? Like a mosquito?"

I raised a brow. "Not sure what that is, but yeah, let's go with that."

"Vox," the royal said, startling me. I shifted on my floating pedestal to give him more of my attention. Sunlight struggled to shine in through the translucent barrier to the classroom, but it seemed to bow and waver uncertainly around him, his power a little too *wrong* for this place. He shivered as if sensing how much he didn't fit in here.

"I asked the professor to pair you with Claire. Consider

183

this an audition."

Claire. I'd only heard her referred to as "Halfling" on campus, but I rather liked her unique name.

However, what I didn't care for were Exos's words.

"An audition?" I frowned. "For what?"

He didn't elaborate, instead reaching out to the Halfling to stroke her wrist. "Air was one of the first elements she manifested. After fire, of course. We've been working on controlling her elements, but with her access to all five..." He shrugged, leaving the rest unsaid.

Gods. All five elements in one beautiful, fragile package? I couldn't even begin to imagine how this Halfling had managed to stay in one piece this long.

He couldn't possibly mean for me to be her mentor during her classes on the Air Quad. I must have inferred that wrong. After mentoring Sol for so long, I should have felt like I was capable of anything, but this? Surely not.

My hesitation didn't go unnoticed. Claire moved away from me, just the slightest fraction that most wouldn't have caught, but I did.

"Exos, if he's not comfortable partnering with me, we can find another," Claire mumbled. "Or I can work alone."

Her uncertainty and distrust gave me pause. I didn't know what she'd been through, but I'd never seen such torment in someone's eyes.

Okay. I could handle one class. Maybe not an audition for the future, but today was fine. We'd discuss the rest afterward.

"Claire, is it?" I asked, closing the gap she'd created and rolling my hands on my knees so that they were palm up. A nonthreatening posture to help her feel at ease. "I've heard a lot about you."

Apparently, that was the wrong thing to say.

Heat flared on an invisible breeze that made her golden hair fly back over her shoulders, and her vibrant blue eyes danced with the dangerous spirit powers that sang with the royal's. I sensed that she couldn't manipulate will—or perhaps the royal kept that part of her powers dampened—but a wave of nausea swept over me as she shared a taste of her emotions through the fragile look she gave me.

Pain.

Guilt.

So much *guilt.*

Gods, how was she not splitting at the seams?

"I meant to say, I've been looking forward to meeting you," I amended, realizing the poor girl had likely been swamped with threats and cruelty. While I didn't believe a daughter should be held accountable for her mother's actions, I knew it was a popular opinion.

She narrowed her gaze at me, distrust in every line of her beautiful face. "Why is that?"

I didn't have a good answer for her. For over two weeks, something had put me on edge, so much so that I'd sought out the latest Academy rumors, only to find that there was a Halfling on campus. Ever since I'd known about her, I'd wanted to find her. For what purpose, I couldn't say; I just knew that I had to learn more about her.

That sounded so pathetic. I couldn't tell her the truth, so I opted for what I was best at in these situations.

Divert.

Evade.

Escape.

The class assignment was to conjure air spirals, so that was what I did. The task was easy enough for a fae with my power and control. I let out a soft whistle, and a spiral of air scented with my innate gift colored the element blue. Each Air Fae favored different hues when they worked their powers, but mine seemed to fluctuate with my mood.

This shade of blue meant I was intrigued. And not in a platonic sort of way.

My power is attracted to Claire.

Fuck.

I glanced at the royal to see if he somehow knew. Maybe he could read my mind. I mean, who knew what kind of powers a Spirit Fae like him truly possessed.

However, he didn't react other than to glance at the air spiral flitting around my hand before looking back to Claire.

Her wide gaze was locked on the spiral. I expected her to be afraid, but she seemed fascinated.

An unwanted heat crept over the back of my neck, making me grateful for my warrior's tail and beard. Displaying her effect on me, even if she didn't understand it, was far too intimate for two strangers such as us.

"Go on, you make one," I offered, taking the opportunity to disperse the air spiral.

Her eyes snapped up to mine, making me suck in a breath. Her powers rested just underneath the surface as if they could burst out of her at any moment. So many elements tangled with the beautiful swirling power that was kindred to my own. I sensed her wavering control over her air element and tugged at the wild, snapping strands before I could stop myself.

Her chest leaned forward at the motion as if I'd pulled on her heart. "Oh," she said, the sound more of surprised pleasure than pain. "That's, uh, pleasant."

"What are you doing?" the royal demanded.

Now that I had ahold of her wild power, I didn't dare let go. Each strand was so frayed on the end that I wondered how she wasn't in acute pain.

"Why didn't you come to Air Quad sooner?" I asked before I realized that I was chastising an all-powerful Spirit Fae who could make me squawk like a chicken if he wanted to. "She needs guidance," I clarified.

The royal straightened his spine and narrowed his eyes, then surprised me by uttering a single word. "Continue."

* * *

"Does that feel better?" I asked, hoping Claire could sense what I was doing.

She shifted closer to me until our knees touched. Her

skirt ran up her thighs from the motion, giving me a better view of her skin that glowed with power.

Not just power, but also the sweeping blue electricity that was scented with my magic.

Imagining her skirt inching up just a little more had the aura turning a deeper shade of blue that matched her eyes. She sighed, making me slightly dizzy. "Yeah. Actually, it does."

I cleared my throat, my hold on her power tightening. If I let go now, her control would snap, hurting us both. However, the only way to truly strengthen her grasp on air was to provide her with an anchor. She needed an Air Fae in her circle, likely as a mate, to truly master her powers.

Someone strong enough to balance her.

Someone like me.

And, uh, yeah, that was not going to happen. I'd never been interested in courtship, and I barely knew this girl. Attraction was one thing. A mating, entirely another.

She needed another fae. Someone who wanted that kind of connection. I'd mention it to Exos after class.

"Try to conjure an air spiral like I showed you," I said, hoping my tone sounded encouraging. We'd been trying this for several minutes, but she'd yet to create one.

Claire hummed as her eyes fluttered closed.

My power coiled around hers on instinct, the contact intense.

She leaned forward, her shirt dipping with her and providing me with an agonizing view of her graceful neck and cleavage. A better fae would have averted his gaze, but I was weak when it came to a fae who tugged at my strings like this one did. She demanded my full attention.

Then I noticed it—a fire brand.

Fuck, I knew I'd sensed something else off about her. Her fire was too passionate, too practiced and perfected for a Halfling who'd been rumored to kill and injure multiple fae.

She'd bonded with a Fire Fae as well.

Two courtship bonds, one for each element.

That wasn't unheard of for a Spirit Fae, but it was definitely rare. Given what I'd seen of her powers, it seemed necessary to maintain her balance and control. However, I didn't know of a single Air Fae who would be willing to go up against such competition.

Yet, I also knew she required one. Exos had one hell of a challenge set out before him.

"Just focus on that place inside," she said to herself. "I'm a fae," she continued, half chuckling. "I have magical powers. I can summon little air spirals."

"Like the hot chocolate," the royal offered. He kept his touch light and coaxing across her arm. "You're doing great, Claire."

Her brow wrinkled as she focused, and her powers fluctuated beneath my senses. Something new blossomed, a strange, dark force that felt wrong, corrupted.

What is that? Or better yet, who *is that?* It wasn't a power I recognized, the taste of it bitter on my tongue.

Wait, no, I do know that power. It's familiar.

I frowned, trying to identify the owner because it wasn't Claire. "Hold—"

She summoned the air spiral before I had a chance to stop her. I immediately latched on, trying to quell the conjuring, but the angry power reared at the scent of my magic. It was as if the power multiplied by a thousand, hell-bent on wreaking death and destruction to any who dared to get too close to the Halfling.

This wasn't right. I'd mentored other fae before, and I was good at it because I could visualize their inner strength, contain it, and hold on to it until they could contain themselves. Yet when I reached out to grasp the strand of power that burned hot and angry, it wouldn't listen to me.

This magic doesn't belong to Claire.

The air spiral danced over her hand, causing her to smile at the perceived achievement. An innocent expression that morphed into horror as the energy sprung from her grasp.

"Dispel it," I commanded. "Dispel it now!"

Claire's eyes widened and snapped up to mine in confused terror, but it was too late.

The spiral exploded.

Shrieks sounded, and the pathetic air pixie was the first to be sucked in by the wild vortex that crashed through the classroom, sending delicate pedestals catapulting through the thick glass meant to contain even the worst projectiles.

Professor Helios cast a wave of power to try to contain the vortex, but even the ancient fae was no match for whatever the horror had unleashed.

"*You*!" the Professor shouted as his black eyes trained on Claire. "I will not tolerate violent elements in my classroom!"

As if Claire had a choice in the matter. This wasn't her. I was certain of it.

Despite her lack of involvement, I'd seen the kind of power she possessed. She could dispel this, if only I could guide her on how to use it.

The royal braced himself against the winds, and power shimmered around him as he anchored himself to the ground with invisible threads of life. My lips parted at the display of power. I'd known he was strong, but not that he was creative.

"Claire!" he shouted over the roar of the whirlwind that rained down chaos on the classroom. Determination was etched into every line of his face as the cyclone spiraled out of control.

Professor Helios grunted, trying to shove the winds back as a projectile flung dangerously close to his head.

"Claire!" Exos tried again, this time winning her wide-eyed stare. He braced a hand on her shoulder. "Remember what we taught you."

A desk soared through the air and caught him against the shoulder, throwing him to the ground, silencing him.

Ah, shit...

CHAPTER SEVENTEEN
CLAIRE

EXOS!

I'd been so careful, so determined to master my fae elements. But of course, I fucked up again.

And now I'd injured Exos.

I started to kneel, to check on him, when the Air Fae—Vox—grabbed my shoulder. "We can dispel it. But I need you to focus."

Exos had told me this Air Fae might be a good mentor, his ability to control elements and help others noted in his academic records.

The wind whirled around us, catching Exos in its tunnel and dragging him across the floor. *No!* I latched onto him and yanked him back with a strand of fire that had Vox jumping away from me.

The professor screamed words I couldn't hear, causing the tornado to whirl toward him, plunging straight ahead, as though vexed by the command.

What the hell am I going to do?

"Exos!" I shouted, shaking him.

Vox was suddenly there, kneeling beside me. *When had I fallen to the ground?* I'd somehow landed beside Exos, my arms tight around his neck to keep him away from the destructive windstorm roaring through the room.

Oh God...

We're going to die here.

Air was the one element I couldn't seem to master. It always threw me off, always—

"Take my hand," Vox demanded, holding out his palm. "We need to stop it before it destroys the building."

"How?" I asked, raising my voice above the bellowing vortex. The professor seemed to have it contained to an extent, but it was throwing projectiles left and right.

And if one hit the professor...

"Claire!" Vox shouted. "I need you to trust me. You have the power to kill that thing, and I can help you harness it."

Of course I did. Because I fucking created it.

Damn it!

I'd been doing so well with Titus and Exos, and now—

Vox grabbed my wrist. "*Claire.*"

I blinked at him, startled. "What...?" I swallowed, my throat tight. "What can I do?"

"Can you feel the darkness?" he asked, his voice too calm for the chaos flourishing around us. "The power? Can you locate and isolate it?"

More shouts came, then screams followed by a crash, and I winced.

"Claire," Vox insisted, demanding me to focus on his voice. "Try to latch onto it. Together, we can destroy it, but I'm not strong enough to do it alone. I need you to try to lasso it with me."

Lasso a tornado.

Right.

Yeah, a walk in the park.

"It's picking up speed!" someone screamed.

"Shit!"

"Run!"

"It's going to take the building down!"

My blood ran cold, the insanity spiraling out of control and trying to tug Exos from my grasp. "No!" I shouted, but the word was lost to the howling winds. My hair tangled before my eyes, the lethal tunnel sucking everything into its inky abyss.

Like a black hole, I realized. *Oh God…*

Vox screamed something over the roar of sound, but I couldn't hear him.

I need to focus.

I need to stop this.

By calling the elements to me.

Just like Exos and Titus always say.

I can do this.

I have to.

Or I'll lose my Spirit, my Exos…

Closing my eyes, I searched within myself—the way Titus and Exos had shown me—and called forth my connection to air. Only, I didn't recognize the whirl of power dancing before me. It felt foreign, tasted wrong, as if it hadn't come from me at all. Not like in the courtyard yesterday when Exos helped me calm my out-of-control elements.

This didn't feel like *me.*

But my power located it, caressed it, explored it, searching for a way inside, trying to find a weakness to exploit.

There, my instincts whispered. *Punch a hole there.*

Using a gust of wind shaped like an arrow, I sent the sharp end into the core, locking onto the heart of the darkness, and gave it a tug.

Sweat dampened my brow from the effort, my breathing escalating, but my gifts took over, leading my every move. I punched another hole with a second arrow, then a third, all while keeping a mental rope tied to each.

Then I yanked them simultaneously with the force of all my power, shredding the vortex from the inside out.

I collapsed from the intensity of it, the back of my head somehow landing on Exos's chest. We'd whirled around from the force of the tornado, landing on the opposite side of the room.

Only, it wasn't my arms around him but his arms around me.

His breath rattled out of him on a sigh that sounded like my name, but the voice was wrong.

I glanced backward to find a handsome face with gray eyes and a head of long, dark hair. *Not Exos.* The arms around me were leaner, too, but still strong.

What in the world?

I tried to move, to shift away from Vox and find Exos, except something heavy held me down. My hands fluttered over the solid muscle, relieved to find my Royal Fae. He didn't move, still unconscious, but breathing.

I sighed, relaxing my head, causing Vox to inhale sharply.

Shit.

How did I keep finding myself in this position? Sandwiched between hot men?

"Exos," I muttered, giving him a shake.

He didn't move.

Vox's arms loosened beneath my breasts, sending a wave of heat through my body. "Are you okay, Claire?" he asked, his deep voice a rumble beneath me.

"I, uh, yeah. But Exos is—"

"Suffering from a splitting headache," Exos finished for me, his voice low. "While also rather enjoying lounging between your legs, princess. I think I'll stay."

Vox chuckled beneath me. "I think he's fine."

"More than fine," Exos murmured, slowly sitting up and cracking his neck.

It granted enough room for me to squirm out from between the two men, not that either of them seemed too keen on moving, if their matching smiles were anything to go by.

Smiles that quickly shifted to frowns as shrieks sounded from across the room.

Vox was on his feet in a second, his long hair loose around his shoulders. Whatever tie he'd used to secure that thick mass of beautiful brown strands was long gone, thanks to the tornado. Now it billowed in the breeze being cast from Professor Helios—a breeze aimed at me and carrying words of accusation.

"Your Highness," he said slowly. "I suggest you get Claire out of here."

Exos joined him, surveying the mess of the room before holding a hand out to help me up off the floor. My limbs shook with the effort, causing me to frown. Taking down that vortex had exhausted me more than I realized. I actually felt a bit woozy now that the adrenaline of the moment had subsided.

The nausea only worsened as I took in the massacre of the room.

"Oh God…," I whispered, finally *seeing* the destruction. Bodies littered the floor. Some of them were moving. Most were not.

And the one screaming was Ignis's friend. The one with wiry blonde hair who'd joined Ignis in the courtyard where I caused the fire.

Her violet eyes found mine and widened in horror. "*You!*"

Great…

"She didn't do it, Aerie," Vox said, startling me. "It wasn't her magic."

Exos glanced at him in question while my eyebrows rose. *Vox felt that, too?*

194

The Air Fae—Aerie—screamed, the sound causing me to flinch and my knees to buckle beneath me. Exos caught me by the waist as I pressed my palms to my bleeding ears.

What is that? The shriek had knocked me off-kilter, splitting my head in two, and worsened the ache in my gut. It left me dizzy and unstable, Exos's arm around me the only thing keeping me upright. And even then, the room seemed to be spinning.

I winced as the shriek deepened, worming into my mind. It knocked the air from my lungs, leaving me floating in a cloud of confusion and deafness.

My hands fell as I tried to find them with my eyes.

Why is everything so fuzzy?

I blinked, trying to focus.

"Enough!" Vox roared, a whoosh of wind following the command and sending Aerie into the wall. Or, at least, that was what appeared to have happened. I couldn't really tell. It was as if my vision had shrunk into a teeny, tiny point.

"I'll talk to Professor Helios, but you need to get Claire out of here." Vox's voice registered, but it rang with an authority that surprised me. He seemed like such a nice fae. Not a bossy one. Not like my Exos.

"You and I need to have a conversation," Exos replied, causing my lips to curl. That was my bossy fae. And why did I find that so amusing?

Vox sighed. "Oh, we'll be talking all right. But for now, focus on Claire. She's about to collapse."

I am?

Oh.

Exos hadn't just put his arm around me but had also lifted me into the air. No wonder it felt like I was floating.

Dude, I'm drunk, I realized. Like the entire world was spinning in a mist of intoxication. When did that happen and how?

"Relax, Claire. I have you," Exos vowed.

"Oh, I know," I replied, smiling. "You definitely have me."

"It's the wind tunnel," Vox said, his voice warm and far away. No, close. Wait, where was he standing, again? "Fucks with the sense of balance and thought. She'll be fine in an hour. Just get her some water." Another whoosh followed his words. "Do not move, Aerie."

I swore she growled in reply. Or someone did. And then more yelling ensued, but I couldn't see any of them or anything. The carnage of the windstorm lay dormant beyond my vision. Or perhaps not so quiet. Panic filtered through the air, words I couldn't understand, and chants.

I curled into Exos, craving his familiarity, his security. I didn't want to be drunk anymore, but I couldn't see beyond the fog of my mind. Everything mingled in shades of blacks that were riddled with sounds.

I whimpered.

Lips pressed against my temple. "You'll be okay."

Exos?

Yes. I snuggled into his heat, his scent, his strength.

"What happened?" a new voice demanded, one I recognized immediately as my Titus. I couldn't say when I started thinking of these two men as mine, but I did. They were mine, and I intended to keep them if they let me.

Their tongues and hands, mmm...

"Is she drunk?" Titus demanded.

"Yes, I took her to the bar to celebrate her destruction on Air Quad today. Sorry for not inviting you." Exos set me on a cloud of amazingness. So, so soft. But not warm enough. I reached for his hand, longing for his heat, and found Titus's instead. My lips curled, my fire instantly engaged, and I tugged him toward me.

"Fuck, Claire," he muttered, collapsing on top of me. Or maybe beside me. I really couldn't tell, this wave of confusion shadowing my judgment.

"Yeah, you entertain her there while I go find some water. According to Vox, that'll help cure this wind tunnel messing with her mind." Exos sounded amused, which made me giggle. I liked him amused. He had the best smile.

Like the sun. Except he rarely showed it. Maybe he lived in a cloud, too. Like me. Because I couldn't see a damn thing. But I could definitely *feel*, and I really liked the heat coming from Titus. So muscular. Hard. *Hot*.

"You and I are going to have a long talk about your conversational skills, Royal," Titus growled. "Claire, sweetheart, can you stop—No. Stop that." He grabbed my wrists, causing me to pout. I wanted to pet him. To revel in his *fire*.

No more of this kissing and orgasm crap. I wanted more. To really, truly *feel* him.

To fuck… yes!

"Claire," he warned. His voice turned to a hiss as I arched into him, signaling with my body what I craved since apparently my mouth no longer worked. Or my eyes.

What is wrong with my head?

So fuzzy.

Oh, but the heat…

"*Claire.*" The pain in Titus's voice had me stilling against him. Had I hurt him in some way? All I wanted was to roll in his flames, to let them bathe over my skin and light my way out of this insane darkness.

"Here." Exos was back. My Royal Fae. My spirit half.

These men were my fae. My Titus and my Exos. Forever mates. Lovers. Oh, but without the fucking. I scowled at that; they really needed to sort this out—

Oh.

Cool liquid slipped over my tongue, exciting my nerves and calming me at the same time. I sighed, my head pillowed against Titus, my hands now being held by Exos.

Sandwiched yet again between two men.

How had this become my life?

"Maybe we should invite Vox," I mused. *Wait, had I said that out loud?*

"He'll be by later," Exos said softly.

Yeah, said that out loud.

Oh, but hey! I had a voice again.

197

Still can't see, though.

"What the hell is this?" Titus asked as more water slid over my tongue. "Start talking, Exos."

"In case it's not clear, I've had a very rough afternoon and I'm not in the mood for your petulant demands."

"Oh? I'm sorry. You bring home a very drunk Claire, who seems hell-bent on fucking me, and you'd like me to just accept that. All right. Care to leave while I indulge her?"

"Fuck you."

"No, *fuck you*. Now tell me what the hell happened."

I giggled, their banter amusing the hell out of me. And they kept saying *fuck,* which was exactly what I wanted to do. But they had some sort of no-fucking rule going on between them that was driving me *crazy*. Like, how many nights could a girl go to bed naked between two hot men and *not* get fucked?

"Try being one of those males and having to rely on your hand for weeks," Titus growled.

Oh, I said that out loud… My brow crinkled. No. I didn't feel bad about it. "I want sex."

"Dear Elements, we are not having this conversation in your current state," Exos snapped.

"Then busy us both by telling me what the hell happened," Titus suggested, his tone doing this sexy, deep, demanding thing that made my lady parts tingle. "Claire, stop doing that."

Exos sighed. "Here." He gently began massaging my temples, which sparked glimpses of light in the darkness but didn't relieve the ache building between my thighs. I'd much rather have his attentions focused elsewhere. I opened my mouth to say just that, when a tongue slid between my lips, eliciting a groan from deep within.

Which one of them was kissing me?

Exos, my spirit whispered.

Yes… I recognized his dominance, his minty taste, his command.

But rather than excite my nerves and caress the heat

building inside, it made me sleepy. Oh, how he drained me. Such a virile, powerful man. I pressed into him, accepting his gift, his presence, his being, and felt my limbs relax.

Such a soft, fluffy world.

Warm.

Safe.

Mmm.

Yes, I would sleep. Just for a little bit. And when I woke, hopefully I'd be able to see again.

CHAPTER EIGHTEEN
VOX

EXHAUSTION WEIGHED HEAVILY ON ME. Dealing with Aerie had been child's play.

Professor Helios, however, had been another matter. Once he'd regained consciousness, he'd been hell-bent on seeking justice for his classroom. And Claire had been the focus of his wrath. Thankfully, Exos had whisked her off to the safety of the Spirit Quad before that could happen.

Of course, now the Royal Fae would have to deal with the repercussions and face the Council. Which meant I'd need to intervene.

That tornado did not belong to Claire. I felt it in every fiber of my being, and not just because my inner air considered her to be a potential mate.

Not happening, I told myself for the thousandth time.

Helping her I could do. Falling for a woman with two other mates already? No.

Except all I could think about was how her essence had called to me.

Fuck.

Fuck.

Fuck.

I was mad to even be thinking of her right now. The entire Academy was in an uproar after yet another series of deaths surrounding the Halfling.

Except this wasn't her fault.

"By the Elements," Sol huffed as he stormed into the Earth Dorms carrying a bag. "Vox, what are you doing here?"

Yeah, about that…

I squirmed on Sol's unforgiving excuse for a couch and glowered at the dusty layers of glass that needed a cleaning. There should have been a beautiful view of the shifting gardens, but Sol sucked at housekeeping.

"You really need to get a more comfortable couch," I complained, ignoring his question. "It's not inviting at all."

Sol rolled his eyes and plopped the cloth bag onto the table and began to unfurl it. Steaming, leafy edges of meat pie made my mouth water. Sol tore one of the leaves and broke me off a chunk, handing it to me with a knowing look. "You don't often mope, Vox. Didn't see the Halfling today like you'd hoped?"

I glared at the offering and took a small nibble, not having much of an appetite even though my stomach was roaring for sustenance after the power I'd expensed kicking Aerie's ass. "Quite the opposite," I admitted around the small mouthful.

Sol's brown eyes raked over me as if noticing for the first time that my usually kempt suit was tattered and torn. "Don't tell me you were there for the maelstrom?" His eyes widened when I didn't respond. "Elements, Vox, you could have been killed!" He leaned in and lowered his voice, glancing around as though someone might somehow hear us in the room of solid rock. "Was the royal there, too?" He waggled his fingers at me. "Did he mind-control her to do it?"

I nearly choked on the morsel. "Fuck, Sol. No."

Sol distrusted all Spirit Fae, but Exos more than most. I still didn't know why, but tonight wasn't the night to ask. Nor did I have the energy to prove his thoughts wrong. It would require talking about what happened with Claire, and I wasn't ready to face that yet.

My best friend scoffed at me and wrapped a leaf around a larger chunk of meat, then tore it off with his teeth. He gazed out through the dirtied window, not seeming to care that he couldn't really see through it. "Well, it won't matter much either way," Sol said.

"Why's that?"

He chewed thoughtfully before answering me. "I heard that if there was one more fae death at the Academy, then the Halfling would be expelled and banished to the Spirit Kingdom." He shrugged. "Not a bad thing, because that bastard royal will go with her and I won't have to keep tiptoeing around my own damn campus. She has power over all five elements, you know so she would eventually have earth classes." He shuddered as if horrified by the idea.

My heart skipped a beat. *Banished? Spirit Kingdom?*

No fucking way.

She's innocent.

And fuck if I was going to let anyone send an innocent girl to a damn wasteland.

I slammed my fist on the table, sending dust flying. "For one, *Sol*, you don't fucking tiptoe anywhere. You shake the ground like a beast that can't be contained." I held up two fingers. "And secondly, don't judge someone you've never even met. The Halfling is innocent."

I didn't give Sol a chance to digest my outrage. Instead I caught a glimpse of his wide eyes—and perhaps a little hurt in his gaze—before I tore open the front door with a gust of wind and marched out of the Earth Dorms.

I should have returned to my own quarters, but I found the breeze taking me straight to the Halfling, who I knew would never harm another living soul and didn't deserve the fae's wrath.

Everyone on campus knew she was living in—or rather, *banished to*—the Spirit Dorms. Now I just had to figure out which room she'd chosen in a wasteland of nothing.

* * *

No one ever encroached on the Spirit Quad, and for good reason. The wasteland looked like a scar across the otherwise beautiful grounds. A stark line grooved out in the dirt where the barriers between majestic energies bordered each other. The lively, shifting rock of the Earth Quad kept its distance from the cold, gray, and lifeless dirt that made up the majority of the Spirit grounds. I drew in a deep breath, as if I could gather my air element inside of me in a protective bubble, before braving a step forward.

There.

Ouch.

Okay, yeah, it hurt. It felt like crossing over from life to death because I wasn't meant to be on the Spirit Quad. I hadn't received an invitation, and there wasn't even the slightest breeze here to make me feel at home.

Lifeless, colorless buildings wrapped in dead vines boasted what had once been classrooms teeming with bright-minded students. There was, however, one pop of color that stood out against the corpse-like dirt.

A white flower.

I leaned down to inspect it and grazed it with my fingertips.

Claire.

Another flower marked the path just a few paces down, so I went to it and squinted until I spotted another. Then another still, until I was so deep into the Spirit Quad that I swore I was starting to hear the voices of the dead that had once roamed these grounds.

Oh, not the dead—that's a fae.

I tilted my head to the side and allowed a sliver of my power to carry a breeze to catch the sounds.

There, the dorms.

I ventured in without knocking, not because I meant to intrude, but because I was so intent on discovering what kind of fae might be here other than Exos and Claire.

"You have to fucking do *something*," a muscular fae demanded. Auburn locks licked with tiny flames, and embers burned in the fae's eyes as he challenged the royal that leaned heavily against the wall. He was shirtless, his hair damp, maybe from a recent shower.

"And *you* need to calm down," Exos ordered. He pushed off from the wall and startled me by pinning me with his gaze. "Ah, Vox. Finally, you're here." He waved me over as if he'd summoned me here. "Come in and make yourself at home."

My eyes widened. I was an Air Fae adept in the skills of stealth. I'd passed every shadowstep and secrecy class with outstanding marks, to the point that I was well on my way as a spy for Air Kingdom if I so wanted, yet the royal had noticed me without any effort at all.

The Fire Fae glared at me, causing me to reconsider coming here. I recognized him. Everyone on campus would. He was a renowned fighter. A champion. And lethal as fuck. "Well, you heard Exos," Titus said. "Don't just stand there, Vox. Join us."

Swallowing hard, I entered and awkwardly adjusted my ruined suit. I probably should have changed into something more presentable before venturing over here. "Ah, so, is Claire okay?" I asked.

Smooth, Vox.

"Yes, she's having a nap," Exos said, then gave Titus a raised brow. "And shouldn't be left alone, Titus."

"Should I expect her to wake up intoxicated? Or did

your little mindfuck fix that?"

Exos narrowed his gaze. "Did you prefer the alternative?"

Titus growled. "This isn't working."

"I know."

"Then fucking do something about it, *Your Highness*."

Exos sighed and ran his fingers through his light hair. "Sorry, Vox. You've caught us in a rather *heated* moment, one Titus can't seem to let go." Those last two words were directed at the Fire Fae.

Titus flipped him off in response.

Okay, then. I'd clearly interrupted something. "I can come back…"

"No," they both said at once.

"We have to talk about what happened," Exos added. "About what went wrong."

"She didn't kill anyone," I blurted out, feeling the weight of their stares. "I mean, I felt it. I'm a mentor, and I can sense energies. The energy that created that maelstrom wasn't Claire's."

Exos smiled. "I know. But thank you for confirming my suspicions."

"Again, that whole communicating thing?" Titus waved between himself and Exos. "Still sucking. Now tell me about these *suspicions*."

"Had you given me a moment earlier instead of throwing a fit, I would have."

"Well, fucking tell me now."

"Who is the royal here, Titus?" Exos asked, cocking his head to the side. "Me or you?"

"Oh, this again." Titus threw his hands up in the air. "Claire is passed-out drunk—from something you've still not explained, by the way—and you want to play the superiority game instead of telling me what the hell is going on. Typical."

"What's typical is you losing your temper over nothing."

"*Nothing*?" he repeated, pointing to a door at the end of

the room. "*That* is not nothing."

"Aerie sent a target shriek of air into Claire's mind. Specifically, the frontal lobe, causing temporary, well, incapacitation," I explained, hoping to dispel some of the tension. "It's a classic Air Fae attack mechanism. Renders your opponent incomprehensible for an hour or two. Essentially, it makes the victim feel very, very intoxicated."

Titus gaped at me while Exos scratched his chin.

"She'll be fine," I added. "Sleeping it off is the best for her."

"Who do you think manipulated her spiral?" Exos asked, changing the subject.

"I don't know. But I can help you find out."

He arched a brow. "How?"

"By tracking the energy source." It wouldn't be hard. After trying to dismantle the maelstrom myself, I had a pretty good understanding of what it felt like. "As I said, I have a knack for sensing energy." It was what allowed me to help Sol with his affinity for earth.

"You're saying you want to help," Exos translated.

"I'm saying I can, if you need it." I wasn't about to assume a powerful Spirit Fae required my assistance. As he already pointed out, he suspected Claire wasn't the source of power.

He nodded, then glanced at Titus. "I think we found our Air Fae."

"You're assuming he can keep up." Titus folded his arms and looked me over. "You up for the task?"

"Of tracking the energy source? Yeah."

"No." Titus smirked. "I meant, are you up for the task of managing Claire?"

"Oh, uh…" I swallowed. "To help manage her air?"

Titus nodded.

Exos said nothing, his gaze assessing me.

"I just came by to tell you it wasn't her and to offer assistance in tracking down the culprit." No, that wasn't entirely true. A part of me had longed to check up on her.

But that was just my mentor side requiring me to make sure the student I'd failed earlier today was all right. "However, yes, she needs a mentor." I'd meant to say that to Exos as well, but the banishing comments from Sol had derailed my focus. All I'd cared about was expressing her innocence so they didn't send her away.

Why do I care so much?

Because she's innocent.

Right.

"She needs *you* as a mentor," Exos replied. "You're a good match for her. I felt it during class. And so you'll mentor her."

He uttered the words as if they were a done deal. "I'll help you find one," I offered. "A mentor, I mean."

"No need." Exos turned, walking down the hall. "She already has one, Vox. You." He paused on the threshold, his blue eyes meeting mine. "Don't leave. I'm just going to grab some proper clothes for us to hunt in."

"But—"

"And I need to wake up Claire. Give me twenty minutes, Vox."

I gaped after the Royal Fae as he disappeared through a door, leaving me unable to argue.

Titus chuckled. "Yeah, he does that. But you'll get used to him."

"I can't mentor her," I blurted out.

"And why's that?" Titus asked, cocking his head to the side.

"I… It's just… I have Sol and classes and…"

He arched an auburn-tinged brow. "I don't know what a Sol is, but so far, all I'm hearing are weak excuses. Sort of disappointing, if you ask me. Exos is clearly wrong. Claire requires someone stronger. Don't worry; I'll talk to him. I mean, he won't fucking listen, but if you're not up for the task, then he'll have no choice. Right?"

"No, that's not what I mean." *Fuck. He's right. They're all just idiotic excuses.* I shook my head and pinched the bridge of my nose. "Her power calls to mine." The truth sort of fell out of my mouth on a breeze of words I couldn't catch. But what else could I say? Another bullshit excuse? No. She deserved better than that. And so did I.

Titus smiled. "Well then, welcome to the team, Vox. I hope you enjoy cold showers."

CHAPTER NINETEEN
EXOS

I RAN MY FINGERS through Claire's thick hair, reveling in the silky texture while I slowly removed my hold over her elements. Manipulating others was the darker side of my ability, and that included being able to put someone to sleep at will.

For Claire, it'd been necessary. Her eyes had been unseeing—*wild*—and her powers had taken on a will of their own. She probably didn't even realize the sheer force with which she'd pulled Titus down onto the bed or the way her fire engulfed him in a sea of hot desire.

Clearly, all of us had some pent-up passion issues at the forefront of our minds.

I sighed and joined Claire on the bed, wrapping my arms around her as she began to stir beside me. Hopefully, her nap had cured the drunken spell Aerie had woven through Claire's mind.

I could kill that Air Fae, I thought, furious. She'd attacked Claire in a moment of weakness, after she'd taken down that maelstrom.

A maelstrom Claire absolutely did not create.

I'd felt the presence of another just before it erupted, stirring chaos throughout the room. There'd been a dark note to it, a sense of spirit that I didn't recognize.

But I knew with certainty that it didn't belong to Claire. My power had tuned into hers over the last few weeks, braiding our essences together and merging our spirits. I *knew* her now. And that destructive energy dancing through the room had possessed an entirely different elemental pattern.

"Exos?" she murmured, her eyes still closed.

"I'm here, princess." I pressed my lips to her forehead and held her tighter. "How do you feel?"

She seemed to consider for a moment before saying, "Hungover. Like, really, really hungover."

I chuckled and reached for the water I'd left on the nightstand for her. "Here." I pressed the rim to her lips and helped her take a few sips while brushing my spirit over hers in a way that had become second nature these last few weeks.

She stretched beside me, a low moan of approval emanating from her throat. "Thank you," she whispered, snuggling into me more.

I returned the glass to the table and folded my arms around her again. "You did well today, Claire." Unfortunately, while I believed that, the Council would disagree. The incident on Air Quad had Claire's fingerprints all over it, which they would most likely use to banish her from the Academy.

"Today?" she asked, her voice sleepy. Then she went stiff. "Oh no…"

"Shh," I soothed. "It's going to be okay." *Because I'm going to figure out who actually created that spiral and break the culprit's neck.*

It occurred to me as well that the other incidents may not have been Claire at all, but the person who had interfered today. The fire and water episodes happened before I fully understood the extent of her powers, so it was hard to say for certain. But given the events on Air Quad, it seemed likely.

"I didn't do it," she blurted out, squirming backward to stare at me. "I mean, I thought I did. I created the spiral, but I don't know how it blew out of control. And when I tried to stop it, I couldn't find my essence inside of it. Like… like… you know, yesterday? With that energy ball in the courtyard? You told me to wrap my fire around it, remember? And I could because I recognized my own powers. But this time…" She trailed off, her expression falling. "I sound crazy, I know, but I swear it wasn't me, Exos."

I touched her chin, gently nudging it upward to capture her gaze. "I know, baby. I felt it, too."

She must not have remembered the part where Vox also claimed it wasn't her. How fascinating that he could sense it without a bond. Either it proved him to be a potential mate for Claire or it was related to his own incredible gifts.

Regardless, it made him perfect for her team.

Which was why he would be joining—with or without his approval.

"You did?" she whispered.

I kissed her softly before pressing my forehead to hers. "My spirit knows yours, Claire."

"Because of the bond," she translated.

"And the last few weeks of training. But, yes, mostly as a result of our connection." I licked her bottom lip and continued to stroke her spirit with mine, eliciting a contented sigh from her. "It's deepening," I told her on a hush of sound. "Can you feel it?" There were different levels to the mating bond, and ours was teetering on the edge of something more permanent.

"I don't really understand it," she admitted softly. "But yes, I can feel it. Is sex what pushes it over the edge?" Her cheeks flushed beautifully with the query, her blue eyes sparkling with life. "That came out wrong. I just... I've wondered if that's why you and Titus are holding back—so we don't accidentally intensify the link."

Her confession surprised me. "You think we don't want to take this to the next level?" It applied to both sex and the mating.

"I, uh, well, yeah." She swallowed. "I mean, I get it. There are two of you, and that just makes this even more confusing, right? And you never really had a choice in our bond, since I kissed you without permission. Not that I knew this would happen. Oh, wait, that came out wrong, too. I don't regret it. What I mean is—"

I captured her mouth with my own, silencing her little rant. While it was adorable, I didn't want to hear her second-guessing the nature of our connection.

Was it my choice? No.

Did it bother me? At first, yes. But now? No.

No, now I wouldn't have this any other way. Her gift for spirit rivaled mine, making her an ideal princess in my court. Apart from the other competing elements, what we had was so unique, so different, so much more powerful than anyone would ever understand.

And it was with that knowledge in mind that I rolled her to her back and worshiped her with my mouth. I unleashed all the emotions I hid from the world, including how I felt about her. Oh, Titus had an idea of how badly I ached for her. But his knowledge only skimmed the surface to the depths of what I kept locked away inside.

A warrior couldn't afford a weakness.

Yet, at some point, Claire had become mine.

She gave new meaning to my heart.

My hips settled between hers, my cock throbbing against her hot center. "Sex is a merging of the bodies," I murmured, my lips moving across her cheek. "The connection is between the elements, and ours is a dance between our souls." I pressed my arousal into the sanctuary between her thighs, providing an introduction to my lustful cravings, and smiled at her resulting moan. If only we were naked, then I could truly demonstrate my yearnings.

Alas, I had a task to complete. One that would hopefully secure her place here and pacify the Council.

To find the one framing my Claire.

My teeth grazed her pulse on my way up to her ear. "You can deepen a bond without sex, Claire. It just has to be a mutual agreement between the fae to continue exploring opportunities. I think, in your terms, it would be the equivalent of going from a few casual dates to dating seriously, or maybe even an engagement. Because once our elements move on to the next phase, it's showing a promise for the future and speaks of a serious intent to mate for eternity."

"How many levels are there?" she asked, her nails scratching down my back as she arched up into me.

I smiled against her neck. "Four."

"And we're on the first?"

"Yes."

"But close to the second?"

"Yes." I took her mouth again—because I could—and slid my tongue deep inside, possessing every inch of her. She groaned, her body vibrating with need beneath mine. I longed to give in, just for one more moment, and so I did.

I gave her everything.

My frustration.

My yearning.

My adoration.

My worries.

The Council would be meeting later tonight, and if I didn't give them a sound argument against expulsion...

No.

I refused.

That was not going to happen on my watch.

Claire's arms wound around my neck, holding me tightly as she reciprocated in kind, her feelings exploding across her tongue. I felt her confusion, her strength, and, most importantly, her craving not just for a physical connection but also for an emotional one.

With me.

A sign of her mutual affection.

She couldn't know that was what it meant, but my power reacted in kind, dancing with hers on a plane only spirit had access to. "That's it, isn't it?" she whispered, awe in her voice.

"Yes." Apparently, that was my word of the night because not only did I keep saying it out loud but my soul repeated it as well.

Claire's energy swirled around mine, causing the hairs along the nape of my neck to stand on end. This was why we didn't need sex to graduate to phase two. The bond required elemental compatibility, coupled with the passion for more.

And there'd never been another fae more for me than Claire. "You're sure?" I asked her softly, nuzzling my nose against hers. "Because if we push this one inch forward, we'll be in the next level, Claire."

"Dating exclusively, right?" she asked, sounding dreamy. Then the words seemed to register, because she froze. "Meaning I can't see Titus…"

"No." I cupped her cheek, pulling her back to me before panic could truly set in. "It would mean you can't see another Spirit Fae. This is about elemental bonding, Claire. You would essentially be declaring your spirit as betrothed to mine."

"Like marriage."

"It's similar, but different. Consider it more of a long-term commitment to ensure that our pairing is what we truly desire. By escalating to the next phase of the bond, you'll have more access to *me*. To my mind. It requires trust,

Claire. And then from there, you move into the third stage, in which our elements mingle and flourish off one another—where you could borrow energy from me as I could from you. And the final level is eternity."

She swallowed, some of the alarm melting into curiosity. "Were my mother and Mortus a three or a four?"

"A three," I murmured. "When you reach that phase, there's no going back. The elements are locked into one another—indefinitely."

"Then why the fourth stage?" she asked.

"It's more of a formality, a pledge of fealty that binds the souls. To join your elements, but not the souls, can be quite painful." Which explained Mortus's rage. But I didn't add that part. I could see from the flare of her pupils that she inferred it anyway.

"The third step is binding, similar to an engagement without an escape route if you get cold feet," she surmised. "And the second is a more serious level of seeing someone, like moving in with them. While the first is temporary—like dating—to see if the person your power is attracted to is someone you might like as well."

I kissed her gently, loving the way she'd gone pliant and soft again beneath me. "Very accurate summarization, princess."

"And we're already living together," she continued, her mouth moving against mine. "So, we should move up a level." Her tongue licked across my lower lip. "Right?"

"If that's your desire."

"Is it yours?"

I pulled back to meet her eyes, my palm still resting against her cheek. "Yes." *There's that word again.*

Her blue eyes brightened. "Really?"

I pressed my arousal into her hot center and cocked my head to the side. "You can feel how much I want you, right?"

She slapped my shoulder. "You said this is about emotions."

215

"It's about everything, Claire," I replied with a laugh. "Do I want to deepen our bond? Yes. Absolutely. But I also very much want to fuck you. The two are not mutually exclusive, but again, the connection isn't about sex. It's about power. And it also happens to heighten the sensations, or so I've heard."

"You've never connected with anyone?"

"Only you, Claire. On any level." I went to my elbows on either side of her head, wanting her to see the sincerity in my expression as I gave her the ultimate truth. "I never wanted to bond with anyone. Nor did I think I would actually find someone who suited my power. I'm one of the strongest fae in the world, and that's not me boasting; it's a fact. Finding a partner who can handle my gift, one my spirit is actually attracted to, was a very impossible notion. Until you."

Tears pricked her eyes, causing me to frown.

That was *not* the response I wanted. At all.

But she pulled me down to kiss her, and the sensation she poured from her mouth to mine floored me.

She didn't just accept the bond; she kicked the fucking door down and yanked me into the next level with her. I felt it in the way our powers snapped together, as if a lock had tied her spirit to mine, securing her place in my heart and mine in hers.

"Claire," I whispered, returning the embrace and worshiping her with my tongue. She clung to me as if she needed me to breathe, her legs winding around my hips, her fingers in my hair.

This kiss sparked a new beginning.

It carved her name into my very being, marking my element as hers and hers as mine. Flowers blossomed around us, the creation of life filling the room with the fragrance of our heightened connection and shaking the very foundations of the building.

That it occurred on Spirit Quad only intensified the moment, bringing all ounces of life back to the formerly dead campus.

The trees rejoiced.

The grounds cried out in pleasure.

And the meadows bloomed.

That was the power we possessed together—a life energy no one could ever touch. *Ours.*

Claire shuddered beneath me, her blue eyes luminescent with vitality. "That's…"

"Amazing," I finished for her softly. "And something we will definitely be exploring more." I laved her plump lip before pressing a kiss to her cheek. Now more than ever I felt a duty to protect her, and that required me to leave her, to find the one trying to cause her harm. "Vox is here," I whispered.

"Why?" she asked, her voice breathy, her expression soft.

"He knows you didn't create that windstorm today, and he thinks he can track the energy signature back to its owner." I drew my thumb beneath her eye, catching the tear she'd shed only moments ago.

Tears of joy, I realized. I sort of liked that. I licked the drop, deciding to taste her emotional gift—*mine. Just like Claire.*

Her gaze widened. "He thinks someone created that thing on purpose?"

"Yes, to frame you. And I suspect the first incident in the courtyard, as well as the water in the dorms, may not have been you, either. So I'm going to go with him to see if we can find the person who created the tornado."

"Me, too," she said, her hands on my shoulders as if to push me away.

I refused to move. "No. You need to stay here with Titus." I pressed a finger to her lips before she could protest. "Claire. He needs you."

This wasn't about my trying to shelter her. If anything, it would be a good lesson for her to learn how to identify the essence of others—especially as Spirit Fae could control

217

them.

No.

This was about Titus.

"He's on edge," I continued. "And to properly protect you, I need him focused. There's only one way to fix it." I'd realized it this afternoon after witnessing the true pain in his features, the barely concealed fire.

While I, too, felt the aching need inside me to claim Claire, my elemental control far outweighed his, and I didn't have a tendency to burn shit down when in a rage.

If we were going to go up against someone powerful enough to manifest powers on Claire's behalf, then I needed everyone focused. Not to mention the general security required to keep our little fae princess alive. Too many people wanted her dead.

I almost liked that she needed more than one mate. *Almost* being the key word. But I couldn't deny that it helped from a bodyguard standpoint.

"Are you telling me to…?" She trailed off, her brow pinched.

I bent to kiss the pucker between her eyebrows before dragging my lips lower to her mouth and whispering, "Yes, Claire. I'm telling you to indulge him while I'm gone. I don't want the details. Although, I'll likely feel it through the bond." I flinched at the thought but quickly swallowed my instinctual reaction.

No one could touch our spirit bond.

Not even Titus.

"It feels… wrong… after we just…"

I silenced her with another kiss, this one coaxing and holding a promise. "You're still mine, Claire. But you're also his. And I respect that, just as I know he'll respect our bond. It's the way of life." I tilted my head to the side, amusement touching my chest. "You're not in the human world anymore, darling princess. We're fae. Our rules are different."

She stared at me for a long moment before yanking me

to her once more and rewarding me with her mouth. "Don't do anything without me," she said softly. "If you find the person doing this, I want to know. I want to be there."

"Of course." I brushed my nose against hers. "Reconnaissance only."

"Promise?"

"I vow it." I pecked her lips once more and shifted back to my knees as I sensed a new presence enter the room. I ignored him and decided to have a little fun instead. "Now that I've let Titus and Vox get to know each other, I think it's time we join them to make sure they're both still alive."

Her eyebrows rose, the innocence in her features telling me she'd not sensed Titus's entrance yet. Likely because I'd distracted her with our bonding and other more arousing activities.

"They don't like each other?" she asked.

I lifted a shoulder. "As I said, Titus has some pent-up anger issues. But Vox strikes me as the calm, collected type. Maybe they can be friends."

"As he doesn't harbor a penchant for bossing me around, I think we'll get along just fine," Titus deadpanned.

Claire froze while I chuckled. "Our Claire is awake, by the way."

"I can see that," he replied, the possessive growl in his voice no better than before. The Fire Fae seemed ready to combust, and while I trusted him not to harm Claire, I didn't necessarily trust him not to hurt me.

Leaning down to kiss her one last time, I rolled off the bed and grabbed a shirt from the closet. She hadn't moved, her wide gaze on a glowering Titus. He clearly sensed the heightened bond within her, and his clenched hands said how he felt about it.

I pressed my palm to his chest to back him up a few paces into the wall and caught his fist before it could meet my face. "Vox and I are leaving to track the energy signature. Claire wanted to join us, but I suggested she spend some time here with you. *Alone.*" I lifted an eyebrow with the final word, ensuring he followed my insinuation. "Does that work for you?"

Flames danced in his gaze as he studied my features. Then his shoulders seemed to relax as he gave me a stiff nod.

"I promised Claire we won't act on any information without her. And I imagine we'll be back in a few hours."

Another nod. "Okay."

"Okay." I released him and went to retrieve my shoes. Claire had sat up on the bed during our discussion, her lower lip snagged between her teeth. I bent to tug it between my own, giving her a little nibble. "Try not to burn the dorm down, baby."

Her cheeks flushed an adorable shade of red, causing me to chuckle. It physically pained me to leave her in the hands of another man, but while Titus might not be my favorite fae, I couldn't deny his compatibility with Claire.

And as such, I trusted him implicitly with her life.

He stopped me with a hand on my forearm, his green eyes holding a touch of gratitude in them as they captured mine.

No words were spoken.

Not even another nod.

Just a brief look of understanding before he released me.

"Be careful," Claire called after me, causing me to pause on the threshold.

I glanced back at her, amused. "I'm a Royal Fae, baby. There's no one on this campus who can touch me. Except you." And with that, I met Vox in the hallway. "Let's go, Air Fae. I want to see what you can do."

CHAPTER TWENTY
CLAIRE

TWO MEN.

Fae.

Both mates.

Watching them interact was… *hot*.

Mainly because Titus had this sexy glower thing going on while Exos still managed to alpha him with that shove against the wall. It provoked all manner of inappropriate thoughts, ones that only seemed to intensify as Titus gazed at me from across the room.

"Are you hungry, Claire?" he asked, his voice low.

I couldn't tell if meant for food or for him. But the answer was a resounding "Yes" either way. Mostly for something of the sexual variety, considering Exos had spent the last however many minutes heating me up, just to leave.

His essence seemed to swim through my veins, his scent forever clinging to me. Because of the bond. He'd been right about it deepening our connection. I could almost sense him in my mind, his resounding amusement at leaving me hot and bothered in his wake.

Or maybe that was my imagination. But it didn't seem too far-fetched a notion.

Titus leaned against the wall. "Are you going to assault me again if I come over there?"

"Again?" I asked, confused.

"You don't remember pulling me onto the bed and rubbing that delicious body all over me while mewling?"

My jaw dropped. "*What?*"

He snorted. "I see Exos failed to mention that part of your drunk little episode." He straightened. "You should eat something."

I frowned as he left. "Okay…"

Is he mad at me? Because of the bond with Exos?

Shit.

I slid off the bed and trailed after him toward the apartment kitchen. Titus stood by the refrigerator, his ass looking mighty fine in a pair of snug jeans. He'd changed out of uniform attire and into casual garb, while I still wore my skirt and sweater—two things that were slightly worn and torn from the Air Quad incident earlier.

My mouth twisted to the side. I remembered taking down the monstrosity and that it wasn't something I created, but I couldn't recall anything after that. *How did I end up passed out in bed? And what did Titus mean about assaulting him?*

"Have I done something to anger you?" I blurted out when he didn't acknowledge my presence.

He glanced over his shoulder with his eyebrows raised. "Do I feel angry to you?" he asked, the question holding a hint of genuine curiosity.

"Uh, well, no, but you're being all… *stiff*." I couldn't come up with a better term.

His lips curled. "That, yes, I definitely am." He returned to his task of placing odd items on the counter. The food in this world was foreign and leafy, and while none of it appeared appetizing, it was mysteriously delicious.

I hopped up onto the counter beside his preparations, wanting to see his expression while we spoke. "What did I do? I don't remember anything after the, uh, tornado."

His emerald eyes flickered up to mine briefly before he pulled a knife from the block behind my back. "Aerie sent a targeted blast of wind into your head. It's meant to incapacitate an attacker."

"Oh." I noticed her in the class earlier, just hadn't realized what she'd done. I almost asked him why she targeted me, but I already knew. "She thought I created the tornado."

"That, and she's just a bitch. She's lucky Exos was there and not me. I'd have lit her ass on fire." The conviction in his tone had me grinning. "Vox said she targeted your mind, something about the frontal lobe. It essentially made you very drunk."

"And I assaulted you?" I pressed, wondering what the hell he meant by that.

His dimples flashed as he finished slicing up the items on his board. "You practically forced me to join you in bed." He tapped me lightly on the nose with the edge of his blade before turning to deposit it in the sink. "Which is why, Claire"—he rotated once more and grabbed my hips—"I'm *stiff*." He tugged me to the edge of the counter, forcing me to wrap my legs around his waist for balance.

I moaned at the feel of his hot arousal aligning with my center and clung to his shoulders as he rocked against me.

"I thought you were mad at me," I admitted, arching into him.

"Oh, I am," he said, his mouth brushing mine with the words. "You drive me crazy, sweetheart. Grinding all over me, telling me to fuck you when you know I can't. It makes me very, very mad. For you."

"I… I told you to fuck me?" It came out on a squeak.

"More like demanded." He nipped my lower lip, then dipped his tongue inside to seduce mine in a dance that left me writhing against him. "Mmm, I'm going to drive you wild, Claire. Taunt you until you beg me to slide inside your slick heat and claim you in a way no other fae has."

Fire licked up and down my arms, eating through my Academy sweater and wasting the fabric away to ash. I gasped as the flames reached my breasts, destroying the fibers along the way until I sat topless on the counter before a smirking Titus. Even my bra was gone.

"Shall we begin, sweetheart?" he asked softly.

"That wasn't the beginning?"

"Not even close," he murmured.

Embers swirled around my nipples, causing them to stiffen beneath the heat. Part of me recognized that it should hurt, but my inner fire caressed the one Titus created, and welcomed the resulting singe.

Just like with Exos, I felt our connection teetering dangerously on the edge of something more. I couldn't explain it, not outwardly. It simply existed. A tangible presence between us, an unspoken contract of fate, just waiting for my mental stamp of acceptance.

"Titus…" I grasped his shoulders, my skin prickling with energy from the wisps of smoke smoldering against my skin. His hands remained on my hips, holding me tightly against his groin.

He smiled. "More?"

I didn't get a chance to reply.

My skirt and panties went up in a whirling blaze of heat—gone in a flash.

I gasped. He'd undressed me before, but never like this. Never with his power roaming over my body, prickling at my nerves, caressing me in sensuality, and destroying all the fabric on me. Even my socks were gone.

"Mmm, that's better." He slid me backward on the counter. "Don't move."

His index finger brushed my knee as he stepped out from between my legs. I shivered at the sensation of electricity humming over my thighs from that little touch, then noticed the flickering energy slowly crawling up my skin.

It held me captive, my eyes refusing to lose focus.

What is he doing?

He's not...

No.

He can't be...

Oh God...

The heat slithered along my inner thigh, the intent clear. And then it caressed my sensitive, damp flesh, inflaming my insides. "Titus..."

"No moving," he repeated, having returned to his food preparations.

"But—" *Fuck, that's intense.* I grabbed the counter to keep from falling over, or running, or jumping, I didn't know. But that little flame circled my clit in the most dangerous kiss, calling my own fire out to play and creating an inferno in the last place I ever thought I'd desire it.

"Beautiful," Titus praised, his green eyes burning with unrestrained desire. "But you need more, sweetheart. I want you so hot that you can't see straight."

I opened my mouth to protest, when the embers grazing my breasts whirled into fiery clamps that pinched my nipples. A scream left my throat, one born of fierce pleasure. Titus's hand against my lower belly was all that kept me upright, my eyes glazing from the rapture his fire had unleashed on me.

"Don't combust on me yet, Claire. I have plans for you." He pushed me backward to prop me against the wall, then returned to his preparations while flames hummed over my skin, skirting over all the places I desired it most without providing any sort of relief.

"You're killing me, Titus."

"Good." He threw everything into a bowl, then drizzled

some kind of dressing over it. "You need to eat first."

"Fuck food."

He smirked. "I'll fuck you after food, sweetheart. Trust me." Heat sizzled between my legs, stroking me in a way that reminded me of his tongue and stirring stars behind my eyes.

This was nothing like the other fire play I'd experienced. This was *hot* and full of promise. One that equaled the very heavy erection barely concealed by the zipper of his pants.

Which gave me an idea.

Two could play this game.

I locked onto my elements—an action that was beginning to feel like second nature to me—and pulled my inclination for flames to the forefront.

Subtle, I whispered to the energy swirling inside. *Let's sweep over the jeans and incinerate in one warm wave.*

Titus froze as my power rolled over him, eating through his pants in a thorough sweep and incinerating the fabric to ash. His boxers disintegrated with it, revealing his gorgeous cock.

His eyes narrowed. "Claire…"

"What?" I asked innocently, my flames dancing across his silky skin to form a grip around the base. He nearly dropped the bowl as I stroked upward with my mind.

"*Fuck.*"

Heat spiked in my center as he returned the sensual assault against my sex. I gripped the counter for balance, my vision blacking out for a moment, and then his lips were on mine.

Hungry.

Punishing.

Devouring.

I returned the ferocity in kind, nipping and sucking and moaning. My arms looped around his neck, my legs closing around his waist. He lifted me against him, then slammed my back into the wall beside the fridge, placing his erection right where I wanted it.

"Naughty little fae vixen," he accused, his voice harsh. "You're going to regret not letting me feed you first."

I slid my center against his hardness and sighed, "I doubt it." The last few weeks felt like unending foreplay. Yes, Exos and Titus had gotten me off—*a lot*—but not being able to return the favor had been the ultimate tease.

This was my first time seeing or feeling Titus bare down there.

And oh, how he didn't disappoint.

I clawed at his shirt, needing him to be completely nude, and dropped it on the floor.

Solid muscle pressed against my curves. So hot. So strong. So *mine*.

The connection between us snapped into place without thought, a feeling of finality settling over me as Titus's fire welcomed mine with open arms.

It sent a shudder through him.

Through me.

Through our bodies where they almost joined.

And then he was there, sliding home without warning and completing us on a level of existence foreign to us both.

His name left my tongue to travel over his, and he returned the favor, whispering words of worship out loud and directly into my mind.

What I felt with Exos was incredibly different from this. Still amazing. Still absolutely perfect.

Yet, Titus carried a note of finality, of unbridled promise for always, and I accepted him with a flourish. It felt right. Perfect. Absolute.

Oh, and the manner in which he moved within me... *Mmm.* My head fell back on a groan, the sensation of utter fulfillment thriving through my veins.

Titus's lips fell to my neck, his hands roaming my sides, tweaking my breasts, memorizing every inch of my skin. My nails raked down his back, slipping back up to touch the tendrils of his thick auburn hair.

This was so much more than sex.

Passion fueled the air, our breaths mingling in hot pants, an inferno engulfing us both. But fuck if I could stop it. I let it overwhelm me, shoot me over the edge into a field of stars and light and *bliss*. A place where only Titus and I existed. An embrace overflowing with our kindled energy.

"Claire..." His mouth found mine again, his tongue a benediction against mine, his touch the life connection I craved.

The eruption building inside me seemed tied to him in an impossible way, as if I couldn't explode without him. But his continued thrusts, his strokes, his ministrations, built a maelstrom of sultry power that vibrated through my limbs.

"Please," I whispered, needing a release. He'd created this insanity, this blaze of ecstasy that lurked on the precipice of *more*.

His teeth sank into my lower lip, his hips driving harshly into mine.

Oh, there would be bruises.

My back bore the brunt of his force.

But my legs clamped even harder around him, begging him to increase his speed and drive even deeper.

And he did.

Oh, how he did.

I clutched his shoulders, my body screaming with the need to ignite.

One. Two. Three more...

"Titus," I breathed, detonating from within into the hottest orgasm of my life.

Fire. Everywhere.

A sea of red and orange and some blue.

Amazing.

Overwhelming.

Consuming.

Titus joined me, the force of his eruption sending me into another state of being. Rapture unlike anything I'd ever felt poured over me, spiking my heart rate, cascading my vision into darkness, and sending me down a black hole of oblivion.

Something soft touched my back several seconds, minutes—hours?—later.

A warm voice cooed in my ear.

My heart thumped in time with another.

Complete. Mine. Fire mate.

Cool air flooded my lungs. Warm lips brushed my cheek. And a tear slid from my eyes. *Home*, I realized. *I'm finally home.*

But not in the home I thought I desired.

Not Ohio.

Not with humans.

But with my fire. With my Titus.

"I love you, too, Claire," he whispered, his lips against my ear. I didn't know if I claimed to love him out loud or if he gathered it from my mind. Either way, his resulting endearment made me smile. "Rest, sweetheart. I'll bring you something to eat, and we'll do that again."

Yes, I thought back at him. *Yes, please.*

CHAPTER TWENTY-ONE
EXOS

MY LIPS CURLED. "Mmm, Claire's happy." I could almost taste her joy on my tongue, something that warmed me from the inside out.

Vox glanced at me, his hands loose at his sides as we walked. A natural warrior. He arched a brow. "She's happy?"

"Yes."

"You can feel her? Even from here?"

We were wandering the Air Quad, searching for the familiar energy signature. "I can always feel her," I confessed. "Our spirits are intertwined."

"And you're not bothered by another male, uh, you know... making her *happy*?"

"Maybe at first," I admitted. "But she has five elements.

230

I can't satisfy them all, and her fire calls to Titus." As was evidenced by the fact that I'd just felt their very permanent bond snap into place. They'd skipped the second level entirely, landing squarely on the third.

"I guess it's not unheard of for a Spirit Fae to take more than one mate," Vox said. "It's just never something I've considered, and you're a Royal Fae, too. Like, you're expected to, well, you know."

"Procreate?" I offered, smirking. "Claire can still have children, Vox." Although, he did bring up a good point. It was one I intended to discuss with her at length, including all the other complexities that accompanied a Royal mating. Fortunately, I had my mother's experience to lean on when it came to managing multiple mates in a Royal setting. She may have passed years ago, but I remembered the toll it took on her, especially after Cyrus was born.

"Right. Of course. I know. It's just—"

"Becoming my betrothed impacts more than just her," I finished for him. "Yes, I know. That's precisely why she and I won't be moving into the betrothed state anytime soon." I envied Titus for being so much easier on her senses. She would have nothing to consider where he was concerned, and everything to worry about with me.

"And Titus?" Vox pressed.

"Is officially engaged to her fire," I said, smiling. Around anyone else, I would have kept that detail to myself. But as I suspected Vox to be one of Claire's future mates, I divulged the detail.

"Like, as in, right now?"

I turned the corner of the Air Quad and nodded. "Yes."

"You can sense that?"

"Yes. Her spirit is linked to mine, which means I can see her potential bonds to all fae." I narrowed my gaze at him. "Such as you, Vox."

His light eyes widened. "Oh, no. I'm not. I mean, yeah, her air is similar, but I'm not getting involved in that mess. I've never… It's just not… Look—"

"What's more, I feel a duty to vet any potential mates for her other elements. Because only those who are strong enough to protect her should be allowed into the inner circle. I'm sure you understand, right?" I didn't give him a chance to reply, my mind already made up where Vox was concerned. He could try to fight it all he wanted, but we both knew his power had flirted with hers earlier today. And the Air Fae had liked what he felt. "Now, tell me about this energy signature."

We'd been tracking it for almost an hour, but it kept coming and going. Vox had commented on how it didn't feel right.

Based on what I sensed earlier, I agreed. Something about the essence seemed manipulated or forged, yet familiar. I just couldn't put my finger on it.

He cleared his throat and pointed at a nearby dorm. "It honestly reminds me of Aerie's affinity for air. But not quite. As I said—"

"It's been manipulated somehow," I interjected. "I know."

"But that's not possible, right? Like, I should be able to follow it back to the source."

"Could you identify it earlier?"

He shook his head, his long hair escaping the clasp at the back of his neck. "It was dark and ominous."

"And not at all like Claire."

"Exactly."

"But you couldn't determine the source?" I pressed.

"No. Not exactly. But I memorized it."

"Because you intended to hunt it later?" I would admire him greatly if that was his plan. It would show promise in his intentions for Claire.

He pinched his lips to the side. "No, more because I am constantly mapping out signatures."

Ah. Well. Still a useful trait. "Which is why it reminds you of Aerie."

"Right. She has this spirally air wave around her that I

sensed in the vortex, but she's not strong enough to have created it. Her aura is also not that *black*."

I leaned against the wall of the dorm he'd pointed at moments ago, scratching my jaw. "Maybe she's working with someone?"

"It's possible, but she seemed just as alarmed by that tornado as everyone else."

"Could be an act," I pointed out. "Gave her cause to attack Claire."

"True. But..." He shook his head again. "It's not completely right."

I understood what he meant. My instincts said we were missing something important, some key component to the explanation. "We need a trap," I decided, thinking out loud. "Now that we know we're dealing with someone manipulating the elements to frame Claire, we need some sort of event to prompt them to act while we observe."

"You want to use her as bait."

"She'll have guards." I looked pointedly at him. "Right?"

"You're really not going to take no for an answer, are you?"

"I only accept viable responses," I told him. "*No* is not reasonable."

He pulled out his hair tie and shook out his long mane of dark strands. Then fixed it up again. A nervous tell, one he seemed to be using to buy time while he puzzled over a response. We both knew he'd already made up his mind. Why else would he be curious about the dynamic between me, Claire, and Titus?

Oh, they might not have an initial bond yet, but their powers had already begun dancing around each other. "You're interested," I said, amused. "You just have to embrace it."

"It's complicated."

"Yes. And fun." I pushed off the wall and glanced up at the star-dotted sky. "Our elements drive us, Vox. Listen to your air, see how it feels, go from there. But in the interim,

I need your help in setting up a trap."

"What kind of trap?" he asked warily.

"One where we entice the guilty party to come out to play, then nail his or her ass to the ground. You game?"

His pupils dilated. "You're giving me a choice?"

"No, I just want to know if I need to make this a command or not." Because he would help either way. But I'd prefer him willing. If he had a stake in this game, he'd care more, and I needed to surround Claire with those who *wanted* to protect her.

Vox considered me for a long moment, his expression radiating a mixture of uncertainty and concern. Then he sighed and resolve settled over his features. "All right, Royal Fae. What do you need me to do?"

"So you're in?"

He gave me a look. "I think it's pretty obvious I joined whatever the hell this is when I showed up at the Spirit Quad tonight."

I smiled. "I knew I liked you."

"Yeah, yeah. Tell me what you need."

"For you to whistle around a rumor," I replied simply. Then gave him the words I wanted him to repeat. "Tell everyone. Or better yet, say it in front of Aerie and let her weave the web for you."

"That's one hell of a tale to be telling."

"It's what convinced you to venture over to the Spirit Quad, right? A rumor about Claire's upcoming expulsion?" I hadn't actually spread that one, the students doing it for me. But when I heard the rumor flying about, I wondered how Vox would react. And he had sought me out, as I'd hoped he would, proving he cared and wanted to protect Claire.

"You did that?"

"No, I was too busy caring for Claire. But I was aware of the comments flying around, and I saw the panic in your expression when you arrived. You thought the Council voted to expel her." Which wasn't the case at all. We hadn't even convened yet. Although, a few of them were definitely sending notes of wrath and consequence through the air.

"That's what I heard, yes."

"And you rushed over to proclaim her innocence." Not a question, but a statement. Because that was exactly what he'd done.

He stared at me for a long moment, then laughed without humor. "You're good, Exos. I'm not sure if I like that skill or fear it."

"Stay on my good side and you'll have no reason to fear it." End up on my bad side, well… that'd be another conversation entirely. "So you'll spread the gossip?"

His lips twitched. "Yeah, I'll get it to the right ears and meet you at the gym tomorrow."

"Excellent." I clapped him on the shoulder. "Good to have you along for the ride, Vox. I think you'll make a fine air mate for Claire."

"That's not—"

"Spread the rumors elsewhere, Vox. We both know the future here, and there's no sense in denying it. But good luck with your inner fight. I give you a week, tops, because you will cave."

His spine straightened. "You know nothing about me or my resolve or my desires in life."

"I don't need to, Air Fae." I leaned in, lowering my voice. "All I need is to know Claire, and trust me, you don't stand a chance. None of us do."

* * *

Claire's bare breasts peeked up at me from the sheets as I entered the room, her eyes closed in blissful unawareness. Titus lay behind her, lazily alert and observing my entry.

"Find anything?" he asked softly.

I shrugged out of my shirt and tossed it onto a chair in the corner. "Not really, no. We'll discuss it more in the morning. Did she eat?"

He pressed his lips to her neck and nodded. "Yes."

"Good." I unbuttoned my slacks and kicked off my shoes. "Congratulations, by the way."

His green eyes met mine. "You feel it?"

"Yes."

No hint of guilt or regret entered his features, only pure male pride. "She's amazing, Exos."

"I know." I pulled off my socks and finished removing my pants just as her eyes opened. "Hello, princess."

Her nostrils flared as she took in my black boxer briefs, her lips parting in appreciation. "Exos."

I smiled as I slid into the bed beside her, cupping her cheek. "There are burn marks in the kitchen." I'd noticed them immediately. "But well done on not destroying the dorm."

Claire's skin darkened to a delectable shade of pink. "Thanks, I, uh, think."

Pressing my mouth to hers, I indulged her in a deep kiss meant to arouse. She responded with her tongue and wrapped her palm around the back of my neck to hold me to her.

Titus chuckled, his palm sweeping up her side and back down. "I told you—amazing."

"Mmm," I agreed against her lips. And kissed her again, this time with more fervor than before, allowing her to feel my approval at bonding with Titus and also to provide her with a glimpse into how much I craved her. She needed to know that this arrangement worked for me, that I accepted her as my Claire regardless of the others.

Her spirit was mine.

And only mine.

Just as my spirit was hers.

"How did it go?" The words were a breath into my mouth.

I slid my fingers into her hair, holding her to me. "Vox will make a fine mate when you're ready for him," I admitted. "But I didn't come to bed to talk. We'll do that in the morning." I met Titus's gaze over her shoulder. "You're welcome to stay, but I'm going to kiss her until she falls asleep."

He drew a line of fire down her bare arm, sending a flicker across her skin. "That's fine. I don't mind finding other ways to relax her while you do that."

"Careful, Titus, or I'll start to think we make a good team."

He chuckled and pressed another kiss to her neck. "Where Claire is concerned, I believe we do."

I smiled, pleased by his reply. It proved my suspicions from earlier accurate. All he needed was a little alone time with our Claire to work himself out. Now that he'd regained his focus and staked his true claim, he would be a formidable ally in protecting our heart. I approved.

"I like it when you two get along," Claire said, a grin in her voice.

"Yeah?" I kissed her again—long and deep. "Shall we show you just how well we can get along where you're concerned?"

She shivered, her blue irises glazed with lust and adoration. "Only if you let me play in return."

"Maybe," I whispered, knowing full well it wasn't our time yet. Not until she fully understood what it meant to mate with a royal. "But I should warn you, Claire. My goal is to make you come so hard you can't do anything other than sleep afterward. As Titus has you all warmed up, it shouldn't be too difficult."

His flames intensified, sliding downward to the apex between her thighs. "I approve, Your Highness."

I nibbled her lip, then started licking a path downward toward her breasts. "Teamwork, Titus. Now let's make our princess scream."

CHAPTER TWENTY-TWO
CLAIRE

"YOU WANT ME TO GO TO GYM CLASS?" I asked, incredulous.

Titus and Exos were sitting at the breakfast table wearing severe expressions. So very different from the ways they looked at me in the bedroom.

My seducers were gone, and in their place were two sexy-as-fuck warrior fae males.

Both taunted my hormones, driving me wild beyond my craziest desires. Just thinking of all the orgasms these two had given me had my face going up in literal flames.

Titus arched a brow. "Does the idea of finding your captor turn you on? Or is it thoughts of last night?"

"Could be this morning," Exos pointed out.

And now my entire body was on fire. "Stop."

238

"But we like you wet, Claire," Titus replied.

"It's true. We also enjoy your screams."

I gripped the counter and glowered at them. "You were talking about gym class," I reminded them through gritted teeth.

"Your mind went to the bedroom," Titus replied, smirking. "Can't fault us for following."

"Oh my God, you two are impossible." I pinched the bridge of my nose while they both chuckled. Only seconds ago I'd been thinking about how stern they appeared and almost longing for my playful fae mates. Now I wanted to go back to the serious topic. "Tell me again why this is a good idea."

"Fucking you? Or the trap?" Titus teased.

Exos took pity on me and replied, "Because now we know what we're looking for. By luring the culprit into an arena where you can be framed, we can in turn catch the guilty party in the act."

"What if all hell breaks loose and it comes back on me again?" I pressed.

"That's where this comes in." Titus lifted a bracelet. "You'll wear this the entire time. No one will be able to accuse you as a result."

"And what is that?" I asked, eyeing the silvery metal.

"It's what all Powerless Champion fighters wear in the ring." He slid it across the breakfast bar. "The metal works similarly to cuffs in fae prisons—it dilutes your power."

"Meaning you can't create a tornado or firestorm," Exos translated. "So if one occurs at the gym, which I highly anticipate will happen, no one can blame you."

"Okay, but doesn't that also mean I can't stop it," I pointed out.

"Yes. That's why you'll have a team of fae with you during class. Some will be more obvious than others." He smiled. "River and Vox will be incognito but helping."

"And if we have to, we can remove the bracelet," Titus added. "Trust us, nothing is going to happen to you."

Exos folded his arms, eyes narrowed. "However, the same cannot be said about the person framing you."

Titus snorted. "No shit."

"So you want me to attend a gym class and—"

"It's technically an intramural sports activity," Titus corrected. "It's one of the few classes where all fae mingle."

"Right. So gym class," I said again. "And I'm just supposed to roll with it? Go along with whatever we're doing?"

"Yes, but I also want you aware of your surroundings. It'll be a good lesson in defensive magic." Exos pushed away from the breakfast bar and rolled his shoulders. "Ready?"

My eyebrows flew upward. "We're going now?" We'd just finished eating some sort of fried pancake thing. I thought we had at least a few hours to work out the full plan, not minutes.

"We overslept," Titus murmured.

"Is that still the right term when we weren't sleeping?" Exos asked.

"Fair. We overfucked?" he offered.

"Oh my God..." My face was on fire again. "Can we stop?"

"Is that what you want? To sleep alone tonight?" Exos asked, sounding far too serious.

"Ugh!" I threw my hands up in the air. "You know what? You're right. Let's go to gym class."

"See, now I knew she'd be eager for this," Exos said conversationally.

Titus started nodding enthusiastically. "You did. You really did."

"She'll be great."

"Because she's amazing," Titus added.

"Very, yes."

"Are you two done acting like I'm not standing in the same room with you?" I demanded, hands on my hips. "Or are you trying to give me a reason to sleep alone tonight?"

Exos gave me an indulgent look that made me want to

punch him. "Oh, baby, you know that'll never happen. If this morning's performance is anything to go by, you'll be begging us to come by midnight."

"I'm leaving now." I started marching toward the front door of the building, their laughter trailing along behind me in a taunting wave of heat and sound.

These men—*fae.*

My mates.

Why had I agreed to this madness, again?

Oh, right. The pleasure. Their sexy energy. The way they knew how to touch me perfectly. Their hypnotic eyes. Gorgeous smiles. Teaching skills. Irresistible bodies. And well-endowed—

I shook my head, needing to clear it before I marched back into the Spirit Dorm and guided them both to our bedroom.

Finding the asshole trying to get me expelled was far more important.

Right. Yes. Focus.

Time to make a fae pay.

* * *

Fae kickball, I thought with a snort. That was essentially what they wanted us to play in gym class today. Except no one wanted me on their team.

It reminded me of a first-grade popularity contest.

With a glare at Exos and Titus—who stood off to the side, watching with those damn serious expressions again—I joined the blue team with Vox and River. Neither of them acknowledged me, which, I suspected, was all part of the plan.

Or, at least, I hoped it was.

It took considerable effort not to pull Vox aside and apologize to him for yesterday. Though it wasn't my fault, but I felt obligated to say something. Maybe even to thank him for believing in me enough to visit last night and going out to search with Exos.

241

Yeah, that would be good.

I could express my gratitude for what he'd done, for helping again today, and for supposedly joining my mentor team.

All normal-ish things to say. Nothing too emotional or strange, just typical conversation.

Why am I nervous about talking to Vox?

I glanced at his profile. His crisp features definitely drew the female eye, and while I didn't usually like long hair on a man, he definitely wore it well. Lean, athletic lines. Handsome. Okay, so maybe I found him a little attractive, but that shouldn't deter me. I had two equally good-looking men watching from the sidelines. Clearly, my docket was a little full.

But something about Vox's energy called to mine. Like he soothed me in a way the others didn't. Because he understood my chaotic affinity for air? That seemed to be the one element I couldn't master. It ebbed and flowed and fought me at every turn.

Yet, I'd managed to hone the energy under his guidance just yesterday.

That had to be it. I felt a strange connection to him as a result, sort of like he resembled an antidote to the insanity building—

A ball slammed into the side of my head, sending me sideways a step.

"Ow!" I shouted, glowering at the approaching blue-haired bitch to my left. Sickle, if I remembered her name right. "What the fuck?"

"Earth. To. The. Halfling."

Seriously? "What?" I demanded, half tempted to pick up the ball and throw it at her bitchy little face.

Her resulting smile was all teeth. "I asked if you're ready to go to the Spirit Kingdom, where you belong."

I blinked at her. "Wow. That's your taunt?" I glanced around, meeting the gaze of several of my *teammates*. They all appeared as welcoming as she did. Great. I shook my head on a laugh, deciding to play this one low-key and not let her get to me. "Sorry, I just expected more originality in the Fae World. But that wasn't much better than my high school bully."

"You'll wither and die there," she continued.

I rolled my eyes. "Okay."

"And disappear for good."

"Uh-huh." I refused to let this bitch bother me. "Still not impressed. But please, continue. I could use some entertainment."

Ice clouded her blue eyes. "You tried to kill my friends, and you think this is funny?"

"I haven't tried to kill anyone." I folded my arms, bored. "I'm just trying to learn about my fae heritage. That's it."

She snorted. "Your mother was a whore who fucked a human and caused a plague that killed off most of the Spirit Fae. An abomination. And you're the product of it all, a walking reminder of Ophelia's atrocities."

Okay, those words stung a bit. Mostly because they were right. But... "I'm not my mother."

She spit at my feet. "You're right. You're worse. Taking a Spirit Royal for yourself to, what, destroy him, too? And Titus? And how many others? You're an even bigger slut than your mother!"

My palm itched to meet her face, but I swallowed the urge and forced a smile. "Anything else?" I learned a long time ago that the best way to deal with a bully was to not react.

"Yes. I hope they banish you," she seethed, ice forming around us. It prickled against my skin, raising goose bumps along the way. A few of the students stepped back, eyes widening. River, however, stood firm, gaze narrowed.

It couldn't be Sickle.

That would be too obvious.

And she couldn't control air or fire.

Although, the two girls glaring daggers at me from across the gym were capable of controlling those elements.

No.

That couldn't be it.

I'd literally done nothing to them, apart from apparently stealing Titus from Ignis. But he claimed they were never in a relationship.

Hmm, though, she did try to drug him into one. So she clearly has a thing for my mate.

The whistle blew loudly, calling all the players to their respective locations. Our team was in the field first. And that, apparently, was a literal location because grass grew across the floor with each step, bathing the gym in an exterior appearance.

Lily-pad-shaped bases formed a diamond configuration, denoting our field positions, and another whistle sounded.

Sickle maintained a distance—thankfully—leaving me to guard third base. My competitive drive was piqued as a ball shot over my head. I jumped to catch it, then threw it to the first baseman.

He caught it with a surprised look, then grinned at the growling fae who halted mid-run.

"Nice," Vox praised, having skipped over to my side in anticipation of the kick.

"Thanks." Maybe this would actually be fun.

We went a few rounds with me catching more balls, completing several throws, and generally pissing off the other team while enthralling my own.

Several fae even smiled in my direction.

Considering how this started out, I took that as a reasonable sign that at least a couple of fae might actually begin to like me.

At least, until Ignis nearly slammed into me during a field-to-base transition. She tossed her long red hair over her shoulder and sniffed. "You reek of Titus."

"Thank you," I replied, smiling. He winked at me from across the room. "As I'm very familiar with his scent, I'm taking that as a compliment. Now, if you'll excuse—"

She shoved me back with her hand on my shoulder,

causing me to stumble. "You might have him fooled, but I see right through your little innocent act. Your mother's blood runs thick through your veins. And soon, you'll end up just like her. *Dead* in the Spirit Kingdom."

My lips parted on a reply as ice drizzled across my skin, forming a ball in my palm.

I gaped down at it, confused.

This isn't mine.

I glanced around, searching for the culprit, and found several people backing away. Including Ignis.

"What are you doing?" she demanded, her eyebrows rising. "Stop that."

"I'm not—"

"You're insane!" she jumped backward, her hands up. "Everyone sees this, right? She's an abomination that needs to be banished!"

"What are you doing, Claire?" some random chick in a skirt demanded.

"Noth—"

"This is how it started yesterday!"

"In the courtyard, too."

"She's unstable."

"A monster."

Energy crawled over my skin, foreign and cold, and began to spiral into a voracious ball of energy.

"River…" I searched for him, finding him too far for comfort.

The mean girl brigade began to approach their team captain, their expressions alarmed, but a sheet of ice blocked their path. Ignis leapt sideways on a yelp, her terrified gaze flickering over her shoulder at me. I did nothing but watch as frozen blades appeared around the room, spiking up from the floor.

Fae screamed.

The instructor—whose name I didn't even remember—shouted.

My name rent the air.

Accusations flew with a fervor.

Stay calm, I told myself. *Exos and Titus are here. It's fine.* I stole a deep breath from within and willed my body to remain warm despite the arctic drop in temperature flooding the room.

Vox was suddenly at my side, his palm on my shoulder. "Do you feel it?" he asked softly. "The negative presence?"

I swallowed, trying to search for whatever he meant and shook my head. "I can't feel anything."

He glanced down at the metal bracelet clamped around my wrist and nodded. "Then the cuff is working."

"Is that a good thing?" I asked, shivering as a frozen sheet blanketed the ceiling of the gym.

"Yes." He nodded toward Elana standing just inside the door beside a man with shockingly white hair. "Looks like Exos invited some of the Council members to the show— Elana and Vape."

Vape. That must be the lanky male with the long, stark strands. Power seemed to emanate from the male's gaze as he studied the room with a serene expression. He said something to Elana before glancing at Exos and giving him a nod.

Something seemed to pass between them. An understanding. Unspoken words. I opened my mouth, ready to ask Vox if he knew what was happening, when an ominous crack sounded through the air.

Golf ball–sized hail fell from the ceiling, crashing into the ground around me. I screamed, falling to my knees, and covered my head just as a lethal ice pick sliced through the air toward Exos's head.

"No!" I made to move, but a wave of fire went up in a flash, incinerating the approaching weapon and leaving a very livid Royal Fae in its wake. He sent waves of power through the gym in a show of dominance unlike any I'd ever seen or felt.

Fire mingling with spirit—the royal declaring his right to the throne.

Everyone froze.

Then several fae fell to their knees on a whisper of sound, his name a chant on the wind.

CHAPTER TWENTY-THREE
CLAIRE

I STOOD GAPING AT EXOS, unable to speak, unsure of what to do.

"Who dares to threaten me?" he demanded, his blue eyes scanning the gym. "The last of the Spirit Fae line. A royal."

Several heads turned in my direction, causing him to scoff.

"You all discredit my ability to sense my own mate's power? You think I wouldn't be able to feel any malevolence coming from the future Princess of the Spirit Kingdom?" He tsked. "Such an insult requires punishment, perhaps in the form of a reminder of what a Spirit Fae can truly do."

Shudders rolled through the room, palpable and fear-driven.

248

"She did it!" someone shouted.

"Who?" Exos demanded.

A petite male with curly dark hair stood slowly and pointed at Sickle. "I felt her water energy roll over me just before it surrounded the Halfling."

"He's right," Vox added, still standing at my side. "I felt it, too."

"Same." The high-pitched voice came from the fae I'd first thrown the ball to at the beginning of the game.

Sickle was frozen on her knees, her expression one of shock. "I... I..."

"I recognized the signature as well," the white-haired male said from the doorway, his voice carrying over the crowd. "It flooded the room. And as you've put the distinctive Powerless Champion cuff on your mate, Titus, it most certainly did not come from Claire."

Several gasps filled the air as Vox lifted my arm. He tugged up the sleeve to reveal the bracelet underneath while I stood stock-still beside him, unable to properly breathe.

Sickle did this?

That just seemed too obvious somehow.

"I didn't do this," Sickle said, her head rotating back and forth. "I would never... I mean... I'm not... This can't..."

"What about the vortex?" Aerie asked, her wiry form shaking beside Sickle. "And the fire? Sickle didn't do those."

"Yet they targeted both me and Exos," Titus broke in. "Odd, considering we're the only two fae helping Claire. Why would she try to harm us?"

"Because she's insane," Ignis muttered from across the room.

"No, I suspect something else is at play." Elana stepped forward in a pristine white outfit, her hands clasped before her. Energy seemed to ripple around her as she moved, the air shifting beneath her, the grassy floor rekindling with life beneath her feet.

Several in the room gave her a wide berth, their reverence palpable as they kept their heads bowed for both

Elana and Exos. Even Titus and Vox appeared to defer to them, making me wonder if I was supposed to be kneeling or bowing instead of gaping.

But I couldn't stop.

I couldn't look away.

I needed to see what the hell was about to happen, hear whatever she intended to say. This woman—the Chancellor of the Academy—held my future in her hands. Exos never said that; it was just something I *knew*. And now she seemed to be considering her options, weighing the events of the room in her mind, and stroking the guilty parties with her spirit.

It slithered over me, a darkness that surprised my senses—there and gone in a flash. But it left an inky texture in her wake, confusing my ties to my inner elements.

Wrong.

Intrusive.

Reject.

Exos moved to stand beside her, his hands tucked behind his back, his spine erect in a distinctly regal manner. Titus remained at his station near the side of the room, unmoving, gaze downcast.

But the white-haired one strode forward with purpose, his eerily light gaze sweeping over everyone he passed.

"Stand." Elana's command sent a shiver through the air, but only three obeyed.

Ignis.

Aerie.

Sickle.

"Chancellor El—"

Elana silenced Ignis with a wave of her hand. "No speaking unless I ask you to." She strode around the trio, the atmosphere moving with her as a twirl of pixies appeared on her shoulder. "Mmm, yes, do."

They took off in a swarm, dancing over the three girls who appeared frozen in time, unblinking. I gaped at the display, concerned and confused, while everyone else in the room appeared to be incapable of observing.

What is happening? I wondered.

She's searching their minds for memories, Titus whispered back, causing my head to whip toward him.

What?! She can do that?

As a Spirit Fae, you possess the same ability.

I gaped at his prone form. He'd remained tucked into a revered pose, his eyes hidden from my own. I learned last night that we could somehow communicate in our minds now that we'd mated, but I didn't realize how clear our conversations could be.

Am I supposed to be bowing? I asked, wiping my palms against my skirt.

If you were, you would be. She's controlling the entire room right now, apart from you and Exos.

Why? I wondered. And how did he know she wasn't controlling me? I'd felt her energy slither over my skin. Just thinking about it made me tremble in foreboding. I *never* wanted to feel that again.

Because she can and she's pissed, Titus replied. *But most importantly, because it's a way of exerting power.*

Oh. And you're telling me she's able to search everyone's memories? Why didn't she—or Exos, for that matter—do that before? It would have saved us a lot of trouble, and me a lot of grief.

Who's to say they haven't? he countered. *But from what I understand, it takes a lot of energy. And to dive into someone's mind requires a conflict worthy of the intrusion—such as witnessing a fae using elements inappropriately.*

Hence, today's trap, I realized.

Exactly.

"Interesting," Elana said as her pixies began to chatter. "Very interesting." She clapped and the creatures disappeared. "It would appear none of the incidents were Claire at all, but the three of you trying to sabotage the new student out of petty jealousy."

"That's not—"

"Silence!" Power thundered through that softly spoken

word, making even me want to think twice about ever speaking again. Ignis visibly shuddered, her fiery hair falling in a wave over her shoulders as she bent even lower. "What was it you three desired? Oh, yes. For the Halfling to be banished to the Spirit Kingdom. Well, I do find that to be a suitable punishment for knowingly trying to destroy the reputation of an innocent student. Thoughts, Exos?"

"Perhaps a temporary visit," he suggested flatly. "They are students, after all. And the Spirit Kingdom is not kind to outsiders."

"Temporary," she mused, tapping her lip. "Vape?"

The white-haired male lifted a shoulder in a slight shrug. "As it is an affront on the Royal Fae and his intended, I would defer to his choice on the matter."

"And you, Mortus? I sense you lurking in the corridor. What say you?" she called.

My heart skipped a beat as the tall male with familiar dark features entered the room, his hands tucked behind his back in a similar fashion to Exos. "Does my opinion even matter?" he asked, his tone emotionless.

"As I request it, yes." She gave him her full attention. "Ignis is one of your students, after all."

He glanced at the redhead. "One of many."

"Then you should care what happens to her."

"As I said, one of many." He considered Ignis as one would an inconvenient mosquito. "Well, I suppose a temporary punishment would be adequate. Though, I'll also note that I surmised something like this would happen. The Halfling is not necessarily well liked, and if she is to survive in this world, then she should get used to being attacked."

Ice slithered through my veins at his callous words. Even Vox flinched beside me. But Exos merely chuckled. "I wish anyone luck who attempts to touch my intended betrothed. Not only will they have me to contend with, but also Titus. In fact"—he paused to address the room—"allow this to be a warning to you all. For while I may suggest a temporary sentence to be served in the Spirit Kingdom, I'm also requesting they be stripped of their elements during their stay. As they've proven to use them wrongly, it only seems fitting. Wouldn't you agree, Elana?"

The girls began to cry—silently—while the elders observed, and I wondered what all that would entail. Cuffs like my own? Or something more dire?

"Yes, that suits the crime, indeed," she agreed, a note of admiration in her voice. "Care to do the honors?"

"I do." He shifted forward, hands still behind him but gaze focused on the three bowing females. "As I said, consider this an introduction, for I will not be so lenient on a second offense."

Swirls of energy laced through his words, stringing through the air and wrapping around the women in wispy vines of magic. Their mouths opened on soundless shrieks at the contact, tears streaming from their eyes as Exos weaved the power through them and over them and around them.

Can you see that? I asked Titus, then remembered he couldn't look up.

No, but I feel it.

What is he doing?

Binding their elements, he whispered back to me. *He's essentially making them human.*

I flinched. *Fae can do that?*

Spirit Fae, yes.

Which meant *I* could do that to someone. Take away their will. Control them. Which, of course, made sense. Spirit represented life and death, and apparently, that included a fae's essence as well.

The girls collapsed as he finished, their tear-streaked faces leaving me slightly unsettled. Not that they didn't deserve it. With their little tricks, they'd almost sentenced me to an entire existence alone. And they'd tried to hurt Exos and Titus.

Yes, they more than earned this fate.

"Mmm, I believe justice is to be served, then," Elana

murmured, calling on her pixies again. "Take them to the house. I'll escort them personally to the Spirit Kingdom later." She flicked her fingers with the words, and the horde of little fairy things took hold of the trio. They practically dragged the three fae from the room by their hair and clothes while Ignis pleaded after them with her eyes. When she met mine, there was a note of urgency in them that I didn't understand.

Panic that she'd been caught?

Frustration?

A hint of revenge?

But it was too quick for me to study, the girls yanked from the gym with a vengeance.

Elana sighed dramatically. "Well, now that we've settled that, I believe apologies are in order. Claire has been wrongly accused and should actually be commended for her efforts in *stopping* the dangerous elements. I witnessed each account with my mind now, through the eyes of the guilty, and I must say, I'm impressed with your control." She smiled at me. "You've come a very long way in such a short time. I suspect there will be great things in your future, young one." She cocked her head to the side, then peered at Exos. "I have an idea."

"Yes?" he prompted, his expression one of deep admiration. This woman was clearly well loved by the fae. It seemed appropriate. From what little I'd observed of her, she'd earned her status.

"How would you feel about me helping with some of her instruction? Given your recent bond and her attraction to all five elements, she has the potential to help—if not *lead*—our elemental peace initiatives. Thoughts?"

Gasps filled the room, including one from Vox.

But I was too busy trying to figure out what she meant by *peace initiatives* to comprehend the entirety of that statement.

"I think it's up to Claire," Exos replied. "But I agree that it would be an excellent—and very generous—

opportunity."

"Might help make up for her rocky start as well," she mused before grinning at me again. "I'll touch base with you next week on what a tutelage beneath me would require, then you can decide for yourself if you're interested. Yes?"

I swallowed. "Um, thank you. Yes, I would be interested." *I think...?* This was not at all how I expected the day to go. But I couldn't necessarily complain about the turn of events, and from the awed noises in the room, she'd just offered me a status of some kind. I only wished I understood what.

"Excellent." Elana clapped her hands once more, eliciting several sighs of relief throughout the gymnasium. "Well, it's been lovely, my beautiful children. I hope we all learned great things today. Should anyone require an audience with me to discuss today's events, you know where to find me."

She left with a flourish of vitality, the ground sprouting wildfires in her trail and a clutter of those pixies forming around her like a guard.

Vape smiled and followed, but not before nodding once at Exos.

And Mortus merely slinked back into the shadows, his presence an ominous shade in the back of the room as everyone seemed to bounce back to life.

I met his dark gaze, felt a chill of ill intention traverse my spine, and suddenly found myself wrapped up in Titus's arms. "You did it," he whispered, his lips at my ear.

"I didn't do anything."

"You remained calm, sweetheart. You didn't let them goad you. And you're one hell of a Faeball player." He cupped my cheeks in his hands and kissed me lightly. "Why didn't you tell us you knew how to play?"

"You mean kickball?" I asked. "Humans play that in, like, elementary school."

His eyebrows shot up. "Really?"

"I told you that," River put in, joining us. "I've said that, like, ten times."

"You did?" He gave him a look. "When?"

"One of the many times you were apparently ignoring my comments about the human world," River grumbled.

"Hmm. Fair." Titus draped his arm across my shoulders, pulling me to his side. "Well, Claire's a natural at it."

I snorted. "It's not a hard game."

"She's really good," someone agreed from the side.

"Yeah, she is," another said.

I frowned after them. "I don't know them."

"Ah, but they know you." Titus pressed his lips to my temple. "Actually, I think your position around here is about to change."

Exos joined our circle, his gaze brimming with pride. "Mortus just gave us permission to move back to the Fire Quad, if you want."

"He did?" I glanced around, trying to find that ominous energy, but he'd disappeared.

"He did," Exos confirmed. "But I told him we're having too much fun on Spirit Quad to move." He lifted a brow. "Unless you disagree?"

I considered it and smiled. "I think the Spirit Quad could use a little life."

His lips curled. "My thoughts exactly." He stepped in to brush his lips over mine while Titus's arm remained solid across my shoulders.

My two fae.

It felt good here.

Felt even better that Vox remained on my other side. I didn't know what that meant, but I would investigate later. For now, I was just glad to have my name cleared of wrongdoing. I still had a lot of work to do to get my elements under control, but at least I could do so without worrying about hurting others.

As Elana said, I'd helped.

No, I'd more than helped. I'd dismantled the bad energy with my own gifts.

"I want to know more about the internship," I whispered to Exos. "What does it mean?"

"It means Elana wants to tutor you personally. Like she did with your mother." He tucked a strand of my hair behind my ear and pressed his forehead to mine. "It would be good for you to have a second spirit instructor, and she's extremely powerful. She could also tell you more about Ophelia."

My heart slid into my throat. "Because she mentored my mom." The gravity of that realization floored me, making me uncertain of how to proceed.

Part of me didn't want to know my mother at all, especially after everything I'd learned. The other part desired more information on what happened, who she was before her relationship with Mortus took a turn, and what similarities I had to her that I should avoid.

"Yes." Exos pressed his palm to my neck, angling my head back to meet his kiss. "Think about it, princess. You don't have to decide now."

"Okay," I whispered. Although, in my heart, I already knew my decision. *Yes.* Because I had to know what she was like, to avoid ever becoming her.

I refused to ever hurt Titus in that way. Exos, too.

"Mmm, we'll discuss it more tonight," he murmured. "I need to go call my brother to update him on our situation, but I'll be quick."

"Promise?" I asked, gazing up at him. "Because I was hoping to get a few sparring lessons in this afternoon."

"Sparring, hmm?" He glanced at Titus. "Seems she wants an upgrade."

Titus snorted. "She just wants to play with spirit because I gave her too much fire last night."

My eyes rolled upward. "Please don't."

"That sounds like a challenge, Fire Fae," Exos replied, looking over him. "Let's see how exhausted my spirit makes her tonight."

"Ugh, seriously—"

"You're on, Royal." Titus smiled. "We can make a game of it—who can exhaust Claire more."

My cheeks were officially inflamed. "Guys…"

"Sounds like a fun way to spend the rest of the week," Exos agreed, his grin positively wicked. "You ready to join yet, Vox?"

Oh God…

The Air Fae merely shook his head. "I'm just here to teach."

"Teach," Titus repeated. "Right."

"I am."

"Uh-huh. Exos is just here to lay out commands. I'm here to light Claire on fire. And you're going for professorship." Titus shrugged. "Works for me."

"You're incorrigible," I growled, shrugging out from under his arm. "And if you keep it up, I'll be sleeping alone later."

"Sure, sweetheart," he said, snagging my waist and pulling me back to him. "Then you'll just dream about us, but I assure you reality is better."

Reality, I thought with a laugh. What a strange word. Because my reality? Yeah, it was nothing like my dreams, or even my fantasies.

No, this was better.

Even with the teasing, the sharing, the constant confusion, I wouldn't trade my current existence for anything in the world.

Exos winked at me, either hearing my thoughts or seeing them in my expression. "See you in a bit, princess."

It was as he disappeared from view that I pondered over his words. *Call my brother…*

Using what? I wondered. I hadn't seen any phones in the Fae Kingdom. Probably some sort of tree or a bird.

"You ready to go home, sweetheart?" Titus asked, his arms tightening around me.

Home. I smiled. "Yeah." I liked the sound of that. "With you." *And Exos.*

My new world filled with odd mating rules, elements, and, most importantly, love.

A girl could get used to this life.

A girl like me.

EPILOGUE
EXOS

I DIDN'T WANT TO LEAVE CLAIRE, but I needed to talk to my brother. Something about the setup felt off. Too easy. Too obvious. And the energy signatures felt tampered with and wrong somehow.

With quick steps, I ventured across campus toward the nearest communication tower. Fae didn't have technology the way humans did. We used something simpler—our minds. But it required the right condition, hence the tower.

I took the stairs two at a time, the air calming with each step upward. So much energy on campus, all spiked by the mingling of elements. Moments like this, I missed the simplicity of the Spirit Kingdom.

The thought had my instincts itching again.

Did those girls deserve their fates?

Yes, I'd made an example out of them, wanting everyone to know what fate lurks for them should they decide to fuck with my mate. But my spirit had sensed something foul inside them as I wove my energy through their skin—a presence that didn't belong.

One that reminded me of someone.

But who?

I glanced around, the hair rising on the back of my neck.

An essence had just joined mine. Subtle. Dark. Familiar again.

No one stood on the stairs. So where was it coming from?

I turned in a circle.

Nothing.

What is that? I crept upward, already reaching out to Cyrus with my mind. He wouldn't answer me right away, would require time to find an appropriate location, but the subtle shimmer of his mind told me he'd received my message.

While I waited, I took in my surroundings once more.

That nagging energy of wrongness thickened. Was it all in my mind? A consequence of that gymnasium? Had I banished those girls wrongly?

No, they were awful beings. I knew that, had sensed it in their auras as I disintegrated their bonds to the elements—one of the worst punishments known to fae kind.

That had to be it. I just felt bad about hurting another, even though those women deserved it. The Spirit Kingdom would not be kind to them—a fate they more than warranted.

Exos? Cyrus whispered through my mind. *Is everything all right?*

I'm not sure, I answered him honestly. *We discovered who was targeting Claire, but I have this odd feeling we accused the wrong fae.*

How so?

I told him about the setup, how Elana used her magic to extract the truth—an exhausting form of spirit magic—and how I sensed a falsehood. *Something isn't right, Cyrus.*

Do you need me?

I think... I trailed off as the dark essence grew around me. No one stood nearby. The sky remained clear. But I *felt* the menacing presence like a scar against my back. *Someone's here.*

Listening?

No. My mental walls were impossible to breach. *But here with—*

A flash in my vision sent me stumbling backward. Harsh. Strong. Quick.

The culprit moved too fast, too unexpectedly. My energy was exhausted after the gymnasium, not yet replete enough for defense. I threw up a wall, but he ghosted through it, startling me. Then struck me upside the head so hard my vision clouded behind a sea of black dots. A second strike forced me to my knees. And a third sent me face-first to the ground.

Exos! someone screamed. Maybe Cyrus. But it sounded mysteriously like my Claire...

Only then I did I realize *who* had joined me up here, the smoky figure taking corporeal form.

But it was too late.

The assailant's name was but a mere whisper in my mind just as everything went dark.

Run, my Claire...

Run.

To Be Continued...

Elemental Fae Academy: Book Two

Someone wants me dead.

Worse yet, my link to Spirit is dying. Why? Because Exos has been taken by a new enemy. Now I have to rely on my other elements to find my missing link before it's too late.

Oh, and I need a guard to protect me while I learn how to defend myself. No big deal. Master the elements, find my lost Spirit, and identify the bad guy.

Yeah. Easy.

Except Titus is tired of playing by the rules of others.
Vox just wants to be friends.
Sol is pissing everyone off.
And Cyrus, well, he's a force of nature and very much in charge.

I'd better solve this puzzle quickly before my heart starts making choices on my behalf. Because all of these fae are beautiful, cunning, and perfect in their own ways.

But how can I feel complete without my Spirit?

The hunt is on, and whoever is out to hurt me and mine will pay.

Note: This is a medium-burn reverse harem paranormal romance, and book two of the Elemental Fae Academy trilogy.

ABOUT LEXI C. FOSS

USA Today Bestselling Author Lexi C. Foss loves to play in dark worlds, especially the ones that bite. She lives in Atlanta, Georgia with her husband and their furry children. When not writing, she's busy crossing items off her travel bucket list, or chasing eclipses around the globe. She's quirky, consumes way too much coffee, and loves to swim.

www.LexiCFoss.com
https://www.facebook.com/LexiCFoss
https://www.twitter.com/LexiCFoss

ABOUT J.R. THORN

J.R. Thorn is a Reverse Harem Paranormal Romance Author.

Learn More at:
www.AuthorJRThorn.com

Addicted to Academy? Read more RH Academy by J.R. Thorn: Fortune Academy, available on Amazon.com!

Welcome to Fortune Academy, a school where supernaturals can feel at home—except, I have no idea what the hell I am.

Made in the USA
Middletown, DE
08 August 2019